Lady Jaided's
SEXY SMILES

MICHELLE BARDSLEY
S.L. CARPENTER
MARLY CHANCE
CIARRA SIMS
CHRIS TANGLEN
SAMANTHA WINSTON

ELLORA'S CAVE
ROMANTICA PUBLISHING

*W*hat the critics are saying...

ဆ

Betty and the Beast

"Filled with Mr. Carpenter's twisted sense of humor, BETTY AND THE BEAST is a fun ride. Don't expect a serious love story, but if you enjoy slapstick, madcap scenes, you'll love this latest "Quickie" from Ellora's Cave. An unexpected plot twist near the end will have readers howling with laughter. Fans of the outrageous should definitely snatch up this tale." ~ *Sensual Romance Reviews*

Deadline

"This Quickie is funny, sexy, and erotic. I was very impressed with the humor of it all as well as the mind blowing sexual contact between Ryan and Alexis. It's sweet and to the point while encouraging the reader to read on. Great job."
~ *Fallen Angel Reviews*

The Phallus from Dallas

Recommended Read "This was the hottest, sexual short story I have ever read. It was packed with the best humor and sex. I drove my husband nuts reading him the funny parts. I have already recommended it to several of my friends who love to read. It was very well written and has me wanting more. On my scale of 1 to 10, I give it a 15. It's that good."
~ *The Best Reviews*

1-800-SEX4YOU

"*1-800-SEX4YOU* is an erotic story that is sure to make romance lovers curl their toes and giggle at the characters actions. Readers get to experience both his and her outlook throughout the story, letting us see how Arissa and Derek both viewed what was going on. It was funny to see how they disagree about how events actually happened. If you are looking for a quick read that is both sensual and funny, than this Ellora's Cave Quickie is perfect for you." ~ *Fallen Angel Reviews*

Redial 1-800-SEX4YOU

Highly Recommended Read! 5 Angels! "*Redial 1-800-SEX4YOU* is a very erotic quickie that is hot enough to melt butter! Enjoy this his-and-her outlook throughout the story that is sure to have you laughing one minute, while quickly making you hot, and sizzling with desire the next. It was very comical to read how both Drae and Kevin could have such various point of views on what really happened during their night of passion. If you are in need of a raw, sensational, quick-fix then, *Redial 1-800-SEX4YOU* is just what the doctor ordered." ~ *Fallen Angel Reviews*

Frog Prince of Planet Marecage

"THE FROG PRINCE FROM PLANET MARECAGE is a cute, sexy story. I really enjoyed this novella and definitely recommend it. You'll be shocked at the inhumane treatment of the Teres princesses and will applaud at the perfect ending. Ms. Winston has written an erotic twist to a classic fairy tale. If you haven't tried Ellora's Cave's series of Not-So-Grimm Fairy Tales yet, this is a great one to start with." ~ *Sensual Romance Reviews*

An Ellora's Cave Romantica Publication

www.ellorascave.com

Lady Jaided's Sexy Smiles

ISBN 9781419954917
ALL RIGHTS RESERVED.
Betty and the Beast Copyright © 2004 S.L. Carpenter
Deadline Copyright © 2004 Marly Chance
The Phallus from Dallas Copyright © 2003 Samantha Winston
and Ciarra Sims
1-800-SEX4YOU Copyright © 2004 Chris Tanglen and Michele
Bardsley
Redial 1-800-SEX4YOU Copyright © 2005 Chris Tanglen and
Michele Bardsley
Frog Prince from Planet Marecage Copyright © 2003 Samantha
Winston

Cover art by Darrell King.

This book printed in the U.S.A. by Jasmine–Jade Enterprises,
LLC.

Trade paperback Publication September 2007

LADY JAIDED'S SEXY SMILES

හ

BETTY AND THE BEAST
S.L. Carpenter

 හ

Dedication

❧

As with everything, this book is dedicated to my wife, who tolerates my weirdness. It is also dedicated to my partner, who kicked my butt to let myself go and have fun with this story.

Chapter 1

ಬಾ

Betty tossed her blanket across the tall grass of the meadow and set her picnic basket down. She had taken this long walk before and loved sitting in the grass amongst the animals. She was unseen by others and could eat her lunch while reading books and daydream about the time that she would find her true love.

Betty was what every man desired but couldn't have. A blonde bombshell with big tits, and she was still a virgin. She lay back on the blanket and gazed at the sky above her. It was chilly out, but she didn't mind the cold. Her nipples seemed to pay attention, though, as they became sensitive in the cool air.

Betty laughed at how her body reacted to the simple changes. Cold, heat, ice, carrots; everything affected her in a different way.

She heard the tall grass rippling in the breeze while the birds chirped in the old oak tree beside the meadow.

The clouds that scattered across the blue sky made different shapes in her eyes. Over there she saw a rabbit. Those two made a fluffy sheep and that big one reminded her of her pussy.

Her pussycat, Jasper.

Why everything reminded her of animals was a mystery.

The clouds seemed to float right over her as the grass swayed back and forth in the brisk wind. Betty again began to daydream of a *knight in shining armor* to take her from her drab boring life with her father.

Betty closed her eyes, taking in the feel and sound of the beautiful setting. It was peaceful, relaxing, and a perfect day.

Her head filled with fantasies of faraway lands. Dragons and a valiant knight risking his life to rescue his damsel in distress. The knight was strong, stunningly handsome and hung like a horse (again with the animal metaphors). Their fate was set in destiny. Books could be written about their love and many generations would hear of them. Women would be green with envy as she became a princess to her wondrous prince. The entire countryside would attend their wedding and they would spend a fortnight making love in his spacious stone castle.

She would become a woman that night. Many times. One orgasm in every room of the castle. The number 69 popped into her head. That was the number of rooms in the enormous spectacle of architecture. Their love would have no boundaries that night. Or in the morning while cooking breakfast. Or once more, after an afternoon walk. Or later, in the barn, lying in the hay. The thoughts flowed through her mind, making her milky white breasts flush with excitement.

Hopefully they wouldn't find the needle in the haystack that would prick her bottom. The only thing she dreamed about being pricked by was her man. Her prince with the long steel-hard sword that would slay her virginity with a piercing thrust.

A damp plop on her forehead awoke her from the daydream as a sparrow had taken aim on her from above, hitting her like a bull's-eye.

Cursing the bird like a sailor, Betty wiped the bird droppings from her skin and hair on a small cloth napkin. Feeling a little down, she began to take stock of her life, or the lack of it.

She was of age for marriage, in her nineteenth year. She waited on her widowed father. She did everything for him because she would feel too guilty to leave him alone. There wasn't much time for herself, so she never really had a suitor.

Except Ralph. He was the butcher's son and would bring meat to the house and stay for dinner. He was the town idiot, but he was a huge man. Being a butcher fit him because he was a beefcake. He was six feet five inches tall, had a wide chest, was strong as an ox and hung. Betty had watched him shower a few times before he went on the long trip back to town. The peepholes in the wood helped her see things. The images of him were good for her fantasies and times alone with the vegetables.

Masturbation was seen as a sin but she did love the feelings it caused in her body. She would always fall into the same dream about her prince being a magnificent lover — not like the time Ralph shot his load on her thigh. It was a sticky mess. His constant pleads of how it tasted like honey and was full of protein wouldn't convince her to try the oral explorations for which he begged. Not at first. She may be blonde but she wasn't stupid. Well, not too stupid.

They had played in the barn horse stalls. It was always just coy teasing and an occasional feel of his manhood. The phrase "hand job" was used a few times but Betty wasn't too keen about the look on his face when she would squeeze the swollen tip between her fingers. A mixed look of pain and anguish, like being constipated from eating too much goat cheese. There had been small deposits on the tip that Betty had wiped away, and she had felt her own arousal rise as she stroked Ralph's pulsing cock in her hand. She did think of him in a sexual way, but never dared to cross the line.

He was truly a gifted man in the anatomy area. Betty loved the firm feel of his cock against the fabric of her undergarments. When he would pull her close, their flesh would touch and the constant burning of desire made her pussy ache to give in to him. They would roll around, semi-nude, in the hay but she didn't want to be seen as a town whore and get pregnant, so she never let him violate her pussy. This was going to be the pure present she would give to her prince on their wedding night. Technically, she was a virgin.

On one daring occasion she let herself taste Ralph's forbidden seed. He was so needy and aroused. She weakened to his pleas and the twenty minutes of groveling and begging. The warm, pulsing shaft filled her mouth and his groans of pleasure fueled her fire. She sucked him deeply until he touched the back of her throat. When he erupted, the seed spewed out, coating her throat with the hot seed from his loins.

Betty liked her effect on Ralph and his appreciation for a release. She also liked the gifts of chocolate and coffee beans he would bring by.

From the nearby wall of trees she heard someone giggling, breaking the silence. It sounded like a woman. The low murmur of a man's voice could also be heard. The grass hid Betty, but she was a little scared because she couldn't see anything or anyone.

Kneeling, she looked in the direction of the giggling. *Oh, it's just Charlotte and Jacob.* They were a couple she met at church. They must be out here to have their own picnic.

Betty thought about asking them to join her but when she went to say something she noticed they weren't carrying anything except a blanket that they had set under an oak tree.

Betty was close enough to see them and the tall grass hid her from their view. They had no idea she was there.

Charlotte leaned against the tree and Jacob moved in to kiss her. She turned her head, closing her eyes while Jacob kissed her neck. Her long strands of brown hair blew in the breeze.

His large hands searched her body, trying to grasp her bounty. He grasped her breast through the fabric of her frilly blouse and Charlotte's mouth opened as she moaned softly.

A smile widened across her face as Jacob kissed her shoulder and pulled the straps aside to reveal more of her neck and flesh.

Betty sat on her feet, transfixed by the couple.

She wasn't sure if she should watch or run away. Her body was becoming hot even though it was cold outside. Betty would watch, just a little longer. She had never seen a couple make love before. The animals at the farm were her only real knowledge of sexual intercourse. Jacob didn't have Charlotte on all fours while he humped away like a dog or bull.

When Betty stood back up on her knees she saw Jacob kneeling before Charlotte and he had a hand on her breast, massaging it. Charlotte was moaning and her skirt was pulled up and ruffled over Jacob's shoulder. Charlotte's hands rested on the back of Jacob's head. Betty could hear a low mumbling sound from Jacob while he sunk his face between Charlotte's legs. She toyed with his hair and smiled brightly as Jacob continued his nuzzling. He quietly growled and a suckling sound caused Charlotte to quiver.

Betty felt heat caress her body. Her chest felt heavy and the clothing became a restriction to her own sexuality blossoming. Her undergarments were now wet and the familiar ache of desire crept back into her. Her hands felt drawn to her chest. She pressed her breasts tightly to her body, cupping the fullness in her hands. Betty bit on her lip and gulped, wanting to watch more.

She had always wanted a man to make love to her. She longed to know how it would feel to have a cock stretch and delve deep inside the sanctuary of her body. The violation would be welcomed and she believed the pleasure it brought would be worth the initial pain.

Betty's hand found its way between her legs. The wet fabric of her undergarment showed her excitement. She was torn, yet knew what she wanted. Looking back over the tall grass she saw the look on Charlotte's face and envied her.

Jacob stood up, pressing against Charlotte. She slid her hand down his strong, flexing chest and grasped the lump in his breeches. He was aroused and their merging was only a matter of time.

Charlotte tugged at the string of his black pants and finally loosened them enough to put her hand inside. The look on her face showed Betty she had found what she longed for. Jacob grasped her shoulders and kissed Charlotte deeply. Their moans echoed in Betty's mind as she heard the pleasure in their tone.

Betty's eyes fluttered as her finger pressed the outer lips of her wet pussy. They were hot and engorged with the blood that began to boil within her.

Charlotte pulled Jacob's pants over his hips and Betty saw the muscles of Jacob's ass flex as Charlotte knelt to pull them down his strong, muscular legs.

Betty stifled a moan as she saw Jacob's large cock, freed and waiting for the attention it needed. He was definitely a bull. A small trickle of drool spilled along the side of Betty's mouth. She longed to taste him.

Betty could only dream of the feelings. Looking into her basket she saw a hard baked breadstick. It was rolled into a cylindrical shape and was smooth. The hardened exterior made it firm and almost like a normal sized penis. *Perfect*, she thought. It was about the same as Jacob and would suffice for her intention. As she watched Charlotte stroke Jacob in her hand, Betty stroked the breadstick. To her, she was joining in their pleasure.

Charlotte looked up at Jacob, then looked down at his cock. She licked her lips and kissed the swollen tip.

Jacob threw his head back and groaned.

Again she kissed it, then again, until finally she slid the head between her red lips. Betty followed her lead and kissed the breadstick and acted as if it were Jacob's beautiful cock.

Charlotte took extreme care in her attention to Jacob. Slowly taking the tip in and out of her mouth. Her tongue would follow the pulsing vein along the bottom as he withdrew from her lips. Charlotte seemed to love the effect she had on him.

Jacob's face spoke volumes. His eyes were closed tight and a wicked smirk crossed his lips. He was blissful. He held the back of her head as he filled her mouth with his swollen cock.

Betty tried to follow Charlotte's example but gagged as the breadstick tickled the back of her throat.

Charlotte freed him and laid back on the blanket spread across the grass.

Jacob knelt down next to her and smiled as she opened her legs to his admiring eyes. He lay down beside her and caressed the soft slope of her neck and the curves of her bosom. He was still hard as a rock but was enjoying Charlotte's body. Jacob took a great deal of care while his fingers dragged along the creases of her flesh. Her breasts were supple and flushed pink.

Jacob stared at Charlotte's legs, as they seemed to twist and turn at her growing arousal. He looked back to her face.

Charlotte was on the wall of passion, about to fall into the oblivion of ecstasy.

She sat up suddenly and pushed Jacob onto his back. Betty saw that Charlotte had become desperate. Her hand found Jacob's cock and she climbed over him. Charlotte kissed him as she straddled his thighs.

Betty let herself get lost within their passion. The firm breadstick now rested between her legs. She had pulled her undergarment to the side and the wetness had slipped down her inner thigh. The end of the breadstick rested at the opening of her pussy, just like Jacob's cock was set at Charlotte's opening.

Betty became engrossed in watching the reactions Charlotte showed as she lowered herself onto Jacob's cock. A glow of ecstasy radiated from her. She looked so enraptured. A wide smile crossed her face and Jacob groaned when Charlotte wiggled her ass as he filled her.

She pressed the French breadstick inside her pussy, opening the sanctuary of her body. But she longed for the hardness of a real man inside. To have his cock pulse and throb within her was the feeling she desperately craved.

As Charlotte rode Jacob up and down, Betty would push the breadstick in and out. In tandem, they both made love to Jacob. His strong arms, his broad chest and his glorious cock thrusting in and out of both of them.

Jacob began to groan with pleasure and Charlotte pulled at her blouse, trying to open it. Her breasts were begging to be touched. Jacob helped ease her need by groping at her nipples. The gentle tugging causing Charlotte to climb over the edge.

She threw her head back, closing her eyes. She was at her peak and moaned. Like wings, her hair floated in the breeze. Charlotte fell backward. The tight opening of her pussy was stretched with the hard strain of Jacob's cock lunging in and out.

Betty felt the steady ripple of her orgasm approaching and became scared and overly anxious. She hadn't felt this excited before. She looked at her pussy and how it seemed to grip the breadstick as she plunged it in and out. Her finger became drawn to the front of her pussy. The swollen tip of her clit protruded out and called to her. Giving in to her needs, she touched it, and came.

She tried to stifle her moan, hearing Jacob grunt and Charlotte sigh as she collapsed onto him.

Her groaning growl startled Jacob and Charlotte. They looked to the field and couldn't see anything, but the animalistic muffled moan sounded like a wild beast.

"That sounds like a wild boar. Let's get outta here." Jacob yanked up his pants and caught the opened flap on his balls. He closed his eyes briefly. A flash of pain made his eyes water. There was a small, thin, sharp-edged piece of tree bark in his pants and when he glanced down he now understood what the term "piercing" meant.

In a high octave voice he looked at Charlotte trying to pick up her layers of clothes and said, "Come on, I think I need to see Doc Griffith." And they rushed off with Jacob bow-legged and limping.

Betty fell back into the brush and began to cry.

She wanted to be with someone. She was jealous of Charlotte because she had Jacob. Betty just wanted a man of her own. Breadsticks served their purpose but she wanted true love.

Thinking to herself, she wondered what to have for lunch, and she began to eat a breadstick.

Chapter 2

ཉ

Henry had decided to take a trip to the nearby town of San Jose. He had a female friend there that would take care of him for an evening. He couldn't tell Betty he had such cravings of the flesh. To him, she was pure as snow and her memories of her mother would only make her angry with her father to be dishonoring her memories. But being a man, he had needs to satisfy. Basically, he was horny.

Henry had loved his wife but the sheep were running faster and the townspeople all knew him. So he would go to the small town and stay with a woman in private. His own personal getaway.

Of course it was a brothel, so nobody would really care who Henry was.

He loved to walk and enjoyed the solitude. It was also a good reason to drink. He was pretty stubborn and wouldn't ask for directions. Being a typical man, he thought he knew everything. Of course, he was also an idiot and usually got lost.

In the distance a cold wind swept through the hillside. Henry knew a storm was coming and it might get a little nippy out, so he packed a second satchel with necessities. Rum, a small flask of rum and a hip sack with a very old vintage of rum.

Henry was hopelessly lost and alone in the dark, freezing woods. The gallon or so of rum kept his body rather warm but his sense of direction was shot. Through the thick, blinding rain he saw an enormous figure. He waded through the mud to meet the man.

"'Scuse me, do you know the way to San Jose? I mean, where the hell am I?"

Leaning against the figure he blurrily recognized it was a stone statue of a guard.

"Damn, it's colder than I thought. You're frozen stiff." This must be the place, he thought. As lightning illuminated the sky Henry saw the outline of a castle. The loud rumble of thunder hurt his ears; his oncoming hangover didn't help much either.

Crossing the bridge over the moat, Henry hid his face from the fierce rain that blew in the wind. He came to the door of the castle. There were two huge round doorknockers; Henry stood in awe of the great pair of knockers before him. *Now I know this is the place. I'd remember those knockers anywhere.* Grasping the globe in his hand he snickered and swung it against the wet wood. After banging on the large wood door, nobody answered, so he pushed it open.

Henry called out, "Is anyone here? I was sent by Marvin. Ollie-ollie-oxen-free."

There was no answer. His voice echoed through the cold, damp air. "Echooooo." Henry heard his voice ricochet through the darkness. Smiling, he yelled again, "AVON CALLING." Henry hesitantly wandered into the castle. He saw a light coming from a room across the entryway from the door. *Ahhhh, must be where the madam of the house is.*

Looking in, he saw a huge fireplace with a dwindling fire. The room was warm and Henry's freezing bones ached. He called out again, "Is there anyone here? I am no threat; I am just a commoner from town. I brought my money for the weekend special." Again there was no answer.

Well this sucks. I go to a brothel and it is closed. Just my luck. Henry was hesitant but the fire was warm. He tossed in a few logs by the fireplace and poked at the fire to get it flaming again. Henry turned around and warmed his ass. He finally got out of his wet coat and leather shoes and sat in the large chair in front of the fireplace.

His large belly gurgled and growled. He reached into his coat he had set beside the chair and grabbed his metal flask. He turned it over and the last few drops of rum trickled onto his dry lips. Beside the chair he saw a large loaf of bread that had been broken and a cup of honey. He was starving and couldn't help but eat the entire loaf. Now his belly was full, his bones were warm and he could relax. Another rumbling echoed through Henry's stomach and he lifted up and farted loudly. The fart echoed through the room, making Henry laugh and made the fire brighten a little. A contented Henry sat in the chair and drifted away to sleep.

* * * * *

Betty became worried because her father hadn't come back from the other village yet. She knew the long night might have delayed him but he usually found his way back by now. Betty had a tendency to worry about her father. The fact that he was an idiot didn't help matters. Her mother had died when she was very young and Betty vowed to take care of her father.

The only problem with that was the fact that she had no life outside her father's house. She did most of the chores and rarely had time for anything except an occasional conversation in town while shopping. Her father was her life and she was afraid of losing him.

Of course, now the burden of taking care of her father would be gone and she could do all the things she wanted. Party time, medieval style. Her dreams of being a singer at the local pub could be a reality. She could yodel better than most and thoughts of the stage and bright candles made her smile. The fancy dresses, the men drooling over her cleavage. Having a real man ravage her nightly for a dollar.

Who was she kidding? She couldn't sing and only yodeled to get the sheep to come for food. Her life sucked more than a fish on dry land.

The first light from the sun caressed the fresh snow, making the powder glow. Knowing his usual path, Betty set out to find her father.

* * * * *

Dreams of women danced through Henry's dreams as he felt his groin being massaged. Half awake, he noticed both his hands were in his pockets. *Mmmmm, I guess the ladies of the house are back from their trip.* He peeked open his eye and saw a large Rottweiler nuzzling his groin and humping his leg.

Henry whacked the dog's nose, which then thrust into his nuts, and the dog scurried off. "Ohhhhhh, I didn't need this. Where the hell am I?" He got up slowly and followed the dog down a long dark hallway. The thumping of a hangover made his eyes squint shut. *That's the last time I do that, until next month.*

The doors were scarred with claw marks. There were no mirrors and a few paintings of a stunning family hung on the walls. There was an oil painting hung with a golden frame on a long bare wall. Henry looked up at it, seeing a handsome man standing strong with an enormous bulge in his breeches. *He must have been very popular*, he thought.

Henry held his head with one hand and tried opening doorknobs with the other. One door at the end of the hall was open and a dim light flickered inside. Henry saw a candle on a nightstand. There was a large bed torn apart. A gold watch and a shiny, golden rod shimmered on the table next to a jar of oils. *Damn, somebody had fun in here.* He picked up the golden rod and it was slippery and warm. There was a golden goblet filled with a red liquid resting by the candle.

Hmmmmm, interesting, Henry thought as he sniffed at the liquid. *Wine...this is what I call being too good to be true.* And he took a mouthful of the bounty of wine.

The door burst open and Henry spewed the wine all over the small table; the candle went out.

Henry stared at a dark figure. It was an enormously large, animalistic beast. The Beast snarled and he began to speak. "I let you stay in my house and you take advantage of my hospitality and try to steal from me," the Beast growled. Its breath was foul and smelled of onions. (It must have just eaten lunch.)

"I...I...I was just looking..." Henry cringed as the Beast leaped toward him. Terrified, Henry closed his eyes and didn't dare look at the hideous Beast. Smelling his onion breath, Henry's eyes began to water.

"Did you plan to pay me for what you have stolen? NO, you were just going to steal from me and go. Just like the others." The Beast's voice cracked and he seemed somber for a brief moment.

"I will find a way to repay you. I am a commoner. I don't have much, but what I have is yours. Just spare my life." Henry was now sober and desperate.

"For this crime, you must die. You have violated my secret sanctuary." The Beast raised his large hand and his razor-sharp claws protruded out.

A voice echoed from the hallway. The Beast glared at the door and watched a woman's silhouette lean in slowly.

"Father? Are you here?" the small voice asked.

Henry, recognizing the voice, pushed the Beast aside and ran out screaming, "Betty, you must leave this place!" He tripped and fell across the wooden floor.

Betty ran to her father, hunched on the floor, and saw the terror in his eyes. "What is wrong?"

The Beast's deep, throaty voice growled from the darkness. "He tried to steal from me, so he shall die! He cannot repay his debt. His crime..."

"My father would never steal from you. He..."

The Beast's loud, thunderous roar echoed through the empty house. Betty and her father huddled, scared.

Terrified she might lose her father, Betty asked in a desperate plea, "If I stay here and be your servant to work off his debt, will you let him go?"

Henry shook his head. "NO, BETTY, you can't."

"I won't let you die. At least I have a chance to help you," she said, holding her father's hand.

"Are you pure of spirit?"

"Yes."

"Are you pure of heart and will vow to stay?"

"Yes."

"Are you pure of body, and your womb untarnished by a man?"

"Yes."

"Then I accept your offer to stay with me for one year," the Beast growled from the darkness. "Now say farewell to your father. He must leave."

Betty stared out the window at her father leaving, not sure if and when she'd see him again. To her, it was worth it. She had saved his life. Also, now, at least, she would be in the world and not stuck in that house. Of course now she was stuck in the Beast's house so there wasn't much difference except the geography.

Chapter 3

ജ

Time passed and Betty honored her vow and stayed with the Beast. Her nineteenth birthday came and went and she started to feel lonesome for her father and her few friends.

Afraid to reveal himself during the day, the Beast stayed hidden in the castle. At night he would come out and talk to Betty from the shadows. Betty didn't mind so much because the Beast never demanded more from her than to cook and clean his house. He was very smart but was in desperate need of some mouthwash and cologne. There was a mystery to this Beast that Betty wanted to discover.

After a long day picking fruit, sweeping the kitchen and various other chores, Betty felt dirty and needed to cleanse herself. She boiled some water and took the washtub to her room and undressed. Her body ached and a nice warm washing would soothe her muscles.

Betty stood naked on the towel and dipped the sponge in the warm water from the dresser. She set it above her bosom and squeezed it. Like a waterfall, it trickled down her body, off of her curves. Her breasts stood full and she relaxed in the sanctuary of her bath. She took the slippery bar of soap in her hand and followed the shape of her body. It slid under the crease of her breasts and her cleavage. She sighed and squeezed the sponge on her chest again, letting herself breathe with the flow of water.

Her baths had become her only solace for the yearning to find love. This was her time to feel free and like a woman. Self-pleasure wasn't supposed to be talked about or pursued, but this was what brought her pleasure.

She soaped up her hand and wiped the foam onto her tummy. Her motion became a small circle, ever widening. She touched the fuzz above her pubis, making her gasp. Widening her stance on the towel, she dipped the sponge in the water and pressed the dripping sponge on her tummy and squeezed out the water. It flowed through the hair of her pubis and between the lips of her already wet pussy. She squeezed the sponge again, making the water wash over her. The water couldn't extinguish the fire burning within her, though.

Betty's eyes closed and she began to rub her pubis with the rough, wet sponge. Her other hand found her breast and she squeezed it in her palm. The excitement made her nipples protrude and become taut, begging for her attention. Her thumb and forefinger plucked at her nipple, causing her to shudder. The sponge was between her legs and Betty became lost in the flickering darkness of the room. The candle was only casting enough light for her to see the gleam of water upon her skin.

She reached to the table and picked up the razor to trim her full bush of hair. The sharp razor reflected the flickering candlelight while she drew it against her tender flesh. Small strands of hair fell to her feet as the straight edge cut through her thick pubic hair but never pierced her skin.

A cold chill swept through her body. She felt someone staring at her. She shivered and the hair on her neck stood on end. The straight edge of the razor was against her pubis. Her arm became stiff and tense, ready to lash out if someone moved toward her through the shadows. Her fear was causing her to shake and she dropped the razor as it cut her. She wiped the small spot of blood from the cut and sucked it off of her fingertip. She heard a whimpering sound and looked into the mirror above the dresser. She saw the reflection of deep, darkened red eyes. She gasped and the figure scurried down the hall.

Oh my God, it was the Beast. Thoughts raced in her mind.

How long had he stood there amongst the shadows watching her cleaning herself? Did it have an effect on him? Why did the thought of him watching her stir emotions and a deep aching burn between her legs? Why was she talking to herself?

Betty picked up the razor and finished shaving. Her pussy was now wet with arousal from thoughts that the Beast had seen her naked and exposed. True, he was a Beast. But beneath that exterior, she believed, beat the heart of a man.

Betty rinsed herself off and slipped into her nightshirt. She still felt a little uncomfortable that someone had seen her bathing. How many times had he watched her? Why didn't he ever tell her? The questions kept popping in her head. She couldn't leave because she gave her word she wouldn't.

Betty needed answers.

She quietly opened the large wooden door and peeked into the candlelit hallway. Only the low tone of the wind outside could be heard in the darkness. Betty felt scared and aroused by her search for answers.

The doors in the hallway were all locked as she tried each one when she passed. Around a small bend a flicker of light could be seen from a single open door.

Betty tiptoed closer and heard a panting sound like that of a dog after a long run. The closer she got to the door, the louder the panting. Straining to listen, Betty could hear a muttering voice breaking the panting.

"Yeah, baby, yeah…who's your Beast, yeah, baby." The panting was followed by a deep rumbling growl.

Trying to be quiet, but desperate to see, Betty pushed the door slightly wider. In a mirror on the wall she could see a silhouette of the Beast with his head thrown back. The room was dark except for the flickering candle on the floor by the door.

Her eyes focused on the Beast's reflection and she could see his hands frantically tugging between his legs.

"Yeah, Betty, you know you want me. Come on, mmm, grrrrrr."

The words shocked Betty but she felt herself cream as she realized what the Beast was doing.

She stepped forward onto something wet and slipped. Falling into the bathroom she fell flat on her face and in front of the Beast. Her candle fell to the floor with a crash and went out. All Betty saw was a large pair of hairy feet. She reached up to grab something to pull herself upright. She found a long handle and pulled on it to get up.

"Ouch!" the Beast grunted.

Betty felt the handle she had in her hand and followed it to where it was based. It was attached to the Beast. It was a very long, stiff handle. The texture caused Betty to cream between her thighs because she may have been in a dumb situation, but she wasn't stupid. Swallowing, she fought the impulse to jerk the handle and never let go.

Scooting back, all Betty saw was the dimly outlined Beast with his hair bristled and standing on end from the candlelight behind him. His eyes were burning red as he stared at her.

Quickly grabbing a towel, he covered himself.

Trying to get a better look, Betty squinted in the darkness. She saw the white towel hanging over the Beast's handle and stopped her own primal instinct to ask if he needed a hand.

"WHAT ARE YOU DOING HERE?" the Beast growled.

Thinking quickly, she said, "I, ummm, I needed to go to the restroom."

Betty thought about grabbing the towel but turned to get away. She never saw the door. It had swung partially closed and Betty hit it full force. Blinking a few times, the stars from the pain in her nose cleared. Betty's nose began to bleed and she started to cry.

Seeing her cry and her nose beginning to bleed more, the Beast handed her his towel and stood dumbfounded and naked again. He took the standard male stance of cupping his genitals and tried to smile.

Betty, embarrassed and humiliated, ran down the dark hallway.

Closing her bedroom door, Betty half-heartedly wanted to go back to confront the Beast. Could he have the same feelings for her that she was beginning to feel for him? Why did he have to have both hands to cover himself? Did a Beast's cock look like a man's cock? Could she have sauerkraut and wieners for dinner?

The Beast was aroused. He was desperate, swollen, and thought if he wasn't careful with his claws, he'd break it. His mind was a storm of emotions. He wanted to vanquish the inner monster growing within him. All the primal thoughts of Betty naked and being ravaged spun like a tornado in his head.

He found himself fantasizing about being with her. Instinctively his hand found the girth of his cock and he slowly began stroking himself like in his dream, where he was sliding within Betty's pussy. Long, deep penetrating thrusts into her sweet, pure body.

"Mmmmmm, Beasty like." A wicked smile crossed the Beast's lips and his fangs were bared as he panted. "Has Betty been a naughty little slave?"

"Ouch, too fast! Damn friction burns." The Beast looked around and found some oil to pour in his palm. The green oil made his warm palm soft and extremely slippery. When he gripped his cock in his hand his vision returned and he could feel the wetness of Betty's hot pussy wrapped tightly around him. Except for the scratching from the tips of his claw.

"Oh Betty, be mine, be mine." The Beast frantically stroked his thickening cock in his hand. "Mmmmm, I didn't know you could move like that." The Beast took his other hand and made a tunnel. His hips were thrusting as he stood masturbating like a wild animal. Actually he was a wild animal masturbating, but that isn't relevant. Anyway, his mind saw Betty roll over, and like most animals, the Beast grabbed her hips and plunged into her doggy style.

"Oh god. This is it."

The Beast envisioned Betty in a submissive state. Bent before him, his rigid abdomen slapping against her tight ass, giving in to his desires. The Beast's eyes closed tight and his hands were vigorously stroking his length. He was freeing himself. A loud howl ricocheted through the castle as the Beast relieved the passion swollen in his heart.

His seed burst from his loins as he bent his knees. Like an elephant's trunk his cock whipped around, spewing seed on the wall, the mirror, across his Beastboy magazine and on his feet.

When the volcano subsided, the Beast let his cock free from his hand. A feeling of relief caressed his body. Except for his cock. It began to burn and ache. His hands also began to burn.

Hurriedly, the Beast rinsed his hands in the water basin. The bowl had fresh water and it didn't seem to help the burn. It only made bubbles. The Beast grabbed the basin and doused his groin, trying to cool the pain. It just made bubbles.

He grabbed the oil he used to smooth his hands and read it in the dim light. For use on bathroom soap scum.

The howls of pain could be heard everywhere.

Chapter 4

ಎ

The next morning Betty sat quietly eating her blueberry muffin and sipping tea. She turned the page in her book and sighed. Looking out the large window, Betty began to wonder how her father was.

The castle was secluded and she never talked to anyone, except the Beast at night. She was lonely.

She glanced toward the kitchen door and saw the shadow of something moving under it. A letter was shoved under the door and it scooted across the slick floor.

She heard the loud thumping of someone running up the stairs.

Stepping over to the door, Betty kneeled down and picked up the letter. Out of curiosity she opened the door to look toward the stairs. Outside was a small pot of flowers. They were all the colors of the rainbow, and the bright spectrum was a treat to the eyes. Betty leaned down to pick the pot up and a bee flew out of one of the purple flowers and buzzed all around her head. In a futile effort Betty swatted at it, banged her head on the swinging door and flopped onto her butt. The pot of flowers fell across her lap and the bee victoriously flew out the window.

Now in a puddle of mud with wildflowers scattered around her, Betty just shrugged and opened the letter she still held firmly in her hand.

The paper was a parchment color and she smelled it, breathing in the scent of the fresh ink.

To Betty,

I am sorry about last evening. I was overwhelmed by the thought of seeing you. I was wrong to watch you bathing. My actions were that of a man becoming desperate and because being so close to you all the time has made me think about you more when we are apart.

Beneath this hideous exterior, I am still a man.

Please accept this arrangement of wildflowers I picked from the garden as an apology. Be careful of the purple flowers, the bees like them because their nectar is so sweet.

Just like you.

Beast

Betty sat back against the wall, warmed by the apology and the compassion of the Beast. For a single moment she was truly happy at the castle.

She reached into her lap, took two handfuls of flowers and nuzzled her face into them, breathing in the freshness.

Later that night Betty sat by the fire knitting. The room was dark except for the firelight. Quietly knocking, the Beast peeked in.

"May I come in?"

"Of cowse you can. Pweese do," Betty replied.

The Beast stepped into the room and looked at Betty smiling at him.

"Oh my, what happened to your nose?" the Beast asked, seeing her left nostril red and swollen.

"Ther wath a bee in tha fwowers. I tuk a big snff an it fwew up my nowse."

* * * * *

A few days passed and the Beast was cordial and polite. Embarrassed by being caught watching her bathe and then relieving his urgent needs, the Beast seemed content with just being friends with Betty.

Deep down his urges and his desires built again. He wanted to possess her. His cravings were an inferno of animalistic urges spawning thoughts of ravaging and devouring her purity with his brute force.

She was a deer and he was a lion. *No,* he thought, she was more like a rabbit and he was a cheetah. Actually a rabbit wasn't right either. She was the beauty to his Beast.

He was driving himself crazy. Constant thoughts of carnal pleasures to free him of his curse flew through his mind. He wanted Betty badly, knowing that he couldn't force her to give in to his wants because it wouldn't be right. *Maybe during her sleep? Noooo, I can't, it would be wrong. Damn, I am horny. Why am I talking to myself?*

Betty lay sleeping peacefully in her bed. The drapes from the window swayed with the incoming breeze. The moonlight shone into the room. Betty was lying on her side and her nightshirt had crept up her torso. Her ass was revealed and the long length of her legs was covered in goose bumps from the coldness of the wind. She rolled onto her back and pulled the covers over her pure body.

From the darkened shadows a large figure crept toward her. His massive frame shadowed the light from the moon on her body. A large claw grasped the blankets and slowly tugged them down to reveal her pristine frame. She was naked beneath the nightshirt and her nipples were affected by the cold and poked into the green fabric. Her trimmed pussy was tightly encased between her legs, like a treasure chest waiting to be opened. The Beast reached out with his claws, placed his hairy palms on her knees and gently pulled them apart. He revealed the wondrous beauty of her virgin sanctum.

A deep growl echoed through the room when the Beast saw her labia open. Her inner pink flesh was so pure to the sight that it made the Beast melt. It also made him so aroused his cock swelled in his pants, looking like a third arm. It pointed at what he wanted. He carefully kneeled down, over her lower torso. His nostrils flared as he breathed in her scent deeply, filling his lungs. His fangs were bare, as he wanted to devour the feast before him. He was torn between the desire to ravage this woman or to admire and relish the sight of her. He knew he had to have her love him freely to release him from his curse.

His desires were becoming more desperate. The Beast lowered his face between her legs and let his long tongue trace the opening of her pussy, just soft enough to not awaken her. Her taste was from heaven. *MMMMM, tastes like chicken.* He closed his eyes and licked her again. A soft moan arose from Betty as she smiled and seemed to be in a blissful dream. Hidden by the clouds, the moon disappeared and the room became black. In the darkness the Beast swept over her pussy again with his tongue. Betty was asleep and moaned again. Her taste was succulent and the Beast savored the sweetness of her. His eyes burned red, as his fury became overwrought in passion. His breathing became more of a growl and his tongue drooled over his meal as he drew deeper, piercing her opening and tasting the juice flowing from within her.

Betty moaned and opened her eyes. She sat up and saw nothing. In the blackened shadows the Beast hid against the wall. Betty wiped her forehead as she sweated. "What a dream," she said. Her pussy was wet and she cupped it in her hand. The clouds cleared as the Beast stood motionless in the corner against the wall. Betty lay back and pulled her nightshirt to her neck. Her breasts were full and she breathed deeply. Her fingers tugged at the lips of her pussy and her other hand cupped her breast.

The Beast became increasingly aroused by the vision he was seeing as Betty massaged and pleasured herself before his eyes. Her fingers burrowed deep within the pink flesh of her pussy. The juices from her passion glistened on her labia and the Beast stared helplessly as she slid her fingers between the lips and groaned.

Feeling safe in the darkness, Betty embraced her lust. Overtaking her in the hidden confinement of her upbringing, she needed to free this fury of frustration. Her eyes tearing with her strain to keep them shut, she imagined her true love feeling her inside. Betty's fingers became his in her mind, probing her. The hardening bud of her sex rose and she rubbed it with her thumb. She put her fingertips in her mouth, tasting her own juice, then rubbed again at the sensitive bud.

The Beast stood silent but his hunger was causing him problems, as was the large bulge in his pants. This woman was the one to free him from the spell trapping him inside this shell of a Beast. Turning toward the door, the Beast's swollen protrusion in his pants knocked the candlestick holder off the small table.

Gasping and oblivious to everything except her pleasure, Betty stroked harder inside of her pussy and pinched her nipples. Her peak of passion approached and she panted. Almost crying, she was consumed with need. The need to let go. Her cry echoed through the room as she came. Her body tightened and stretched. Every muscle enjoyed the bliss of her letting loose her tensions.

A gust of wind swept by Betty as the Beast burst out the open windows to the balcony. He tripped over a small cement birdbath then stumbled over the railing and fell off the ledge into the large sycamore tree. Like a pinball machine he ricocheted from branch to branch until falling astride a large one, causing extreme pain to shoot through his groin area. A tear filled his large red eye and he fell onto the patio with a loud THUD in a crumpled lump. "That's gonna leave a mark," he grunted as he crawled back inside.

Betty pulled the blankets up, rolled over onto her side and enjoyed the refreshing feeling wrapping her in a blanket of relaxation. She gazed out the window at the full moon and heard a loud echoing howl through the castle. Must be the wind, she thought to herself, drifting into a restful sleep.

The Beast hunched in his bed growling. He sat hidden under the blankets, panting and mumbling to himself.

"Yeah baby, that's it, use the feather duster, grrrrr, not there, over here, whoooooooo, ROAR."

The Beast pulled the blankets off his head and tossed a towel against the wall where it stuck. He, too, drifted into a restful sleep.

Chapter 5

ℬ

The Beast was becoming more and more torn by his desires for Betty and his fear of the unknown. Animalistic thoughts crossed his mind as he walked along an abandoned road outside the fences of his land.

His daydreams again turned to the nights he watched Betty sleep, bathe, go to the bathroom, watched her eating bananas. He scratched himself, feeling the urge to adjust his other Beast. He had found some wildflowers that were supposedly aphrodisiacs. An old mythology book he read spoke of them. He had spent weeks making the potion. He patted it in all the appropriate areas, only to have himself break out in a nasty rash. That alone was bad enough, but the damn scent attracted fleas.

His walk became an adventure in scratching. From the scratching of his head to the scratching of his...well...other head. Frustration was taking over. He was lost in his life and just needed something to show him the way. Some kind of light. *A light,* the Beast thought as he looked through the darkness to see a shimmering light behind a row of trees.

The darkness hid the Beast and his large hulking frame. He could make out the faint sound of voices from the direction of the light. Slowly and cautiously he moved toward the sounds.

The Beast spotted a black carriage parked in a small opening of some trees. A horse was grazing, and flickering lamplight illuminated from the front of the carriage. He heard a woman's voice, followed by a seductive moan. Raising an eyebrow, the Beast smiled and stepped toward the rear of the carriage.

Wincing in pain the Beast's eyes bugged out and he stifled a howl from stepping on the sharp edge of a rock. When he stepped back, eyes closed, he dared not scream but a coolness beneath his foot eased his pain. He opened his eyes and looked down, noticing he was standing in a pool of horse urine. The Beast looked skyward and mouthed, *WHY ME?*

Now determined to scare the prowlers off of his land, the Beast walked to the back of the carriage and with the prowess of a lion, bared his claws, hunched his back upward and gazed into the carriage window.

A glistening crossed over his reddened eyes and he stood motionless as he stared into the carriage.

There was a couple in the carriage. The Beast didn't recognize them but they were Betty's friends, Charlotte and Jacob, out for a midnight romp.

Charlotte lay back in the carriage, arms across the red leather seat and her brunette hair scattered across her neck and burning, pink flesh on her chest. The Beast stood frozen in his stance, watching Charlotte glow. She radiated the heat of a blazing fire and when Jacob pulled her corset open her full breasts almost burst free.

Drool slid down the Beast's chin while he stood watching. Jacob groped at her breasts and his groans enhanced her pleasure. His mouth encompassed her taut nipples one by one. They were deep red and erect.

The Beast remembered seeing Betty's breasts when she was masturbating in her bed and he too longed to feed on their fullness. The dreams he had of Betty were now in front of his eyes as the loving couple gave in to their passions among the darkness of the woods.

Charlotte turned her head to the side and moaned while Jacob kissed her shoulder blade and pressed his hands firmly to her breasts. Their bounty filled his palms and Charlotte grabbed Jacob's face and kissed him deeply. Her hunger was overwhelming as her need for Jacob was more passionate and urgent. Their tongues danced in each other's mouths.

Jacob was about to lose control. He stood up and clunked his head on the carriage's low roof. He stood hunched over and fought with the buttons, fasteners and other gazillion layers of clothing he had on.

Charlotte rested her hand on his. With an appreciative look in her eyes, she gently unfastened the last button and set him free.

The Beast stood, shocked by Jacob's size. He looked down at his, then up to Jacob's erect cock and thought, *hmmm, I guess men are small compared to a beast.*

Charlotte pulled her skirt up and Jacob grabbed each of her legs. He smiled wickedly at her and a gleam of naughtiness crossed Charlotte's face. Jacob caressed up her legs to her undergarment. The material was sheer and damp from her excitement and Jacob gently pulled them off of her pale thighs.

Charlotte bit her bottom lip and winked at Jacob while he teased at her ankles with his tongue.

When the underwear was finally to her feet, Jacob nuzzled them to his nose and made a growling sound.

The Beast also made a growling sound. It was his stomach.

Falling forward, Jacob leaned into Charlotte's waiting pussy. His cock sunk deeply until the base of his shaft rested against the wet labia. For a second they both lay motionless, enjoying the feeling of their mutual bliss. Charlotte sighed and Jacob groaned. This was their heaven.

Like a key opening a door, Jacob unlocked the sensual being trapped inside Charlotte. He kept putting his key in over and over again.

The Beast couldn't help but be aroused by this couple's total abandon. They intrigued his emotions and while he stood like a perverse animal, watching the two of them make passionate love, he kept thinking about Betty. How, instead of Jacob and Charlotte becoming enthralled in passion, it could be him and Betty.

Creeping closer and closer, the Beast dared to see more of the couple. He stood behind the carriage and looked inside the rear window.

Jacob's back was bowed and the Beast saw Charlotte's fingers digging into his sweaty flesh. Jacob began to groan and the Beast could see Charlotte smiling.

With powerful thrusts, Jacob began to hammer into Charlotte, causing her to gasp for air. Her fingers groped at his back and his hair.

"Oh, oh Jacob, this is it. Oh Jacob, harder, harder. Say my name, say my name," Charlotte begged.

"What?" Jacob asked.

"She said she wants you to say her name," the Beast replied.

* * * * *

There are moments in time where you lose track of what is going on and where you are. This was one of those moments.

Charlotte's eyes opened wide and she screamed in horror as she saw a big furry face with its tongue dangling out of its mouth, looking at her and Jacob making love.

Jacob groaned and sighed, oblivious to the Beast, and spilt his seed into Charlotte.

"Oh, dear, that was fantastic when you tightened your muscles around me like that and screamed."

Jacob saw the look of horror on Charlotte's face and he turned his head around to see the Beast bumping his head on the carriage ledge and running away.

Embarrassed and horny, the Beast turned to see if they were chasing him. He abruptly ran into a tree branch, tripped

over that damn sharp rock and fell face first into the horse piss.
This was another one of those moments you don't forget.

Chapter 6

❧

The days turned to weeks, and weeks to…well, months. The Beast let Betty see more and more of the things he held dear to his heart.

His collection of animals he had killed and stuffed. The hundreds of books he had in his library. He told her of his love of painting and blindfolded her before revealing the portrait he had done of her.

"What do you think?" he asked, reluctant and afraid she would hate it.

"Oh, it is beautiful. Ummm, I see where you did this as a night pose while I was in bed. But, ummm, what is that right there on my thigh?"

"I took the liberty of adding to it. That's my tongue."

"I see, and are my breasts really THAT large?" Betty raised an eyebrow, knowing she had caught the Beast in an awkward situation.

"Ummmm, you want to go, ummmm, get something for supper?"

They became friends on the night shift. He would appear from his room in the darkness of night, not wanting to frighten Betty with his hideous appearance. They would talk in darkened rooms with just a fire burning.

Betty told him of her childhood and growing up with her father after her mother passed away from a freak accident with a horse and buggy. She had been checking something under the horse and had spooked it, and the carriage ran her over. She was led to believe her mother was checking the horse for a hernia.

The Beast was becoming more and more comfortable with Betty, and their dark talks became a necessity. He was being drawn to her. He wanted to be with her. His palms were becoming hairier than they already were because of his longing to be with Betty in the flesh.

The Beast finally felt it was time to tell Betty of his curse.

He summoned up all his courage and began.

"Betty…I want to tell you something. I need to tell you. I was cursed by a witch a long time ago. Because of this curse I am forced to remain in this form until I find true love and consummate my heart, body and soul."

"Body and soul?" Betty asked.

"Ummmm, you know, ummm, I have to be with someone."

"You mean WITH someone?" she said, raising an eyebrow.

"Yes, I need to consummate my love. I do truly have deep feelings for you, Betty, but am not sure how to go about asking you to free me from this curse. If you free me, I shall return the favor and free you from your vow to stay with me."

"So you will come and I can go?" Betty didn't realize the pun in her statement.

She sat dumbfounded and apprehensive. Betty was still technically a virgin and wasn't sure having a monster deflower her was what she had always imagined her first time to be like. All of her dreams and fantasies were of a handsome knight in shining armor to save her and all the other trite, rehashed fairy tales. She had saved her flower for her true love. Of course, having a massive, muscular, raging Beast take her would be a good over-the-fence story back in town.

"Let me see you," she asked. "Then I will decide."

The Beast stood up and his enormous figure moved toward Betty while she sat before the fire. She stared at his figure as he came into the light. Gasping, she saw the face of a man hidden by hair. He had a mane like a lion. His hair was thick and wavy and hung over his eyes and face. He pulled his cape aside, revealing his massive upper torso. He was a mountain of a man.

Hubba, hubba, Betty thought.

With his claws, he shredded his shirt, exposing his chest.

She saw the muscles of his chest and abdomen flexing beneath a thin fur. Most men have six-pack abs. He had a twelve-pack. She licked her lips. "Let me see all of you," she said, clearing her throat.

Turning away from her, the Beast hunched over and tugged at the strings holding his pants up and pulled them down his hairy legs.

Betty sat staring at the flexing muscles on his legs and butt. Warmth filled her veins. The Beast's immense size and his pure animalistic prowess were arousing her. She gulped and a nervous twitch began to cause her lip to move like Elvis.

He turned to face Betty and she sat mesmerized. Her eyelids fluttered and her upper lip spasmed uncontrollably. All the blood in her body rushed to her groin area, causing a burn. She blinked and tried to speak. "Whhhhahahhhttttt is ttthhhhhaaaatatt?" she stammered.

She had seen other men's penises. Her father in the shower, a few boys skinny-dipping at the lake and, of course, her times in the barn with Ralph. Even *she* knew this was huge. It was like that of a horse or a small elephant. This was truly...a BEAST!

"Why is your penis green?" she asked.

"I had an accident in the bathroom."

After a few seconds of contemplating the Beast's offer...she agreed. "Oh hell yes!"

* * * * *

Betty sat up and slowly pulled her dress up over her head. She didn't wear much except underpants and a thin shirt. Lying back on the rug before the fire, she reached out to the Beast. She was an angel before his eyes.

He knelt before her and stared as she pulled her shirt over her head, revealing her bosom. The fire illuminated her body in a deep orange color. A canvas of color, brushed into a masterpiece of art. His eyes moved down to her underwear.

With his claw he pulled gently at the waistband. The sharpness of his claw cut through the fabric. They fell loose from her and he saw that for which he longed. A shaven patch of hair nested the fruit he desired. Her pubis was fresh and the pale skin made him drool.

He leaned forward between her legs and breathed in her scent. He remembered her taste and he whimpered, wanting to taste her again. Betty closed her eyes and opened her legs to him. A drop of saliva drooled from his mouth as he lowered to eat her. His large tongue spread her labia apart and he dipped his tongue into her. He closed his eyes, wanting to sink his fangs into this feast of flesh before him. Betty held back her need to scream in pleasure. She was so hot her body wanted to burst from her skin. She pulled at her breast and stroked the Beast's mane of hair as he ate her. She could feel his bare fangs sliding against her outer labia. His dense tongue lapped up her juices like wine and he seemed thirsty for more. Betty squirmed and wiggled when his hair tickled her inner thighs.

"Come up here, please," she begged. "I want to feel you inside me."

The Beast licked up her stomach and body with his large tongue. He encompassed her entire nipple and breast with his mouth. She could feel his fangs poking on her breast but didn't care. Betty grasped his large forearms as he raised his body above her. He looked so powerful. He was the king of beasts.

The tip of his enormous cock was pressing against her opening and a fear crossed Betty's mind. *How would she handle this monster inside of her? What would he feel like? Was he going to hurt her?* For a minute she wanted to stop. She looked up to say something and he sank into her tight pussy. The stretching caused her to dig her nails into his arm and scream with pleasure. Her inner walls were filled beyond full. The massive size of this Beast's cock stretched her flesh and the friction was too much for her to handle. He opened up everything in her like a doorway to sin as she came. Her body shook and she felt like she was being split apart.

The Beast tried to pull back but she frantically grabbed at his ribs, wanting more. His hair hung over his face and dangled in Betty's eyes as he plunged deeply into her again. She held her cries back as the pain mixed with the incredible pleasure from the thickness expanding her opening. Her exposed clit was being rubbed by the rigid hardness of his cock against it.

The veins in his arms bulged as the hot blood flowed through his body. He dug his feet into the carpet to give him more thrust as his urges started taking control. The wet warmth of her wrapped around his cock, and made him want this moment in time to last forever. He felt like a man instead of this massive beast. Betty was his destiny and this act of sheer passion would release him from the bondage of his curse.

The Beast growled and he dug his claws into the rug below them. His body slammed against Betty in a brutal rage of lust. She felt the tension within him building. She reached her hand to his cheek and rubbed his face.

The Beast stared into Betty's eyes. In them he saw the doorway to his soul. She made him whole. A tear filled his eye and his body vibrated and flexed. His teeth were bared and he growled loudly. Betty tightened her inner walls, gripping the thickening shaft within her. Her body elevated as she arched her back. She slipped into the oblivion of the orgasm that swept over her.

The Beast stopped, straining upward, and drove deep into Betty and erupted. The hot seed from him burned and filled her. She felt his cock pulse over and over with his essence creeping out of her aching pussy. His chest pounded with the beat of his heart and he rested against her and smiled.

For a second they both felt free. Then reality set in and they looked at each other in bewilderment. The Beast was still a beast. They both sat up. The Beast asked Betty, "I wonder why I didn't change back?"

"Well, what was supposed to happen?" she asked.

"After I had consummated my love with a pure woman I would change back to my original form." He reached up and pointed to a painting above the fireplace to a scrawny man wearing spectacles and having bad teeth. "That is my original form," the Beast said.

"Oh…well, when you said pure, what does that mean?"

"Untouched by another man."

"Hmmmm, well…does anal sex count?"

Epilogue

ဢ

The mail arrived and Henry went to get the weekly delivery. The cold wind rustled through the trees. Henry opened the box down the road from his farm. Inside he found some old time junk mail from a local store. There was also a letter from Betty.

Henry was so excited that he tore into the letter to see the news about his daughter.

Dearest Daddy,

Things are fine here. We just added a new wing onto the castle and I did some decorating renovations. The Beast says hello. He has been doing great and he is on his way to the store to buy diapers and get me some more wine. The kids are fine. All eight of them are doing well but my nipples are killing me. The Beast says he'd like to have some more kids but my body can't handle carrying another litter of beast-pups.

Betty

About the Author

ဆ

S.L. Carpenter is a born and raised California man. He does both writing and cover art for novels as outlets for his overactive libido and twisted mind. His inspiration is his wife, who keeps him well trained. Writing is his true joy. It gives him freedom and expression for both his sensual and humorous sides.

S.L. Carpenter welcomes comments from readers. You can find his website and email address on his author bio page at www.ellorascave.com.

Tell Us What You Think

We appreciate hearing reader opinions about our books. You can email us at Comments@EllorasCave.com.

DEADLINE
Marly Chance

౭ఠ

Chapter One

 જી

Ryan O'Roarke listened to the shrill voice on the other end of the phone and resisted the urge to bash his head against his desk until he lost consciousness. It had been a very long day in a very long work week. *Ugggghhh.* At thirty-eight, he was getting too old for this crap. He kept his voice reasonable despite the jackhammer currently operating with demonic glee behind his eyes. "Jillian, I'm at work, remember? I have a newspaper to get out. I'm sorry but I can't talk to you about this now. I'm not part of an evil media corporate mentality bent on oppression and manipulation of the masses. I'm an editor. I do it because I'm good at it and I have bills to pay and a parrot to feed. And I'm going to be unemployed if I don't get off the phone."

Jillian's voice rose higher and Ryan looked at the clock on the wall to his right with growing impatience. His ex-lover had somehow slipped over the line from hostility to outright lunacy after their breakup, despite all of his efforts to let her down easy. He rubbed his forehead and talked over her. "I'm hanging up the phone now, Jillian. Take care. Goodbye." Hating to do it, but knowing he had no choice, he placed the receiver back into the cradle gently.

He scrubbed his hand over his face, wondering how he could possibly feel guilty over a breakup that had taken place four months ago. Jillian had left him with almost zero choice with her increasingly unstable behavior. And he ought to be tougher with her. He was an *editor* for goodness sakes. He should be able to cut people cold...and yet he found he just couldn't do it. He scowled.

He was getting perilously close to having his good guy personality come to light. If that happened, the next thing you knew, his reporters would be in his office telling him that he was a sensitive, caring boss—right to his face, no less. He scowled harder just as his ace reporter, Agnes, marched into his office.

She was in her sixties and the term "battle-ax" had been invented with her as the prototype. As she returned his scowl with one of her own, Ryan wondered briefly if she could kick his ass in a fight and figured she probably would any minute. Of course, then she'd write a great story on it later and at least he'd have page three done. She was one hellava reporter. Probably boxed middleweight, too.

She pronounced with all the sunny personality of a marine drill sergeant, "The county commissioners are *idiots*. They voted 5-3 last night that the proper spelling of the word 'commission' is with one 's', not two."

Ryan tried to find a logical explanation for that remark but could find none. "They're finally bucking Webster's evil dictionary empire and striking a blow for the freedom of spelling?"

She gave him a glare as if he was in agreement with the notion. "We need a coup. I could write a decent story on a political coup. It's hard for me to write an intelligent article when the commission's collective IQ is less than the total number of members in the group. I need a raise."

Ryan muttered, "I need an aspirin," right as his second reporter, Grace, walked into his office. He glared at her. "Doesn't anybody knock anymore? Hello?"

Grace smiled her bright zealot smile at him, her eyes flashing with excitement. "Hello! You won't believe my story! People should know this, Ryan! It's important! I think it's *definitely* page one material!"

Ryan winced, knowing where this was leading. "Tell me it has nothing to do with Humans for Humanity." The organization was a favorite of hers, and the mayor's brother-in-law headed it so they had plenty of political pull.

Her eyes widened in surprise. "It's a worthy, important organization, Ryan. And they've just received a letter of commendation from the mayor."

Ryan blinked. "Again, huh? Yeah, that ought to have readers shocked to the core when they see that news. What's this...the third commendation for them from the mayor in a year?"

She frowned at him, obviously displeased with his attitude. "The fourth. But it's news! This is a story of hope, Ryan, of humanity, of...of..."

Ryan said with resignation, "Yeah, of humans and of habit. Look, nothing wrong with the organization. It's terrific. But this is not exactly a sexy story."

As he said the word "sexy" he saw the walking definition of it enter his office. Webster's *and* the county commission would agree on this one. He was sunk. Absolutely sunk. He could *not* deal with his third reporter now. She made him crazy on a routine basis and he had spent the last six months torn between banging her brains out and strangling her.

Alexandra Holden stood five feet, eight inches tall and nicely curved in all the right places. Ryan was extremely aware of her and the fact that her body would fit against his perfectly. Well, he was taller... If he just lifted her that extra bit... He shook off the thought but was distracted by her hair.

What had she done to her hair today? The question pounded through his brain in perfect time with his headache. It fell in waves to her shoulders, the rich brown color touchable and shiny even under the fluorescent light. He looked into her face and saw sea blue eyes sparkling with mischief, staring right back at him.

Ohgod. He was too old for this. She was the last straw. He stood up slowly and announced in an overly quiet voice, "Deadline is in forty minutes. Write your articles. Leave my office and pretend we have a paper to put out. Then make fake clacking sounds on your keyboards so that I mistakenly assume you're actually doing as I ask. Please. Go. Now. Have mercy." He sat back down.

The first two reporters flashed him looks of indignation and left, but Alexandra stayed behind, smiling and staring at him with a thoughtful look in her eyes. She reached into her pocket and said, "Your head is pounding. I can tell. Here are two aspirin *again*. You know, you get way too tense."

Ryan reluctantly took the aspirin from her hand and grabbed the coffee cup from his desk. He tossed the pills into his mouth and drank the cold coffee, swallowing them both with effort but unclear on which tasted the most bitter. Then he put his coffee cup back on the desk with a thud. He kept his voice level but it cost him, "Thanks. Again. Now what's the problem?"

Alex regarded him in confusion a moment. The problem? Now, there was an interesting question. The problem had nothing to do with the paper and everything to do with her boss. In a word, he was hot. Oh, he had the reputation as a curmudgeon and she knew he enjoyed making everyone think of him that way. But she liked him. She liked that dark hair and the gleam in his blue eyes when he became passionate about some issue. She liked his smile and dry sense of humor. She liked that charm he must have picked up genetically from some long ago Irish rogue ancestor. When he set out to charm someone, Ryan did a thorough job.

Of course, if Ryan cared about something, he did a very thorough job, period. He was probably just as thorough and passionate in bed. And she *wanted* him. He was making her nuts. The urge to jump him one day was getting irresistible. She banished the thought and tried to focus. He was looking at her patiently. She blurted out, "Can you believe United Express will deliver actual live horses to your doorstep?"

The corners of Ryan's mouth kicked up in a reluctant smile. Trust Alex to find the humorous slant even in a dull story about the increase in parcels shipped this year by the local company. "Good to know."

She said, "It's true. I've confirmed it. I have a list of all kinds of bizarre packages they've shipped this year. Oh, and I got a great quote from a driver who once delivered a baby boy on the side of the road when he helped a stranded motorist. It's the one delivery package he'll *never* forget." She grinned at him. "It's a human interest story, Ryan."

Ryan suppressed a grin at the very familiar phrase. Alex managed to turn nearly everything into a human-interest story. And in truth, her articles were very popular with the reading public. He nodded. "Good. Go with it. We're darn close though. Make sure you have it done quickly, okay?"

She looked at the clock and said, "No problem," but she didn't leave.

Ryan arched an eyebrow. "Anything else?"

Alex gathered her courage. "Uhhh...yeah." Ryan still sat at his desk, looking so formal, so serious. She walked until she was standing directly in front of the desk and then leaned down, placing her hands on the top of it. She saw his eyes wander to her cleavage before he quickly looked back into her face. She felt a blush heat her cheeks as her nipples tightened in response to that look, but it also boosted her confidence. She lowered her voice. "Can we get some conference room time later?"

Ryan stared at her, fighting the pull of that cleavage for all he was worth. He was no Neanderthal. He was a mature adult male. He'd *never* gawk like some adolescent boy over a pair of... She shifted lower and he felt his gaze drop like a magnet... Ohgod...absolutely magnificent breasts...barely contained in a lacy white bra. The top of her blouse gaped open just enough to make his mouth water and his hands itch to touch her.

He wrenched his eyes back up and could have sworn he saw a hint of mischief before her face blanked into an innocent expression. He narrowed his eyes and studied her closely. She was flushed, the color climbing in her cheeks, but those sea eyes were sparkling. She wanted to play, did she? He fought the impulse to give her more than she'd bargained for. He said in a voice that sounded entirely too husky, "Why do we need the conference room?"

Her face remained innocent, but those wicked eyes were a dead giveaway. She said, "I have something I'd like to discuss with you, and it's private and rather…in depth."

Yeah, he had something he'd like to explore in depth, too. He jumped and jerked to attention as he heard a loud crash from someone dropping something outside his office. What was she doing? What the hell were *they* doing? He said gruffly, "We have a paper to get out now."

She stood up slowly, not taking her eyes from his. With a slight nod, she said, "Okay. But I'd like to get back to this later. Eventually we *have* to discuss it. *Soon.*"

Ryan stared at her silently for a moment and ticked off all of the reasons why starting anything with her would be a bad idea. First of all, she was a little young for him. He was twelve years older. Second, she worked for him and he had a firm policy against involvement with anyone at work—especially someone who worked *for* him. Third, she stirred him up too damn much…there was a spark between them that would burn too hot. This would be no casual, light relationship. The strength of the feeling and attraction between them made him extremely uneasy.

He was too damned old to fall in love and deal with this hassle all over again. He was too smart to risk another painful breakup and a potential new stalker, too. He looked into the pull of those wide, sparkling blue eyes and heard himself say, "We can talk tonight at my house over dinner if you want. I'll throw some steaks on the grill."

Her smile could have lit the entire building. She nodded enthusiastically and said, "What time?"

He was so busy kicking himself he almost didn't hear the question, but managed to answer, "Uh...six?"

She nodded and turned to walk briskly toward the door. She paused at the last second in the doorway and turned back, "I'll be there."

He started to say, "Okay," but then remembered she didn't know his address. "Right. I live at..."

She interrupted him, "I know where you live. Deadline's in thirty-five," and rushed out.

Ryan surveyed the empty doorway and tried to process that fast exit. Okay, she knew where he lived. Glancing back toward the clock, he noted the time and realized he'd better get busy. He needed to focus.

She knew where he lived? He'd never told her and it wasn't common knowledge. She was a good reporter and sharp as a tack. She could have found out through research. Then again, she could have stalked him home from work one day. Shuffling papers in front of him, he turned toward his computer.

He stared blankly at the screen. Oh well, at least if this relationship went south, he might have two ex-lover stalkers to harass him in shifts for variety's sake. And Alex the sharp reporter would be excellent at tracking him right down any time, day or night. *Uggggh.* He turned back to his desk and picked up the stack of papers again.

Another angle struck him. Uh-oh. She wouldn't need to track him down most of the time since he would be right here at the office, acting as her boss, and trying to navigate the sexual harassment quicksand issues with her.

Then again, why worry? That was only until the publisher fired them both for fraternization, right? Ohgod. His head hit the desk with a *thunk*.

Chapter Two

ॐ

Ryan ran around the house like a madman, picking up clothes and other miscellaneous objects, barely aware of what he was grabbing or where he was throwing it. When he'd told Alex to come at six, he thought he'd have plenty of time to prepare since he normally got off work at two o'clock. Instead, today of all days, the publisher stopped by his office and kept him in a meeting until nearly five. He was trying to restore order before Alex arrived at six. She was always on time for everything and it was nearly six now. The house wasn't a wreck, but he hadn't planned on company this morning when he left either. He'd barely had time to get the steaks prepped, shower, and change clothes before he realized he had maybe twenty minutes to clean house. He heard his parrot, Pete, croon from across the room, "Ohhhh, Captain Ryan! You naughty pirate!"

Ryan made a beeline for the cage, wondering how in the world he could have forgotten to cover it. His ex had taught the bird a mixture of embarrassing phrases before the breakup, strictly for the purpose of driving him nuts. He glared at the bird, "Do not start with me tonight. It's not too late for barbeque chicken...or parrot."

The bird cocked his head and said, "Ohhhh! Take me captive again, Pirate Ryan. Yar!"

Ryan scowled. "You're *my* bird! Why can't you say the things I taught you, huh?"

Pete regarded him solemnly and said, "Ryan's a big jerk."

Ryan threw the blanket over the cage and waited. Nothing. Total silence. He lifted the corner of the blanket again, feeling guilty.

The bird said, "Pete wants a cracker, puhleaze." Ryan laughed and reached behind the cage for the crackers. He tossed a few in the cage, getting a grateful squawk in response before letting the blanket drop.

The doorbell rang. He felt his heart rate climb instantly into overdrive. Wiping his hands on his jeans, he walked to the door and opened it. Alex stood there in a white sundress, a bottle of wine clutched to her chest like a shield. When she smiled at him tentatively, he sucked in a breath. She was so damn beautiful. And she was here. He moved aside and motioned her forward, "Well, hi. Right on time. Come on in. I was just about to start the gas grill."

Alex felt her nerves jump as she followed him into the house. He looked great. He'd changed into jeans and a tee shirt. It was the first time she'd seen him one-on-one outside of the office and dressed so casually. The intimacy of it was something of a jolt. She was actually at his house, too. Looking around with interest, she studied the masculine décor. It was obviously a guy's place, but she liked the artwork on the walls and the comfortable feel of the room. Holding out the wine, she said, "I hope you like it. I'm not very good at picking out wine, but the guy at the store said this one is great with steak."

Ryan took the bottle from her hand. "It's fine. I'm no expert either. Would you like the two-bit tour or do you want to come with me to light the grill?"

Alex felt her nerves kick at the thought of seeing more of his house. Would that tour include his bedroom? She said, "No! I-I'll just go with you to the grill. To light it. So that we can cook. The steaks."

Ryan heard the nerves in her voice and it somehow settled his own. He smiled at her and said gently, "Okay. Follow me."

The two of them went outside to the backyard and Ryan could feel those wide eyes on him, watching his every move. He strove for an easy tone, "I'm glad you could come."

Alex tried desperately to settle down but for some reason she felt totally out of her depth. She had been carefully planning his seduction for so long now that, with the moment at hand, she was nearly paralyzed with nerves. She took a deep breath and managed to say, "Thanks. You have a great house."

Ryan looked up from turning the dial and grinned at her just as the grill caught fire. He teased gently, "You haven't exactly seen the whole house yet."

She laughed. "Okay, your living room and patio are great. And nice…ummm…privacy fence, too."

He stood up and laughed with her. "Well, would you like to see the kitchen now? I need to get the steaks. Think you can take that much excitement?" He could hear the provocative note in his voice, but couldn't resist the impulse to flirt with her.

She smiled. "Lead on…I'll try to contain my enthusiasm."

Ryan stepped past her. On impulse, he touched a hand to her check in a fleeting caress. "Don't hold back on my account, sweetheart."

He winked and then continued back through the door into the house. Alex knew she should follow but that brief touch on her face and his words stunned her. His hand was so warm. That simple gesture thrilled her more than he could possibly know. She stared blindly at the doorway, thinking of what to say to him next, wondering if and when he would touch her again. Or if she should touch him.

Ryan reappeared in the doorway with two steaks on a platter. He smiled and said, "Changed your mind about the kitchen, huh? That's okay. No rush."

Alex shook her head, feeling ridiculous. "Can I help you with that?"

Ryan stabbed the stakes with easy efficiency and slid them onto the grill. "Thanks anyway. Nothing to it. We've got some time before I need to work on a salad. Would you like some of that wine now?"

Alex said, "Sure, I'd love some." Maybe it would help her relax.

Ryan nodded and walked back into the house. Alex stood there feeling foolish, staring at the cooking steaks. She was a mature, sexually experienced woman and she was acting like she'd never been alone with a man in her life. *But this was Ryan,* the little voice in her head said. *Ryan is different.*

He walked out of the door again with two glasses of wine, handing her one. She took it gratefully, glad to have something to do with her hands. Raising the glass to her lips, she took a sip and felt the warmth of the wine slide down her throat. Okay. Maybe after a bottle, she could relax. Better yet, she should have brought a case.

Ryan took a sip of his wine, wondering why Alex seemed jumpy as a cat. Was she *that* nervous at being alone with him? What exactly was going on with her? Before he could think better of it, he asked abruptly, "What exactly did you want to discuss in the conference room?"

Alex choked on her wine at the question. Tears sprang to her eyes and she coughed. Ryan immediately put his wine down on the nearby table and touched her arm gently. "Sheesh. I'm sorry. Are you okay?"

Alex nodded, unable to speak. She hurriedly placed her wineglass on the table next to his. Finally, she turned and said, "Ryan, I'm sorry. I'm being such an idiot. I have no idea why I'm so nervous all of the sudden."

Ryan watched as her gaze skidded away from him. He placed his hands on her shoulders. The soft skin felt smooth and warm. He was keenly aware of the thin strap on each shoulder holding the dress in place. Torn between tenderness and frustration, he challenged, "Don't you?"

She looked up at him and her gaze fell to his mouth. She parted her lips to speak and it was just too much temptation. Ryan ducked his head until his mouth met hers.

She tasted so sweet, with just a hint of the wine. Her lips moved softly under his, responding with more and more enthusiasm. His heart pounded so hard he thought it might come out of his chest. He traced her bottom lip with his tongue and she instantly opened her lips further. Answering the invitation, Ryan changed the angle of the kiss, exploring her mouth with his tongue, savoring the taste of her. When her tongue tangled with his own, he nearly groaned at the simple contact. He took a step closer just as she brought her body up against his and moved her arms around his neck.

Her full breasts pressed against his chest, the hard nipples a very nice surprise. He wrapped an arm around her waist and pulled her tighter against him. His cock hardened in a rush as he felt the soft curves of her body leaning into him. She was responding with fervor to his kiss. He felt utterly lost in her. The kiss grew hotter and Ryan fought the urge to back her against the wall and plunge inside her. Deep.

He broke the kiss and trailed his lips down her cheek to the side of her neck. She moved her head sideways to give him better access and gasped. At that breathy little intake of air, his pulse leapt. He kissed his way down until he reached the base of her neck and bit gently, then licked. She shivered and moaned, moving her hands from his shoulder up into his hair.

He moved from her neck to the delicate skin of her upper chest, sliding the strap off her shoulder, just as he heard her murmur, "Fire."

Ryan muttered, "Yeah," and kept going.

She said, "Ryan, there's a fire!" and wrenched away from him, pointing toward the grill.

Blinking, Ryan saw that sure enough there *was* a fire. He remembered that he'd turned the heat all the way up as far as it would go in order to warm the grill for the steaks. However, he'd been so distracted by Alex that he'd put the steaks on without turning the dial down to the correct setting. The steaks were now actively on fire, burning to a cinder. He ran toward the grill.

Alex looked around frantically and spotted the garden hose in the grass just one step away off the patio. She grabbed it quickly and hoped the water was turned on. The hose had one of those sprayers on it and she pressed the trigger, aiming toward the grill.

Ryan reached for the dial but before he could turn it, he felt a blast of cold water. He fumbled, unable to see in the middle of the sudden deluge and wondering if this was her way of cooling him off. Finally he was able to turn the dial and hear the gas shut off. He spun toward her, water now pouring over his chest like a mini waterfall, and said, "Alex! I've got it! The fire is definitely out."

Alex's mouth dropped open. She had just sprayed *Ryan* worse than the grill. She rushed toward him, forgetting to release the trigger and too horrified at her actions to realize it. "I'm so sorry."

Ryan reached out and grabbed for the sprayer. His hand blocked the water and the motion sprayed water backward all over Alex. When the blast of cold water hit her, she finally stopped pressing the trigger.

The two of them stood there, staring at each other incredulously. Ryan was soaked. Alex was only marginally better. Ryan blinked and then started to laugh. Alex stared at him a second and then she lapsed into spasms of laughter, too. They looked totally ridiculous. From blazing passion to drowned rats in one minute flat.

Ryan laughed harder. "You tried to drown me. A simple 'no' would have been fine, you know?"

Alex clutched her stomach, still laughing at the two of them. "Hey, I was *trying* to help. And besides, you're the one who torched dinner. I was doing damage control. I never claimed firefighting skills on my resume."

She tossed the hose to the ground and grinned. "You're one hell of a date, Ryan. Next time I'm bringing my bathing suit."

Ryan was enjoying the moment until he realized something. His laughter gradually died. Her white sundress was now soaked down the front and completely transparent. He had a graphic view of her body. He could see the outline of her tight rosy nipples without any difficulty. The dress clung to every curve, every line, even the sweet indention of her belly button. He could see the outline of skimpy white panties, but most of her body was revealed in amazing and erotic detail beneath the newly sheer material. The sight stole his breath and wiped the smile completely from his face.

Alex saw his sudden change in expression and glanced down at her dress in confusion. When she saw the results of their little shower, she was shocked. She had completely forgotten she was wearing white. Ryan's eyes moved back to her face and she swallowed at the look in them. He looked hungry, but not for food...for *her*. Her body heated again as she responded to that look in his eyes, the very male need. She took a step toward him, wanting that hunger.

Ryan met her halfway. Keeping his eyes on her face, he reached out and toyed with the straps on her dress. "You realize this is gonna get complicated."

Alex felt him sliding the straps back and forth, back and forth under his fingers. The anticipation was killing her. She said huskily, "Yeah, I know. I don't care."

He pulled one strap down until it rested on her arm. "We're too different."

Alex kept her voice steady, but it was difficult. "You're wrong. And I don't care."

He pulled the other strap down. "We work together."

She was extremely aware of the sundress clinging to her breasts, barely staying up. She sucked in a breath and said, "I. Don't. Care. I want you."

He smiled, although the smile looked strained. "Be sure, Alex."

Ryan watched tensely as she reached down to the hem of the sundress. With one graceful move, she pulled it up and over her head. The wet dress dropped to her feet. She was left standing in front of him, wearing nothing more than a pair of very tiny white lace panties, sandals, and a smile that stopped his heart. Her next words stole his breath entirely. "I'm sure."

Ryan froze. She had surprised him yet again. Gone was the woman who was too nervous to be in a kitchen with him — and in her place was a temptress. Her body was all gentle slopes and rounded curves. His gaze lingered with appreciation on her breasts before sliding downward to trace her small waist and shapely legs. He put both hands on her shoulders and gently turned her toward the doorway of the house, trying very hard to will the blood from his lap back to his brain — and actually form sentences. "You're so damn beautiful... There's a bed. ... In the house... Sweetheart, this is gonna take a while."

Chapter Three

ဆ

Alex stumbled through the doorway into the living room, eager to feel his hands on her. She stopped after about three steps and turned to face him. "Which way?"

Ryan stared down into her face, caught by the expression of blatant desire. Her eyes were darker now. Her lips were swollen from his kisses, and her hair was wet, curling around her face. He leaned down and kissed her, unable to resist one more taste. She immediately moved her body against him, opening her mouth as if she was just as greedy for the contact. Ryan ran his hands down her back, enjoying the smooth, silky skin, feeling her shudder against him.

He kissed her harder, thrusting his tongue deep, wanting to know every inch of her. His hands moved to the full curves of her bottom and he massaged her gently before lifting her just a little. She went on her toes and the mound of her sex brushed against his cock. Even through the denim of his jeans and her panties, he could feel her. She moaned into his mouth and strained against him. The pressure of her sex against his cock made him crazy to be inside her. Even as he reminded himself to slow down and find the damn bedroom, he returned the movement. The kiss turned hotter, and for several long moments, he was intoxicated with the wonder of her.

Only when desire sped through him like a runaway train did his sluggish mind start to realize they were still in the living room. He needed to get her to the bedroom. For some hazy reason he refused to name, he wanted her *there* that first time—in his room, in his bed. He started walking her backward, still kissing her. She moved with him as if they were dancing, allowing him to lead her backward across the room. They almost made it out of the living room into the hallway, but her elbow struck the birdcage and she yelped.

Pete's voice screeched through the room, "Evil oppressor!"

Alex jerked her head back and said, "What?"

Ryan shook his head and said, "Never mind." Taking her hand, he led her down the hall to his bedroom. When he stepped inside, he turned around and muttered, "Thank you, God."

He kissed her again, running his hands over her back and then bringing them forward to cup her breasts. At his touch, she threw her head back and moaned. He brushed his thumbs across her nipples and watched her face as she bit her lip. Her nipples were stiff, and he captured them between his fingers and gently rolled. She sucked in a breath and arched into his hands. She was responding to his touch as if she'd been made for him. There was no holding back or playing games—just honest, open enjoyment of his touch. It excited him more than he thought possible.

Alex shuddered, unable to believe the pleasure flowing through her. He was playing with her nipples, tormenting them with such perfect skill. Each gentle pull sent a delicious shot of pleasure through her. When he leaned down and circled one nipple slowly with his tongue, she actually felt her knees go weak. It felt so good that she moaned helplessly. Each soft wet lick of her nipple coiled the aching tension in her higher. He switched to the other breast and she suppressed the urge to beg him never to stop. He teased her nipples ruthlessly until she finally pleaded, "Please, suck them."

Ryan made one more slow circle with his tongue and then took her nipple into his mouth and sucked. She moaned loudly then and he felt the sound go through him like a gunshot. His cock was pressing uncomfortably against his jeans, the denim suddenly too tight, too restrictive. He turned her and backed her toward the bed.

Alex pulled away from him just a bit and said, "I want to touch you."

He was more than happy at that notion, but knew he was riding too close to the edge of control at the moment. He moved his hand over her stomach, watching her face as he said, "In a minute, sweetheart." Her stomach muscles jumped under his hand. He reached the top of her panties and slipped his hand inside.

He continued his downward trek, seeing the anticipation on her face, feeling the sudden stillness of her body. As he reached her curls and combed through them, he carefully traced her lips. She literally shook under his hands and her excitement continued to wind his arousal even tighter. She was breathing very fast. As he traced her softness, her eyes went blank and he knew she was focused completely on his hand touching her.

When he found the entrance to her sex, she was wet, very wet. Feeling the slickness against his fingers, he couldn't help the moan that escaped him. He pressed his palm against her mound, putting pressure on her clit for the first time. She jerked and said, "Ohhhh..."

He held the pressure for a second before he lifted his palm. He used his finger to trace upward, sliding easily over her swollen flesh. She was so hot against his hand. When his finger found her clit, he circled it gently, still watching her face to find what motion she liked most, loving the fact that she was completely lost in pleasure. She moved her hips, arching and pushing against his hand in a rhythm as old as time.

Alex muttered in a throaty voice,

"OhgodOhgodOhgod..."

Ryan leaned forward and kissed each nipple before moving downward with small kisses, pausing occasionally to suck or lick. The entire time, he kept his finger moving, sometimes pressing against her clit before returning to circle it slowly, following her rhythm. She was moving her hips blindly now, pressing harder, her motions faster and openly greedy. He withdrew his hand from her panties and went down onto his knees.

She was breathing harshly, frowning in obvious confusion at the loss of his touch. Her voice held the same note of confusion as she protested, "No! Wait!"

He nearly smiled, but he was too frustrated. His cock was actively throbbing now, painfully hard. He reached up and hooked her panties in his hands. Pulling them down, he said, "Shhh... It's okay. Step out of them. That's good."

As the panties reached her ankles, she obeyed his words and stepped out of them. Ryan found the strap of one sandal and pulled it off her foot, and then moved to the other. She was completely compliant, cooperating by bringing her foot up just a bit. Finally, he had both sandals off. He rocked back on his heels and looked up at her.

She stared down at him dazedly. Her breasts rose and fell rapidly with each panting breath and there was a delicate blush stealing from them up toward her neck. His gaze lowered until he could see the nest of brown curls between her legs. Leaning forward, he placed his hands on the back of her thighs and said, "Widen your legs for me, baby."

As soon as she moved, he placed his mouth against her sex and kissed her. She jerked, but he tightened his grip on her thighs to keep her still. He moved his mouth in gentle kisses and then reached out and traced her lips with his tongue. When he circled her clit, she moaned loudly and her head fell back again. Ryan was completely captivated by that sound. He loved the taste of her, loved that moan, loved the way her legs were trembling in his hands. Eager for more, he licked and sucked, wanting everything from her. He ached for her to come against his mouth.

Alex felt the tension in her lower body and knew she was about to go over the edge. His tongue was so wet and warm as he teased her clit again and again. Her entire focus was on the feel of Ryan's mouth against her sex. Each hot, wet lick, each rasping touch of his tongue against her clit made her crazier. She was wild with need, aching and frantic and out of control. As he licked and sucked, she tried to pull away, muttering, "I'm going to… I… Ohgod…"

Ryan murmured against her curls, "Yesss."

Alex screamed as her climax hit her in one long rush. She felt her knees going and grabbed his shoulders for balance. Her body pulsed, clenching and unclenching, as wave after wave of pleasure hit her. She kept screaming, shaking with the pure joy of it, until the last of the pleasure died away.

She couldn't pull enough air into her lungs, and just focused on breathing and remaining upright. Finally, she looked down and saw that Ryan had pulled back, his mouth still hovering over her curls. He stared at her, his expression a strange mixture of hunger and tenderness. She cleared her throat and said in a voice that was barely recognizable even to her, "That was fantastic." And then she smiled.

That smile rocked Ryan to the soul. She was looking at him as if he was the best thing since the invention of chocolate ice cream. The pain in his groin had him nearly howling, but that smile was worth it. She was worth it. He smiled at her and asked, "Want more?"

Her smile widened and her eyebrow rose. "Always! Although I can't believe I'm still standing. That felt *so* good. How is it I was going to seduce you and you seduced me instead, huh?"

Ryan grinned and flashed her a look of mock innocence. "I have no idea. But hey, I'm an agreeable guy. You can try again…anytime you want."

She put her hands on his arms and tried to pull him to his feet. He cooperated with her, wondering even as he stood exactly how much seduction he could take. He wanted to push her back on the bed and fuck her into next week. But then she gave him a sultry look as old as Eve and he decided to see what her first move would be.

Alex reached for the hem of his damp tee shirt and said, "Raise your arms, please."

He obediently raised his arms and she pulled the shirt over his head. Tossing it to the floor, she said, "You don't know how much I want this... And now I can finally touch you like this...day after day of seeing you...wanting..."

She moved her hands over his chest, exploring eagerly. Ryan felt those soft fingers tracing his nipples and focused hard on remaining still so that she could explore. When she leaned forward and traced his nipple with her tongue, he shuddered and knew, without a doubt, there was no way he was getting enough air. His head felt light and he was breathing too hard. She ran her hands through the hair on his chest, moving upward, tracing his shoulders and then back down until she reached the top of his jeans.

She kissed him suddenly, a hard, tongue-thrusting kiss that caught him by surprise. He responded without thought, still focused on those hands at the top of his jeans. When she hooked one finger under the material and traced along the waistband, he groaned into her mouth and brought his hands up to cup her face. He kissed her harder and it was unclear at that point who was in control of the kiss. He only knew he wanted those soft hands on his cock.

She unsnapped his jeans and then brought the zipper down carefully. Breaking the feverish kiss, she looked down just as his cock sprang into her waiting hands. At that first touch, Ryan moaned and hissed, "God, yesss."

She moved one hand into his boxers down to his sac and traced it lightly while the other hand circled his cock in a gentle grasp. Her hand glided down slowly, barely circling him. He nearly put his hand over hers to tighten her grasp but at the last second, brought his hand back up and buried it in her hair. The smile she flashed him was pure temptress as she moved her hand along his length, deliberately teasing. She leaned forward and kissed his neck.

He felt as if his entire body was locked into place. The tension was unbearable. With each downward motion, her hand grasped him more firmly, each stroke surer, firmer. Ryan was going out of his mind at the simple pleasure of it. She was killing him. He was so lost in the sensation, he didn't even register that she had dropped to her knees.

Somehow her hand was just gone and she was suddenly sucking his cock, taking him deeply into her mouth. Wet heat. He could feel her tongue as she worked her mouth slowly up and down. He sank both hands into her hair and stared down at her, watching as his cock moved in and out of her mouth.

He thought he'd never seen anything so erotic in his life— and then she looked up at him from that kneeling position, his cock still in her mouth. It stunned him. That look in her eyes was purely carnal, innately female. He groaned and tightened his hold on her hair without thinking. He felt the pressure building and knew he was about to totally lose it.

He shook his head frantically and said, "Oh, no you don't!" and gently pulled her head back. His cock came free from her mouth with an audible *pop* and he had to shut his eyes for a few seconds to keep from screaming.

He muttered, "The bed, Alex. Right now."

She smiled and hooked her hands into his wet jeans and underwear. She pulled them to his ankles, struggling some, and then rocked back on her heels. She stared at his jeans and said, "Uh-oh. Your socks and shoes."

Ryan just pointed at the bed and said, "I'll deal with 'em. You...head over there."

She grinned. "Deadline's in two."

Ryan smiled. "No problem." He saw her moving toward the bed and reached down. He fought with his socks and shoes for several agonizing seconds but managed to remove them and then kicked off his boxers and jeans. Turning, he strode over to the bedside table. Fumbling the drawer open, he grabbed a condom and quickly sheathed himself, too eager to consider asking her to do it. He turned back to the bed. She was sitting on the foot of it watching him with hungry eyes the color of a storm-tossed sea.

He moved and then motioned for her to scoot all the way up onto the bed. She scrambled back toward the headboard awkwardly and he followed her. When she was positioned on her side facing him, she said, "Where were we?"

He turned until he was lying on his side facing her, mirroring her position. He said huskily, "I believe we were right..."

He moved his hand and cupped her. "About..."

She shifted her legs so that he could cup her more fully. He found the entrance to her sex and slid one finger into it slowly. "*Here.*"

The smile slid from her face and she closed her eyes. Her lower body arched into his hand and she moaned, "Yeah."

She was soft and slick and tight around his finger and he wondered distantly if he'd make it through this without having a heart attack. At the moment he didn't care. He moved his finger in and out of her with increasing speed, using his thumb to tease her clit for several moments. When she moaned long and low, he withdrew his finger. He moved his hand to her shoulder and pushed her gently.

As she landed on her back, he moved over her. He caught his weight on his hands and used his knee to spread her legs wider. His cock brushed against her sex and she drew her knees up just a bit as if asking for his cock.

Ryan pushed into her carefully, his gaze locked on her face. Her eyes were dark now, wide, intent, and he watched as she stared back at him. The eye contact between them felt almost as intimate as the joining of their bodies. He thrust forward, sliding inside her to the hilt in one hard move, then stopped. Her eyes closed and her walls tightened around his cock like a vise. He sucked in a breath.

She opened her eyes and said in a soft, shaky voice, "Oh. Wow. Hi!"

Ryan would have laughed if he wasn't aroused to the point of pain. Instead he choked out, "Hello, Alex," and then eased back until he was almost out of her. Her legs came up and hooked around his waist. Her hands went to his shoulders and she made a little sound of protest.

He pushed back into her, savoring the feel of her around him, so hot and wet and tight. When he was in as far he could go, she moaned and her fingernails dug into his shoulders. That tiny pain was too much. Ryan pulled back and then slammed into her with real force. Her hips rose to meet him. He groaned and repeated the motion even faster and harder.

She moaned, "Ohgod, yes," and tightened her legs around him.

Ryan was past thinking, the demands of his body rode him too hard. He slammed into her over and over, completely lost in the feeling of her body around him. He was burning up, the pleasure singing through his veins now. The tempo grew faster and he pushed harder, wanting nothing more than to sink as deep into her as he could get. She moaned repeatedly, her head thrashing from side to side. He pounded into her and felt his control sliding away. Desperate for release, he gritted out, "Come for me."

She dug her fingernails deeper into his shoulders, moaning continuously. Her eyes were locked on his, but they looked dazed, unseeing. Both of them were sweating now. Ryan leaned down and licked her upper lip, tasting salt and something that was uniquely her, uniquely Alex. He ground his body against hers harder, angling for more pressure on her clit.

As he pulled back from her, he felt her sex clench hard. Then she screamed. He kept plunging into her, feeling her muscles contract around him. He was poised on the edge of his own release, and in total agony, went completely wild. His arms shook violently, and he could feel the pressure building at the base of his cock. Suddenly, release slammed into him with the force of a punch. His froze, buried deep inside of her. Then he came and came, shuddering with each pulse until he thought he'd die from the scalding pleasure of it. Finally, it faded away and he collapsed, burying his head in her neck.

A moment later Alex tapped her hand on his shoulder and he realized he was probably crushing her. It took every ounce of energy he had, but he rolled and drew her close to him. Her head came to rest on his chest as if it was the most natural thing in the world. Ryan worked on getting his breath back and his synapses firing again.

After a few minutes, he moved his hand gently through her hair. She had rocked his world and he had no idea what he was going to say to her now. What had happened between them was more than just the best sex of his life. It was...special, with a wealth of emotion he didn't even want to identify. He wondered sleepily if she'd felt the same thing.

She answered his questions when she spoke. "Sheesh. We are in *biiiiiig* trouble here, Ryan. That was unbelievable."

He paused with his hand above her head at the comment, and then continued stroking her. "Yeah. Lady, you're something else."

She lifted up and looked at him. She had a strangely serious expression on her face, an almost guilty look. "Umm...Ryan, I have a confession to make about the conference room discussion."

He smiled, thinking she was about to tell him that there had been no topic for discussion, she had just been trying to seduce him. "Okay, what's your deep, dark secret, sweetheart?"

Her next words wiped the smile from his face. "I quit."

He was stunned. "What?"

She licked her lips, and he could feel her body tense. "Ummm...that's what I was going to tell you and then I was going to seduce you in the conference room. In two weeks I'll be working for the paper one town over."

Ryan couldn't seem to get a bead on her. "Whoa... Back up... But... But... Why?"

Her shoulders relaxed and she arched an eyebrow, suddenly smiling. "Well, because they're paying me more money. It's a small commute. And, oh yeah...because I have a small rule against sleeping with my boss."

Ryan felt a crushing disappointment at the thought of not seeing her daily, watching her come into his office with that teasing smile and gazing at him with those big eyes. He understood what she was saying, but... "Alex, you don't have to do that. We'll figure something out."

Her smile widened. "Actually, I already did." She shifted her body until she was sitting up and then crawled over until she straddled him. She threw back her hair and said, "I'll miss you during the day of course. Major downside. But...Ryan...I'm realllllly going to enjoy the nights."

He felt the beginnings of a smile bloom. "Yeah?"

She grinned and winked. "Oh yeah..."

Chapter Four
One year later…

&

Alex waved and grinned at Agnes and then turned to knock on the door to Ryan's office. She heard his voice saying, "Come in" even as she opened the door.

Ryan sat behind his desk, papers scattered, one hand running through his hair. His head was cocked sideways as he listened to the phone receiver tucked between his ear and shoulder. He didn't even glance to see who it was, just motioned for her to sit, as he said into the phone, "I'm very sorry, Mrs. Nelson, but as I explained last week, I can't run a front page story about Buttercup's ability to paint abstract pictures with his paws."

He listened for a moment and said, "Uhh-huhh. Yes, ma'am, I realize he's a very talented pit-bull. But the fact remains that we're a small daily paper with limited resources. Yes, ma'am…"

Alex choked back a laugh and dropped into the chair in front of his desk. She studied him as he continued to talk. He looked a little tired and exasperated, but it was already one o'clock, an hour past deadline. News days began in the early hours of the morning. She had deliberately timed it so that tomorrow's newspaper was currently coming out of the presses downstairs and Ryan only had an hour left until his day was done. She watched as he ended the conversation diplomatically, charming the elderly lady as only Ryan could, and then he put down the receiver with a scowl and sighed.

"Passing up a hard news story, tough guy?" She teased him and laughed when he jumped. He'd obviously forgotten he'd told someone to come into his office. She watched as his expression changed completely when he looked at her. The weariness disappeared and his face lit up as he grinned widely.

Ryan shook his head and rolled his eyes. "What a great surprise! How are you, sweetheart? Mrs. Nelson again. Some things never change. Tell me you're here to kidnap me from this awful place."

Alex felt a little secret thrill but kept her voice carefully casual. "Well, yes and no. I have something I need to discuss with you. In there." She motioned a few doors down toward the conference room.

Ryan's eyebrows lifted a little but his eyes began to gleam with humor and interest. "Really? Well, I suppose since it's been so long since we've seen each other, we should at least be able to hug privately without people barging in."

Alex cracked up. "Oh yeah. So very long. Who was it that hogged the sheet in bed then this morning, huh?"

Ryan laughed with her. "Well, fine, if you'd rather stay here."

"No, no." Alex quickly backtracked. She stood up. "This is important." She tried to make her tone solemn and motioned for him to follow her. "We need the privacy, Ryan. I need to talk to you and it can't wait."

Ryan studied her closely but she deliberately avoided looking into his eyes. He was about ninety-nine percent sure she wanted the conference room for a surprise seduction. In the year since they'd been together, the flame between them only burned hotter. His body stirred at the thought of what she might have in mind.

Still, he felt a small trickle of unease. What if she didn't want to seduce him? What if it was something else? Something bad…like….she didn't want to see him anymore. He stood and followed her out, trying to push aside the disturbing thought. He and Alex had grown closer, not just in body, in the last year. He'd never been happier in his life with any woman.

He'd never felt so comfortable or so turned on, all at the same time. Every day with Alex was a miracle and he was still rather dazed at his good fortune.

The thought of losing her was too horrible. He reminded himself of how happy she seemed. They lived together now, had been since about three months into the relationship. They fought occasionally, as all couples do, but overall they got along very well and managed to resolve trouble areas. There was no reason to think she might be dumping him. No reason at all. He walked into the conference room behind her, fingers sliding over the lock, and shut the door. He turned to his left and flipped the light switch. The conference room never failed to amuse him. The rest of the newspaper office building décor was a wreck—dated and cramped and last renovated sometime in the Nixon era, but the conference room was the publisher's little showroom to impress his political friends.

It was nicely furnished, fairly large, and dominated by a rectangular wooden table. The table was sturdy, the dark surface highly polished and gleaming impressively under the office lights. There were seven nondescript, utilitarian chairs on each side but at the head of the table there was a large, plush chair used almost exclusively by the publisher when he presided over meetings with the lesser minions. There was also a huge window along the outside wall for when he wanted to impress people with the charming view of the city square, but the blinds were closed. Ryan watched as Alex walked to the table and leaned on it with one hip.

He paused a few feet away and studied her with appreciation. She looked exactly like what she was—a successful, confident, sexy woman. She had on a white blouse with a red business suit and high heels. The suit skirt was just a tad on the short side, showcasing those wonderful legs. He felt a flash of heat as he remembered the feel of those legs when she had straddled him in bed last night.

Suddenly, she used her foot to push the chair away from the head of the table. It chair had rollers on the bottom of it and the chair moved easily, speeding toward him. Ryan caught it in front of him and rested his hands casually along the top of the high back. "You might have yelled 'incoming.'"

Alex laughed, her eyes sparkling with mischief. "But Ryan, what's life without a surprise or two? Why don't you take a seat?"

The lady was definitely in the mood to play. Ryan felt the tension ease from his chest and travel directly to his groin. He decided to play along. He smiled as he moved to the front of the chair and sat down. "Sure, sweetheart. The ball's in your court. I'm game for anything you have in mind."

Alex felt a deep thrill at his words. She loved this man. She loved him so much that she ached with it. Every day only made her realize how lucky she was to have found him. He was watching her closely, those eyes full of tenderness and humor, and she nearly blurted out, "I love you." She held the words in, but just barely. In the year they'd been together, they'd circled around the word love again and again. It was no secret that they cared deeply for each other, but both had avoided the L-word. She wanted to tell him. She did love him, but each time some flash of insecurity held her back.

She needed to say it, and she really needed to hear it, too. She kept hoping he'd say it first. So far, that hadn't happened. She refocused and realized he'd been waiting patiently while she was off on her L-word tangent. She stood up and walked toward him, conscious of the sway to her hips. She was in the mood to tease and seduce and give Ryan one heck of a surprise.

She walked until she stood in front him and then bent down. Alex pressed the lever to swing the right arm of the chair upward and lock it next to the back of the chair, out of the way. She turned to the other side and did the same. Leaning back up until she was facing him again, she raised her hands to his tie and said, "Darling, I know it's been a long work week. I wanted to talk to you about relaxing. I think you're way too tense." She untied the tie and slowly slipped it free from his shirt collar.

Ryan nodded mock solemnly. "I suppose you have aspirins with you, like old times."

She ran the silky material through her hands slowly. "Nope. Fresh out of aspirin."

Alex hung the tie loosely around her neck temporarily. She sat down on his lap and moved until she was straddling him. The short skirt rode up to the tops of her thighs, exposing the tops of her stockings. She saw the stunned look in Ryan's eyes and nodded. "Yep, silk stockings and garter belt, no underwear. It's amazing how sexy that combination can make a woman feel."

Ryan said huskily, "Alex, you're sexy in a sweat suit." He groaned as she shifted a little in his lap and his cock hardened. "You're killing me."

Alex felt a little feminine thrill at the power she had to affect him so quickly. She smiled and rolled her hips, watching as his pupils dilated and he licked his lips. She nearly groaned at the rush of pleasure when her sex rubbed against his cock. She reached for the buttons of his shirt and began to slide them free. Leaning forward, she pressed her lips to his in a sweet, teasing kiss.

Ryan's mouth moved, responding eagerly to her. She swept her tongue along his bottom lip and his arms came around her suddenly. He changed the angle of the kiss, pressing harder now, greedy heat flaring between them. She dug her hands into his shoulders and fed that heat, nurtured it. She touched her tongue to his and felt the wet velvet glide of his answering stroke. The kiss burned hotter and then hotter still. His arms tightened and she realized they'd been lost in the kiss for some time. She needed to take control and do it fast.

Jerking her head back abruptly, she said, "Wait! Your hands." He obediently loosened his hold on her and she ran her fingertips down his arms lightly until she placed her hands over his. She then moved them gently but firmly, guiding his arms to behind the chair. She said, "Darling, clasp your arms behind the chair, okay?"

Ryan was surprised at the request, but had a sneaking suspicion of where this might be leading. He obliged her. He crossed his arms behind him, around the back of the chair, and waited. He felt incredibly excited already from that kiss and very turned on by the challenge in her eyes. At this point he was eager to see how far she might go.

She pulled his tie from around her neck and then leaned forward, her breasts full and soft against his chest. She reached behind him and slowly but efficiently looped the tie around his arms. She knotted it. Ryan knew he could get loose, but was mildly surprised to find the touch of vulnerability a little arousing. He was her prisoner and he couldn't think of anyone in the world he'd rather have as a captor than Alex.

She leaned back again with a satisfied smile that made his heart beat faster. Then she flashed him a sultry look combined with the sweet charm of mischief. "There. Now I can play all I want without any distractions."

Alex pulled his shirt open and ran her fingertips over the hard planes of Ryan's chest. He was tense under her fingers and that tension excited her. She could tell by his heated eyes that he liked this game. He liked it plenty. She traced her fingers over the hard nubs of his nipples and watched as his eyes closed and he groaned.

She smiled. She brought her head forward and licked a line from one nipple to the other, raking her tongue over each one in a searing caress. When he shuddered, she placed her mouth over his right nipple and sucked hard.

Ryan nearly came out of the chair. The jolt of pleasure shot straight to his cock. He wondered just how much teasing he could stand. Alex continued teasing his nipples, driving him wild, as he breathed harder and harder, struggling to stay motionless. When she shifted off his lap and went to her knees, he began to sweat. He said, "Sweetheart, I'm dying. I want to touch you."

Alex shook her head, pleased at the way he was responding to her. "Not yet, darling. Relax. We have plenty of time." She pushed his legs apart and moved between them. Then she planted tiny playful kisses down his chest, over his stomach. She traced his belly button with her tongue and felt his stomach muscles bunch. Ryan was definitely feeling the heat and she reveled in that fact. When she ran her tongue along his waistband, he moaned quietly and threw his head back.

Smiling to herself, she unzipped his pants. When his cock sprang free she teased, "Commando, huh? Well, since I didn't wear underwear today either, I'm not gonna say a word. *Wellllll...*" She traced her thumb over the spongy tip of his cock and watched as a bead of moisture formed on the tip. She leaned down and whispered huskily. "Maybe one word." She licked that moisture away, tasting salt and Ryan. He arched his back and she said, "Excellent. I think the word is excellent."

She sucked the tip of his cock into her mouth, loving the hard feel of it against her tongue. As she sucked gently, taking more of him into her mouth and then pulling back teasingly, she dimly realized he was saying her name in warning. "Alex. GodAlexOhgod."

She sucked him harder, taking more of him into her mouth. Again and again she tormented him. Her fingers drifted downward and played at the base of his cock. She was so totally lost in teasing him that she missed it when his control snapped. She just heard a muttered oath and then his hands were free and in her hair. He was shaking, his whole body shuddering as if he had a fever. His hands pressed her head back and she released his cock from her mouth reluctantly, surprised that he wanted her to stop.

When she looked up and saw his face, she sucked in a deep breath. Ryan looked...he looked like a man pushed too far. His eyes were dark and dangerous. She realized with a sudden thrill just what happens when you tease a tiger. He devours you.

The planes of his face were harsh with strain and his voice was rough as he said overly quietly, "Stand up, darling."

She stood up slowly, cautiously. When he stood up too, his pants stayed up, his cock jutting from the gap in the cloth. She felt his hands on her shoulders guiding her backward. The table pressed against her bottom. She let out a little gasp of surprise as he lifted her and sat her on top of it. No warning. He just wrapped his hands around her waist and moved her where he wanted her.

Ryan pulled her forward until she was sitting on the edge of the table. He placed a warm, hard hand on the inside of her thigh and spread her legs. The other hand was still on her waist and she realized suddenly that he was holding the tie in one hand. Alex swallowed hard.

Something about the movement excited her tremendously when he suddenly stepped between her knees. Maybe it was the hungry, dangerous look in his eyes. Maybe it was the vulnerability of having him between her legs. Whatever it was, it was intoxicating. She felt breathless and too warm.

Ryan ran a gentle hand down her cheek. "Two can tease, sweetheart." He moved his hand to her shoulder and pushed her backward gently.

Alex was forced to place her hands behind her on the table for balance to remain upright. He quickly looped the tie around her hands and tied it. Her hands weren't really tied together. She had only to move her hands a little closer and the loop would allow her to slip through. But for some reason, even that loose bond felt thrilling and dangerous.

He pulled back a little and said, "Keep your hands on the table." Then he pushed her jacket open and began to unbutton her blouse.

When he pulled the blouse from her skirt and unclasped the front fastener of her bra, she felt the caress of cool air against her naked breasts and her nipples drew even tighter.

Her heart pounded as she tried to stay in control. He leaned forward and swiped his tongue around her nipple in a teasing lick. She shuddered and made a tiny noise of pleasure. She looked down and watched as his tongue toyed with her hardened nipple. The sight was so erotic that she couldn't help the whimper that escaped her.

Ryan watched her the whole time, his eyes intent on her face. He ran one hand along her inner thigh and paused when he felt the condom tucked into her garter. His fingers deftly removed the condom and then lingered, teasing and making her shake with excitement. He placed the condom on the table next to her and then sucked her nipple gently as if in reward. He said, "Have I mentioned how much I love it that you're detail-oriented?"

The tugging pressure sent pleasure through her. She muttered, "Ryan, ohhh, again, please." He pulled her nipple into his mouth, suddenly sucking hard. Jolted, she arched into his mouth, nearly begging for more. It was all she could do to keep her hands on the table. When she tried to move them outward without thinking, the tie held. She moaned softly, struggling to keep the sound inside but not succeeding very well.

Ryan pulled back, hotly raking her nipple with his tongue again, and whispered against her breast, "Careful with the noise, sweetheart. You don't want people to figure out what we're really doing in here."

Alex tensed. How could she have forgotten? They did need to be quiet. She knew most people were busily going about their workday, but they weren't deaf or stupid. If she started moaning, they might come to investigate.

Ryan sucked her other nipple into his mouth and she arched her hips helplessly. Her hands remained on the table behind her, but she was wondering how long she could take this sensual torment. He was making her crazy with need.

After endless moments, Ryan let her nipple go and stood up again. He shook his head as if clearing it. "Alex, you're so damn beautiful. I can never get enough of you. Never."

His hand moved to the table and he grabbed the condom, impatiently tearing into it. He sheathed himself so fast that Alex barely even realized what he was doing. His hand returned to the inside of her upper thigh as he stared hard at her. He toyed with her garter a moment, saying roughly, "You know how wild I feel right now. I could eat you alive. In one gulp."

Alex felt his hand climb higher until it reached the curls between her legs. His fingers combed through her hair. She was wet, incredibly wet, and he touched her with the tips of his fingers, teasing her clit with knowing skill. She choked on another moan and struggled to keep from crying out. When he found the entrance to her sex and thrust one long finger inside, she arched her back harder and let out a muffled moan, helpless to contain it.

The sound appeared to electrify Ryan. He removed his finger and moved his hand. She would have protested but he suddenly replaced his finger with his cock. She felt the pressure as the wide head probed for entrance. When she arched her hips a little more, eager and aching, he thrust forward, hard, all the way to the hilt, claiming her in an instant. Alex gasped and bit her lip to keep from screaming at the nearly painful sense of fullness and pleasure.

Ryan remained still, buried deep inside her, and just rested his forehead against hers for a moment as if he was gathering his control. Then he began to move.

He stroked her deep, but each thrust was slow and deliberate. He was teasing her now in a completely different way. The slide of his hard cock along the walls of her sex rasped her nerve endings, winding the tension in her higher with each stroke. Again and again he moved, thrusting and nearly withdrawing, only to thrust again.

Then he began to speak in very low, rough voice. "Remember Alex, you can't scream. People will hear you." He thrust forward and pulled back. "I hope I locked the door. Tell me, Alex, do you think I remembered to lock the door when we came in here?"

His gaze challenged her to answer and she struggled to think. Hadn't she locked the door? No, she'd entered the room first. He was behind her when they walked in. Surely he had locked the door. Hadn't he? She tensed further and wondered. She stuttered, struggled to whisper, "Y-yes, you did. Didn't you? Ryan..." Her voice ended on a quiet moan.

Ryan sped up, his strokes faster now, harder. "No, Alex, I don't think I did. I was surprised to see you, remember? I just followed you in here without..." he struggled for control and ended roughly, "thinking."

His hands dug into her hips and pulled her onto him harder. He thrust full force now and ground against her. Alex could barely breathe. Her heart was hammering so hard and she was wild now, teetering on the edge of control. The threat of discovery sent a jolt of fear through her and yet it inexplicably excited her at the same time. She struggled not to moan, afraid a scream of pure blazing pleasure might escape at any moment.

Ryan pumped in and out, grinding, struggling not to lose it. Need clawed at him and he said in a voice he barely recognized, "Come. Come for me, Alex. Give me all of you."

Alex's whole body shook. The tension was too great and she felt the first ripple of her climax hit her with a sense of panic. She opened her mouth, helpless in the rush of pleasure, and nearly screamed.

Ryan pressed his mouth to hers and prevented it. What emerged was a muffled sound. He kept kissing her and stroking in and out of her. When he felt the last of her orgasm fade and her scream turned to a whimper, Ryan slammed into her hard once more and let go. He slid over the edge in a blistering surge of pleasure. He stayed pressed to the hilt, buried deep inside her, and shook as the orgasm ripped through him and he spilled into her.

The pleasure was so intense that for long moments afterward neither of them could speak. Both Alex and Ryan remained locked together, panting, dazed by the intensity of their union. In the distance they could hear the busy sounds of the office, but in the conference room the only sound was their labored breathing.

Finally, Alex spoke. "Feeling more relaxed?"

Ryan laughed weakly. "Darling, any more relaxed and you'll have to pour me out of here. You are *good.*"

Alex flashed him a pleased smile. "I'm feeling pretty relaxed myself." A thought suddenly occurred to her. She asked, "Did you really forget to lock the door?"

Ryan leaned back a little and grinned at her. "No, of course not."

Alex began to laugh and choked out, "No fair. You freaked me out."

He gave her a knowing look and laughed. "Sure I did. Freaked out? Yeah, right. If you'd let that scream loose, they'd have heard you three states away."

Alex rolled her eyes. "Whatever. It's a good thing I love you. Otherwise I'd have to kill you for being so smug. You are such a *guy*, Ryan."

When Ryan tensed and blinked, Alex realized what she'd just said. She searched his face, but wasn't sure what that weird expression meant. He was surprised, that much was obvious. Panic shot through her and she moved back a little, clearing her throat. "Ryan...I...ummm..." She looked away from him and tried frantically to think of something to say.

Ryan moved both hands and cupped her face. He turned her head to face him and said urgently, "Say it again, Alex."

Alex saw the joy blooming in his eyes and relief flooded her. She swallowed and said, "I love you, Ryan."

He closed his eyes and then leaned his forehead against hers. She removed her hands from the table, slipping out of the tie, and wrapped her arms around his neck. He pulled back a little and stared at her.

Ryan was struggling hard to find the right words. He was so moved and so happy that he could barely think. He knew exactly what he wanted, but the words jumbled inside him. His heart seemed to have grown too large for his body and he felt dazzled by the sense of rightness and joy of this moment. Finally, the words came. He said simply, "Marry me, Alex."

Alex froze. Now it was her turn to stare at him in surprise. Marry him? Wow. She hadn't expected that reaction. Talk about a shocker. There should be some kind of conversational penalty for leapfrogging from the L-word to the M-word that fast. She sputtered, "Ryan, I…you…we…"

His voice rang with sincerity. "Alex, I love you. I love you more than I can ever say. I want to spend the rest of my life with you. These last nine months? Coming home to you at the end of the day? It's been the happiest time of my life. I want to hold you every single night and wake up every morning with you grousing because I've hogged the covers. I love you. I love you so much. Will you marry me?"

Alex knew there might be someone else on earth who was more overjoyed than she was at that moment, but she didn't think so. She loved him and she wanted to spend the rest of her life with him, too. She'd barely dared to dream that he might feel the same way. She said, "Yes. *Yes.* I'll marry you. Oh Ryan." She leaned forward and hugged him, tears of wonder springing to her eyes. "Oh wow."

He hugged her hard. Then he leaned back and placed a hard kiss on her mouth. "*Yes!* Thank you!" He threw back his head and laughed, the sound mixed with joy and relief. Alex joined him, swept away with that same sense of joy.

They finally grew quiet and just grinned at each other. Then Ryan said, "When do you want to get married?"

Alex felt a dart of mischief as she suddenly remembered a conversation they'd had the day they'd first gone to bed together. "Well, gee, Ryan. I'm not sure. The whole marriage thing is huge. You know, this is gonna get complicated."

Ryan looked confused for second and then the memory hit him, too. He shook his head and smiled as he said firmly, "I don't care."

She said, "We're so different."

He flashed her a look. "You know you're wrong. And I don't care."

She looped her arms around his neck. "We'll be living together all the time, married."

Ryan nodded. "You bet we will. 'Til death do us part."

Alex sobered but her blue eyes sparkled like diamonds and her smile was full of tenderness and promise. "Six months will do for an engagement. But our marriage? I want happily ever after. The deadline on that is forever." She flashed him a stern look edged with love and hope. "Be sure, Ryan."

Ryan looked at the woman he loved and smiled. He ran his hand along her cheek and promised quietly, "I'm sure. We'll love and live happily ever after all the way until forever, sweetheart."

And they did.

Also by Marly Chance

☙

About the Author

&

Award-winning author Marly Chance lives with her husband and young son in a small Tennessee town where truth is always stranger than fiction. She believes firmly in happy endings, chocolate, family, and good friends. When not writing, she stays busy persuading her toddler that the coffee table was not actually designed to be a trampoline or a teething toy. Her hobbies include reading, bowling, and playing poker.

Please stop by her website. Any comments, gifts of chocolate, or new friendships are always welcome.

Marly welcomes comments from readers. You can find her website and email address on her author bio page at www.ellorascave.com.

Tell Us What You Think

We appreciate hearing reader opinions about our books. You can email us at Comments@EllorasCave.com.

THE PHALLUS FROM DALLAS

Samantha Winston & Ciarra Sims

ဢ

Chapter One
A Huge Problem

&

Mitch

Mitch stared at his huge cock. It was the bane of his existence.

Ever since he'd been old enough to get laid, women had run screaming from his monstrous organ. To make things worse, he'd gotten drunk one night and someone had dragged his sorry ass into a tattoo parlor. Written in gothic script, just under his navel, were the words "The Phallus from Dallas". The worst thing about that being, he lived in Austin. If the woman wasn't screaming at the size of him, she was rolling on the floor laughing at the tattoo. And the dark didn't help—the damn words were fluorescent.

If he ever got his hands around the neck of the bozo who'd hauled him into the tattoo parlor he'd… Hell. He'd been so drunk it was possible he'd done it to himself.

That would teach him to go out gambling and drinking. Sure, he'd won the championship. He'd deserved a bit of fun, so he'd gone out and gotten shit-faced drunk. He had a vague recollection of staggering around trying to pick up every gal he saw and being generally obnoxious. He'd acted like a jerk.

But to wake up with the most dreadful hangover of his life and the words "The Phallus from Dallas" written on his lower belly was terrible punishment. After that, he'd never touched another drop of liquor and promised he'd stay away from gambling. He'd sworn that on his knees, and in exchange, he'd prayed for a woman to call his own. Someone to love him and share with him all the joys and sorrows of life.

He wanted a wife and a family, something better than just his two hands to warm his cock.

He looked once more at his colossal cock. There had to be someone out there who wouldn't scream and faint at the sight of it. Someone with a heart to love him, and a body to fit over his—

A nicker brought him back to reality. He reached over the bars of the corral and patted the shiny, red hide of his beautiful mare, Hi Ciarra. "Well, at least I have you," he told her, but his heart was heavy and he sighed. His daydreams were just that—dreams. He'd better get his mind back to tasks at hand. He had a long week ahead of him, and he had to get his farm in order.

Hannah

Hannah Hunt from Houston had a horrible headache as she headed her Honda towards the highway. She had a bit of a drive before she reached the Dallas-Fort Worth area and her destination, the Pro Bull Riding Association finals, but she didn't mind.

It would give her time to dream of that hunk of a man that kept her temperature hotter than the asphalt in the midday heat. She had memorized his face...tanned and lean, his square jaw marked with a sexy cleft, and that smile—lazy and knowing...as if he could be rode all night and put away wet and still come back for more. Hannah's fantasy and wet dream all rolled up in one.

Hailing from Austin, Mitch Winston was known as "The Phallus from Dallas" because when he'd won the Dallas-Fort Worth PBRA bull riding championship two years running, a rumor had started that he was hung like a Brahma bull. The moniker had stuck, and every woman dreamed of sneaking a peek at the lusciously long cock that reportedly had to be shielded by a special cup for the bull riding event.

Hannah wanted more than a peek. She was obsessed with having Mitch ride her the way he clung to the back of those bulls. Only she wouldn't try and buck him off… No, siree, she'd lock her legs around Mitch Winston and feel every inch of that dick slide into her till he was wedged as tight as he'd go, and then she'd make him give her more. She'd clench her cunt around him till he creamed inside her, and still she'd milk him until he'd had the ride of his life.

Hannah had seen how the women buzzed around The Phallus as he exited the arena, like honeybees looking to pollinate. There was no doubt Mitch could have his pick of women but his fast and loose attitude wasn't fooling Hannah one little bit. She was the only woman for Mitch Winston and she'd make him see that!

Mitch

Mitch was heading towards the PBRA roping and bull riding championship with his red sorrel mare. He'd entered in the calf-roping contest and the bull riding, as usual. Calf-roping was for fun, and to give his mare a workout. But bull riding was serious. It was his bread and butter, and if he didn't win this year, his biggest sponsor, CowPoke Condoms, would drop him. Then he'd have to sell his horse and the trailer he'd won at last year's event to pay the rent.

So, his mood as he drove towards Fort Worth was pretty tense. What he needed, he knew, was a spunky filly to tuck into his bedroll and help him relax. Not some dainty little fashion-victim of a city-girl. No, he wanted a real woman—one with good bone and muscle on her frame. One who didn't care if she didn't have makeup on. One who loved to strip off her clothes and plunge into a swift-flowing stream, shouting, "Catch me if you can, and then do what you want with me!" She'd have wide shoulders and long legs, and a butt big enough to grab with both hands. Her tits would be made for sucking, and her cunt would stretch large enough to take all of his mighty cock into her —

Shit. He swerved back into his lane and wiped some sweat off his brow. He had to stop daydreaming about being able to squeeze his dick as deep as it could go into a slick, hot, throbbing pussy while driving. His cock felt like —

Pop! Pop!

Damn. There went the first two buttons as his cock reared up in need.

He pulled over to a handy rest station and checked to see no one was around. He didn't feel like getting arrested for indecent exposure. He thought about putting his ten-gallon hat on his lap to hide his hard-on, but decided the best thing would be to real quick pump himself dry. Then he could get back to driving and keep his mind on the road.

He unbuttoned his jeans the rest of the way and grabbed his cock with both hands. Leaning back in the seat, he slid his hands up and down, all the while squeezing and thinking of a honey of a gal with a mouth as wide as the Rio Grande and a cunt made to hug him tight all the way down. All the way — what he'd give to be able to plunge all the way in.

He had never been able to thrust into a woman without worrying about hurting her, so his sexual encounters had been lessons in control — painful struggles to be gentle and hold back. He'd taught himself the art of slipping just the head of his powerful peter into a woman's pussy and then thrusting ever so slow until she'd reached her limits. His cock had never been more than halfway in. Frustration sometimes made him want to bawl like a roped calf.

But he knew that somewhere out there was a ready and willing woman made by the Creator just for him. He had faith in his Creator, because why make a stallion and not his mare? His filly was out there somewhere, and he would find her. He'd love her and cherish her, and he'd dive into her slick cunt while she screamed with pleasure, *not* pain.

Hair and eye color made no difference to him. He pictured her as a laughing gal, with breasts that bounced when she walked and a swagger to her hips. He wanted spunk and personality, and a slippery, swollen pussy hungry enough to take his whole cock in one big swallow.

He imagined her peeling off her skintight jeans and tee shirt, and tossing them in the hay. Then she'd tease him a little — reaching up and unhooking her bra as slow as molasses, and then she'd take it off, baring those beautiful breasts. She'd touch herself, running her hands down her sides and belly, turning herself on for his pleasure. He pictured her fingers probing into her dark pubic curls, giving him glimpses of a shiny pink clit.

By now his cock was throbbing in his hands, but he held himself back. His dream woman was bending over, showing her whole cunt to his avid gaze. With dancing fingers, she parted her labia and stroked them, spreading sweet juice over her shiny flesh. Her cunt gaped open, and she bent lower, spreading her legs. As he watched, one, then two, then three fingers plunged into her pussy. She wriggled them around, stretching herself wide.

"Come and get me," she whispered.

He pictured himself going to her, taking hold of her hips, and gently pressing the tip of his cock to her cunt. She looked back at him, her mouth curved in a smile.

"Harder!" she ordered. "I want all of it, you hear?"

His hands pumped frantically on his cock in response to his daydream, and the image of a swollen pussy surrounded by glistening dark curls made his mouth go dry. Arching his back and wishing his seat was bigger, he groaned aloud as he imagined her hungry pussy sliding all the way down his aching cock. He tightened his fingers, closed his eyes, and let the vision take over.

She shoved backwards, her pussy opening and stretching. But to his astonishment, she didn't stop halfway. She ground her ass into his hips, pushing against him while inch by inch he slid into her tight sheath. It felt so good. It felt so right! Tight and pulsing, hot and slick—and hugging him right to the root of his monstrous cock. His balls slapped against her ass as he started to thrust. He felt his cock start to jerk in his fists.

"Yeah, baby," he groaned. "Yeah, all the way, that's right. Please, all the way...yah-hoo!" he cried, his hips lifting off the seat with the force of his orgasm. His dream woman cried out with him, writhing as he shot his load straight to her womb. He sighed in relief, then opened his eyes. The vision vanished, replaced by the very startled face of an elderly woman peering through the cum-spattered windshield.

"Are you all right, boy?" she asked. Then she caught sight of his monster penis—her mouth dropped open and tears actually appeared in her eyes. "If only I were fifty years younger," she said. "I could've given you the ride of yer life, sugar."

"I'm so sorry!" stammered Mitch, his face boiling with embarrassment.

"Oh, that's all right. I've seen a bunch of those suckers, and now I can die happy, knowing I've seen the biggest one of all." She shook her head.

Mitch cleaned his cum off the windshield with a tissue, and then started back towards the highway. He caught sight of the old lady in his rearview mirror. She was still staring after him and still waving. He waved back halfheartedly.

The next exit was Fort Worth, and soon he was at the fairgrounds setting up his corral and getting Hi Ciarra settled in.

Chapter Two
The Rodeo

ೲ

Hannah

Hannah pulled her Honda into the parking lot awed by the size of the crowd. Every year this event got bigger and bigger. In the side lot, various trucks and trailer rigs were parked for the weekend event. Was Mitch Winston's one of those? She knew it was likely. She craned her neck for a better view. It was widely known he'd won a loudly painted red-and-black slant load horse trailer for taking the championship. Cowpoke Condoms sponsored his clothing and paid big bucks for Mitch to sport their logo on his jeans and shirts. They never hesitated to supply the championship prizes, either, provided their product name was emblazoned on the side. Mitch proudly accommodated them two years ago by winning the championship and taking possession of the trailer.

Last year Hannah had waited in the slant load trailer, as Mitch finished the bull riding event. But he'd never shown up after all the press conferences and Hannah had ended up waiting in the small trailer dressing room till she damned near froze her ass off. There was nothing sexy about a cramped, bare-bones dressing room anyway and she doubted Mitch and his enormous phallus could have fit in it with her anyway. But damn, it had been her last chance to get next to him for a whole year!

She remembered her frustration at knowing there would be no riding that huge cock she so craved. But Mitch Winston was a prepared cowboy and always carried a spare saddle. In this case, a wide-seated roping saddle with a big horn that rose up sort of like a short, stubby, flat dick. Hannah had sighed with regret and disappointment over the poor substitute for Mitch's own glorious dong but it was a part of Mitch, sort of.

The saddle stood on a metal rack lower than a horse's back but still elevated enough that the stirrups swung free. With a wicked smile Hannah shucked off her boots and jeans and swung on, placing her stocking feet in the stirrups. The leather padding molded to her seat, just right, and when she leaned forward, her labia rubbed seductively against rough, textured leather. *Time for a test ride,* Hannah thought with glee. She rose on the stirrups and leaned forward, rocking herself as if Mitch were under her, his woolly pelt of pubic hair rubbing against her, making her wet and slick.

Already the heady smell of her juices on warm leather made her swoon with lust. Hot leather and the smell of sex were the ultimate aphrodisiac to Hannah. She increased her pace against the saddle seat as she rubbed her labia and leaned forward, bringing the leather in contact with her clit. The worn saddle had little nubs that created delicious friction and made Hannah writhe all the more. She grabbed a long thin piece of leather, the piggin string, attached to the back of the saddle. With a quick snap she was able to bring it down on her thigh like a lover's lash, so lightning quick it caressed her before the sting took over and made her shiver. She alternated the whipping motion from both sides, bringing herself to a frenzy of pain and pleasure.

But she needed more. She wanted a part of Mitch in her— even if it was only a part of his saddle. Hannah raised herself up and parted her nether lips wide. The saddle horn was hard wood covered with leather, wrapped in layers for reinforcement, with slight ridges between the layers. When Hannah stretched her pussy around it and sat down, she felt every nuance of the leather and the ridges against her vaginal walls, stroking her, bringing pleasure to her already creaming body. The thick, hardy stitching on the top of the horn rubbed her clit as she worked herself to and fro, bucking frantically.

Breathless and not sure she could take much more, Hannah smelled raw leather and her cunt juice and, she swore, the manly aroma of Mitch Winston.

With a cry, not far from a scream of primal eruption, Hannah peaked. Her orgasm crashed over her like a stampede of longhorns. A flood of creamy cunt juice coated the horn and ran down the sides. A little gift for Mitch, whenever he used the spare saddle—and he would, to keep the leather pliable and in good repair. On any hot day the sun would heat up that leather and the smell of Hannah would flood Mitch's nostrils.

A keepsake from the very heart of her. She marked her territory, like a bitch in heat, wondering if Mitch would get to know her smell, a subliminal message appealing to his most basic instinct, that of a man looking for his special woman. And when the day came when she got close to him...and she *would* get close to him, his senses would recognize her unique scent and he'd be unable to resist latching on to her and like to a stud, mounting her with his stiff cock sticking straight out ready to mount and plunge its engorged head into her swollen cunt and ride her till her flanks quivered. Hannah sighed. God, she hoped so!

This year Hannah had hatched a new plan, one that didn't contain such a wide margin for error as Mitch recognizing her by smell. She knew the layout of the fairgrounds by heart. Rodeo cowboys were a superstitious lot and since Mitch had won last year, he'd set up in the same corral in the same area this year or as close to it as he could. Hannah also knew Mitch still had his sorrel mare, Hi Ciarra. Hannah had read in the PBRA magazine that he'd trained the mare himself and treated her like a queen. So Hannah had dyed her own shoulder-length hair the same burnished copper shade as Mitch's beloved horse. He had to notice her this year...he just had to.

The standing-room-only crowd was flowing towards the entrance gates and Hannah joined them, clutching her coveted ticket as though it were a lifeline. When she passed through the entrance, the ticket agent stared at her ample breasts in the baby blue stretch knit tee shirt as if they were an ice cream cone ripe for licking. Hannah gave the man a look of pure scorn. She'd chosen the shirt as the color was the exact shade of blue as Mitch Winston's delectable eyes—and the fact the material hugged her luscious breasts and showed the tantalizing top of the deep crevice between her cleavage. No siree, these cones were for Mitch's tongue only!

There were ropes and poles set up to guide the crowd into the refreshment area and bleachers but Hannah knew better than to let herself be trapped in the roiling coil of lookie-loo's who came to the event to eat, drink and watch cowboys eat dust. Years ago, in her teens, she'd been a barrel racer and knew her way around the chutes. Small-town rodeos, big-city championships, it made no difference, the crowds were all the same.

With a sly glance about, to be sure no one was looking, she ducked under the rope and dashed behind the stand selling popcorn, cotton candy and cinnamon churros. She had to skirt around the chutes to get to where the contestants lounged around or stood bullshitting about their past glories. Hannah had never seen so many fine asses packed into Wranglers and Levi's in all her life. If she hadn't had her heart set on one specific pair of overpacked Wranglers she might have paused and admired the scenery longer. But her plan needed to be set in motion and time was a-wastin'.

Behind, and to the right of the chutes, the portable corrals were set up, and right where she knew he'd be stood The Phallus from Dallas, Mitch Winston, petting his horse. Damn it! Hannah had forgotten the carrot! An integral part of getting close to the man was getting close to his horse and now she had come empty-handed. There was nothing for it...she'd have to use her God-given talents—her tits and ass.

And God had given her ample in both departments to work with. Her ass was packed into a pair of stretch Levi's that hugged her generous hips and teased her cleft and her clitoris as she walked, for Hannah Hunt hated panties with a passion. She would have no panty lines obscure her luscious hams — hams just designed for a man to grab onto, begging for mercy, as she rode him to orgasm time and time again.

And *her* man was waiting not more than a few yards away. Suddenly Hannah felt a squish beneath her Justin lizard-skin boots. Damn it! She's stepped in a pile of cow patty that stunk like high heaven and clung like molasses to a piece of toast. Hannah couldn't help it... She was cursed with a temper that let loose like a cyclone. "Hog's britches, son of a bitch! Cattle-whoring piece of shit! Mother fu — "

Suddenly aware she was being watched, Hannah looked up into the baby blues of her dreams. "Can I help you, little lady?" A voice deep and husky that made Hannah's cunt heat up instantly spoke in a tone that was amused and, yes, interested. Cow shit forgotten, Hannah made a show of tucking strands of her coppery hair behind her ears, hoping to draw attention to its vibrant hue.

Mitch rewarded her by staring at her hair and continuing down to her face. She wondered if he found the smattering of freckles on the bridge of her nose alluring, or if he liked the way her chest jiggled with the remnants of her anger. She thrust her heaving bosoms out, inviting him to admire their creamy fullness. She knew she had his attention as her nipples tightened instinctively beneath his gaze, and she swore she could feel his tongue, as it ran over his own lips, tease them till they puckered and swelled. His eyes roamed to her hips and Hannah shifted one leg forward to accent their glorious full roundness that begged to be molded against his own rising bulge.

Hannah's eyes grew huge as she took in the growing cock that should have been firmly encased in denim. But the button fly Wranglers were stretched to their limits, and the serpent was about to burst forth in all its lusty girth and length.

"Oh, God!" Hannah cried as she creamed in her jeans, and the sudden burst of thick liquid that surged from her cunt took her by surprise. How could she deny herself any longer? But she must!

She could tell Mitch Winston was interested. The Phallus from Dallas spoke its own language and it was loud and clear. With an abrupt, demure retreat, Hannah took a step back. She wanted Mitch and she would have Mitch, but he had to prove himself to be worthy of the prize.

"You like what you see, cowboy?"

"Yeah. You know I do. It's obvious."

Hannah watched as Mitch rubbed his crotch as if to relief the discomfort of the tight inseam. He tried to reposition himself gently but there wasn't enough room in his jeans for his hands and his enormous cock. "Give me your hand." He didn't exactly command her, but it wasn't a request either.

Hannah held up a hand that wasn't small and delicate but wasn't the meaty size of Mitch's either. "Now, work it down inside my jeans then take my cock and move it to the left a scootch. It's the least you can do, getting me all worked up before the big event."

"I…" Hannah decided not to argue, instead she tried to get her hand down the front of his jeans. "You'll have to unbutton them. There's not enough room."

"Stand behind me." He commanded huskily.

Hannah complied, noting her head barely came to the big man's shoulder.

"Stand flush against me and give me your hand."

Hannah wedged herself against his hard ass and reached around, rocking herself against him. He grabbed her hand and guided it to his fly, where the buttons were undone.

"Someone will see us!" Hannah protested weakly.

"Honey, I am six-feet-four and two hundred and twenty pounds. Don't matter what anyone sees, they ain't gonna say a thing to me about it." He assured her as her hand dipped into his pants.

Hannah felt taut muscles flinch under her touch, almost quivering in anticipation as her hand slid over thick pubic hair till it encountered the Paul Bunyan of erections. The super phallus was hard, it was silken…it begged to be touched, stroked and sucked all at the same time and Hannah wanted to be the one to make it happen.

Her hand barely fit over the massive love muscle, so she made do with stroking the base then gliding back and forth. Totally awesome! It was like petting a feral beast that longed to be uncaged and free. She fondled the crested shaft further, trying to work it out of the jeans but the large bear-like paw over her own hand stopped her.

His voice was a mere rasp. "Much as I want you, I ain't got the time. I gotta put the big guy in his cup and be ready to ride in fifteen minutes. You be around after the event?" His voice was smooth and didn't betray the anxious hope his mesmerizing blue eyes held.

"Oh, I'll be around." Hannah patted his big daddy dick back into place. "Can you ride with it like that?"

"Sweet thing, I can ride with a hard-on just as natural as I can have sex all night long. It's a part of me just like that butter-melting smell coming from you." His brow furrowed as if he wondered where he'd smelled her lip-smacking, musky mesquite aroma before.

Hannah gulped. Did he recognize her odor as the same leather and joy juice that surely flooded his nostrils on hot days in the saddle? It took all her willpower to withdraw her hand and say the words she'd only dreamed of saying in her mind. "My name's Hannah Hunt. But I'm not easy as you think, Mitch Winston." She tilted her head coyly, then added as an afterthought, "You want to taste that butter you've got to prove yourself to me by winning today."

"Oh, ho! The little lady puts a high price on her favors." Mitch grinned.

"You don't win with a '96' score and you don't get any Hannah." Hannah smiled softly with her best "come hither" smile.

She had the satisfaction of seeing Mitch gulp. "A '96'? Are you crazy? Do you know which bull I drew?"

"Uh-huh. I read the PBRA magazine. You're riding Billy the Kid, the meanest son of a bitch in the chutes."

"Yeah, and also unridden this year."

"So…ride 'em." Hannah shrugged, feigning indifference.

Mitch ran a hand through his thick dark hair and laughed. "Yeah, I'll ride 'em and then I'll ride you."

Hannah let her breath out in a rush. It was hard to think straight, much less breathe, with that hunk of a stud just a few feet away. She watched him walk towards the chutes admiring the way his ass filled out the jeans that touted *Cowpoke Condoms* stenciled on the back pockets. God, she wanted to get into those pants and get a good look at The Phallus from Dallas.

Mitch

Mitch wanted to win the bull riding bad, real bad. He loved his horse, he liked his slant load trailer and had no intention of losing either, but most of all he wanted Hannah. She was pretty, despite the dyed red hair. He didn't mind that though—why, it almost matched his horse's coat. He wondered what her real hair color was. He might be able to tell if he caught a glimpse of her pussy.

He loved a challenge. He loved spunk. And this girl had spunk. Plus, she hadn't batted an eye when she reached her hand into his pants and took hold of The Phallus. Most women swooned or turned white as sheets. Hannah had simply smiled like the cat that had caught the canary. He wanted her beneath him, squirming. And if riding Billy the Kid to a '96' was what it would take to get that filly under him, then that's what he would do.

With his special cup in place to guard his humongous cock, Mitch sat on Billy and wrapped his hand in the rope, tight. Not as tight as he pictured Hannah and her cunt wrapped around him, but tight enough so his hand wouldn't slip out and earn him a no score. He waited for Billy to quit shifting his great bulk. The Black Angus bull, known for his spins, was a hellion to ride. Mitch heard his name announced and took a deep breath.

Mitch knew the bull felt every emotion coursing through him. So not until he'd relaxed, did he nod for the gatekeeper to pull the rope and open the gate. Billy sprang forward and, true to form, began to whip around a yard from the gate. Mitch hung on, feeling the rope around his hand slip. He thought of Hannah and what it would mean if he lost. He spurred the bull and stuck with him.

At seven seconds he felt himself list sideways as Billy ended the spin and reversed suddenly. Mitch threw himself back and clung to the bull tenaciously, his body pitching, spurring hard, riding the bull like there was no tomorrow.

He heard the eight-second buzzer but still rode the bull. He felt a rush of adrenaline as he jumped from Billy and the pick-up rider shielded him until the bull made his escape back into the chutes. Mitch doffed his black hat to the roaring crowd and waved it triumphantly.

He'd done it! He'd rode Billy the Kid till the eight-second buzzer. He felt great.

He waited with bated breath for the score. Had he used enough spurring action? Had Billy's spin been enough to get him the score he needed not just to win but to get Hannah? He heard the crowd roar with approval as his score came up.

'94'.

Mitch knew he should be relieved. It was a great score and hard to beat. It probably had won him the round, but it wouldn't get him Hannah. He felt a gnawing in his stomach like a craving he knew wasn't going to be fulfilled. Damn, but he wanted that girl.

Her coppery red hair and her snapping brown eyes had caught his fancy. Not to mention her curvy body, full hips and breasts, and long, strong legs. He sensed that she was the one for him. But how to convince her that despite his score? '94'! Someone up there was playing a mighty nasty joke on him.

He scanned the crowd hoping to catch a glimpse of Hannah's fiery hair. But the crowd was too dense, and now reporters, fans, and officials surrounded him in a churning, screaming scuffle. It would be ages before he untangled himself to go search for the gal of his dreams.

Hannah

Hannah felt her heart flutter as Mitch rode the bull. As the massive animal twisted and spun, her breath caught anxiously until the buzzer sounded and she released a sigh of relief. He'd done it! He'd rode the bull safely and even bowed to the crowd like the winner he was.

When his score came up she felt her heart plummet. Why the hell had she said he had to get a '96'. It was an impossible goal. Why couldn't she have said '94'? *Damn you, Hannah!* She railed at herself. Now what? She couldn't renege on the deal, but she'd waited so long for that man... She had a decision to make and she'd better make it before the end of the event.

Hannah watched as one after the other, the other bull riders either hit the dust or rode their behemoth bovines to the annoying sound of the buzzer. Mitch won easily and came out to accept the trophy and congratulations. Hannah sighed as she made her choice and slowly made her way out of the stands and headed towards the parking lot.

114

She meant to drive on back to Houston and put Mitch Winston, The Phallus from Dallas from Austin, behind her. She tried to convince herself it wouldn't have worked between them and the life of a rodeo cowboy was too uncertain and hard for Hannah, no matter how tough she was.

She almost succeeded...almost.

You stupid fool, Hannah Hunt! A man like that comes along once in a lifetime...now don't blow it! Hannah pulled the Honda around hard and reparked. It was getting dark but that would make it all the easier. She made her way back into the fairgrounds, the stamp on the back of her hand enough to get her past the ticket monitor. Using the same route as earlier, she was back by the corrals in no time, but there was no sign of Mitch. Either he was doing interviews or out celebrating. Hi Ciarra, his sorrel mare, nickered as Hannah came up to her corral. The mare hadn't been fed yet so that meant Mitch would be back.

Hannah looked about, spotting the barn where the community hay was housed. The cowboys paid extra to be provided with hay for their animals so they didn't have to haul so much with them on the road. With little compunction Hannah headed for the barn. In the gathering dusk she saw bales of alfalfa and straw stacked neatly while a few bales had been cut and loose hay and pale straw strewn about.

She didn't know how long she'd have to wait and there was always a chance others would come in, so as a precaution Hannah ducked behind the bales and sat down. She must have drifted off, because a sound awoke her and suddenly the barn was flooded with fluorescent lighting.

Hannah peered from behind the bales and there he was! Mitch Winston grabbed a flake of alfalfa and headed out into the darkness. Hastily Hannah hurried out to the loose hay, hopping on one leg at a time as she shucked off her boots and pants. Without a thought, she tossed her shirt haphazardly onto the floor. She had to get in position, using the soft natural mattress of the hay to display herself, reclining provocatively.

When she heard his boots scudding on the hard-packed ground outside the barn returning to turn off the lights, she posed herself with her arms behind her head and one leg crooked seductively.

Mitch appeared, the words of a Toby Keith song cut off in mid-sentence, as he caught site of the bodacious vision provocatively displaying herself right before his eyes.

Hannah had the satisfaction of seeing him stunned beyond words. She sighed breathlessly. "Come get your prize, cowboy."

Mitch shook his head as if waking from a dream. "But I didn't make the score."

"You give me a sixty-nine ride and I'll score you a ninety-six, sugar." Hannah laughed.

Mitch was next to her before she completed the last chuckle. Impatiently he tore at his shirt. Popping buttons flew in all directions in his haste to peel it off. He dropped to his knees and knelt over Hannah's lush form. "You sure about this, pretty Hannah?"

"Oh, yeah, cowboy. Show me what you got."

Mitch's lips were brusque, yet soft against her own, feeding a hunger intensified by a hell of a day. His tongue pushed inside her mouth, and she opened her legs so he could lay between them. He was a big man and could have crushed the breath from her but he was careful—she wondered if years of riding the bulls had taught him such skilled weight distribution. So it was a secure feeling Hannah received from his bare chest against her voluptuous breasts, pressing hard and rubbing against the nipples, teasing them, prepping them for his tongue.

When his wet mouth traced a path to her breast and seized the puckered nipple, laving it tenderly, Hannah gained a false sense of gentleness. She only had time to sigh before his mouth fastened on her areola and suckled forcefully until she begged for mercy. With a chuckle Mitch turned his attention on her other full-bodied orb and provoked equally conflicting sensations that nearly drove Hannah out of her mind. As he worked over her, Hannah undulated beneath him, writhing in a tide of naked lust and passion. A large callused hand with long fingers worked its way down her thigh into the dark curls that encircled her cunt. He sifted through the tangle of growth and pulled teasingly at the hair. Even this light love play brought a rush of thick fluid from her cunt, coating Mitch's fingers.

"I gotta get me some of that, darlin'." His mouth left her breast, and without preamble fastened itself against her cunt like a man in the desert slaking his thirst. At first his tongue licked the sensitive lips, taunting Hannah, encouraging her to give up her cream, daring her to do so, making it impossible to keep the flood of liquid from working its way towards his greedy mouth. As if taking a dram of fine wine Mitch dipped his tongue into her and took a taste, but then finding it too intoxicating to be merely sipped, he lapped avidly before thrusting his tongue inside her as far as it would go.

She bucked beneath him but it was nothing for the big man to hold her with one hand and lick her juices till Hannah thought she would go mad swallowing back her screams of ecstasy.

"Don't you come yet, sweetheart. Don't you come till I'm buried deep inside you." Mitch coaxed and Hannah fought the urge to spasm against his tongue. She couldn't hold out much longer.

Mitch's long fingers replaced his tongue. They felt inside her, as if measuring her for what was to come. Hannah clenched around his hand but he only rubbed against her clit enough to make her squirm impatiently, her body begging for the ultimate gift, if she was woman enough to take it. All of it.

Mitch rose up and shucked off his boots. Hannah heard the jangle of his belt and the *whomp* as his champion belt buckle hit the barn floor. At least Hannah hoped that heavy noise was his belt buckle. With a sudden flash of uncertainty she rolled to her elbow and looked at Mitch. He was just rolling down his briefs and—

"Oh...my god!" Hannah couldn't help the words that tumbled from her lips.

His cock was huge! Magnificently engorged, thick and long, the pulsing serpent was a beautiful sight to behold. The moment she had been waiting for was upon her but suddenly Hannah had second thoughts about that masterpiece plunging into her. She found her legs closing of their own volition.

"It's alright, darlin'," Mitch assured her. "I will never hurt you. Only bring you pleasure. Lay back and let me show you. That's a girl."

His low voice soothed and reassured Hannah, and she complied. Mitch's fingers prepped her, moving in and out, his thumb flicking her clit till Hannah writhed again in unfulfilled wanton lust. "Do you want my cock, Hannah? Say when and it's yours but slowly...so slowly...you'll take it in, feeling every inch, expanding so you'll be able to enjoy what a man with a big one can do for you."

He pressed the tip of the big cock against her vulva and moved it inside, stroking Hannah's clit with his finger all the while. "Take a little more. That's it. Raise up."

The big dong parting her cunt lips so wide felt foreign even with just the tip and first two inches inside. Before she could contemplate this Mitch pulled back withdrawing almost completely, but then he rocked forward and another two inches found welcome. The next time when he pulled back, Hannah was ready and met him halfway, taking in a full six inches. She groaned at the bulk working its way inside her, making her want to shriek with uncertainty, yet the feeling was sooo good she wanted more...had to have more.

She wanted a chance to savor the sensation as she contracted around his girth. "Wait!" Hannah breathed.

But he only smiled and gave her another two inches.

Hannah sighed and squeezed her cunt around him, tight. She wanted to milk him...to make him cream but Mitch wasn't finished. He pulled back only a little this time and fed her two more inches. Hannah quivered, thinking she couldn't take any more.

She'd been fondled in the past, nibbled on and pounded into by men whose idea of sex was fumbling and groping flesh or how much noise they could force from her own lips whether it be pleasure or pain or a yawn. But the feel of Mitch sheathed within her was awesome. The way it coaxed her to give from her very apex, to accept his faults into her soul. To accept Mitch fully inside her was to accept Mitch as a person. Could she agree to so much? Her eyes must have communicated her fear and uncertainty as Mitch suddenly became still.

"It's all right, sweet Hannah," Mitch soothed. "Relax and give me some juice to help. Don't grip me so tight. Not yet. Relax."

Hannah breathed deep and let her muscles go lax. She felt a thick slide of cunt juice release and in answer Mitch slid in two more inches causing her to quake like a volcano...quickly Mitch pulled back then hunched over her, bringing her fully against him. He was in her all the way and she couldn't believe how complete she felt and how a woman like Hannah Hunt from Houston could take all The Phallus from Dallas had to give. The fact filled her with pride and she preened, trying to keep from grinning. But Mitch's next move drove all thoughts of self-congratulations from her mind as she felt him nudge against her womb, withdraw, then bury his rigid staff deep inside her again. Hannah felt the huge cock within her as she contracted against it, and it answered by pulsing back...she tingled as it moved, rubbing against the walls of her textured canal like sandpaper against silk.

Hannah watched the myriad emotions playing over his face as Mitch began to undulate within her, his great girth contracting and expanding, insisting Hannah accept its bulging presence. Hannah tried to stifle her cries to prove she was able to handle his unadulterated passion but Mitch wanted to hear her raw moans. "No, baby. Let it out if you want. That's it. Let me ride you like a twisting, turning bull. Feel me. All of me, inside you. Ah, you feel so good, so tight."

A spring inside her begin to uncoil as he moved and churned within her. Her juices gushed but she did not orgasm. She felt it coming but it wouldn't release her. She writhed against Mitch and tried to pull him in further. Her mewling cries seemed to incite Mitch to pull out and push back in, all the way to the hilt. His rhythmic movement caused friction, rubbed her clit back and forth, teasing Hannah mercilessly into following his motions and anticipating his needs. Frenetically Mitch grabbed her generously rounded ass and held her still as he drove into her over and over, then with his balls resting against her anus, he rubbed against her, marking her with his musky scent.

Hannah's orgasm rocketed through her like a speeding train. Her hands clutched Mitch's beefy arms and kneaded the muscles in rhythm to the surging force that radiated through her cunt into her stomach and throughout her body. Even her toes orgasmed as they curled and uncurled spasmodically. The blood in her head pounded with the ringing in her ears as wave after wave rushed over her.

Without warning Mitch bellowed and began to shoot his load, his body clutching hers as over and over they quaked and creamed to a peak. Mitch's cock pulsated within her and caused little bursts of sparks, encouraging Hannah to continue to ride against him, milking his cum greedily.

Almost like a wind-up toy Hannah's motions gradually slowed as the fire faded to embers. Their hearts thudded loudly as Mitch lay, still within her, trying to catch his breath. "You okay, sweet Hannah?"

"Umm. Died and gone to heaven." Hannah sighed with pure, sated bliss. Never in her life had she dreamed such a feeling existed. The whole barn could have collapsed around them and she could have cared less. No heifer in the herd could be as happy with her bull as she was with her cowboy. She'd wanted him, she'd gotten him and if she had it her way, she'd have him again.

She felt his cock, still huge, though no longer engorged, pulling out of her. "Ohhh." She mourned the loss of him pulsing within her, almost like it was a piece of herself he withdrew. "No…"

Already there was an ache in her heart at the thought that it was over. Her cunt felt empty, bereft of the catalyst that had made it slick with dewy cum as it hungered for the hard, oaken rod that was only part of what made Mitch her special lover.

"It's all right, my little cowgirl. I have something very special I want to ask you."

Chapter Three
The Proposal

ഔ

Mitch

Mitch got up and knelt in the hay. His heart was pounding. Not only from the best sex he'd ever had or ever dreamed of, but because he was about to lay his life on the line. He cleared his throat, hoping his voice wouldn't crack like a school boy's.

"Hannah, honey, I have been searching for the woman of my dreams ever since I was old enough to dream about her. I've prayed each day the sun rose and finally my prayers have been answered. Hannah, will you do me the honor of becoming my wife?"

There. He'd said it. He held his breath. If she refused, if she left him, he'd just curl up and die—he knew it.

Hannah lifted her head and stared at him. Her eyes sparkled with tears. "Oh Mitch," she said. "I...I don't know what to say. It's so sudden! We hardly know each other!"

Mitch's stomach clenched with nerves. She hadn't laughed at him, but she hadn't said yes either. Desperately, he searched for something to say. "We have all the time in the world to do that now. I want you by my side, Hannah. I never want to leave you. I promise to be true, and I promise—" Her hand came up and covered his mouth.

"I have to think about this."

She got up, and to Mitch's dismay, started to walk away. Oh no—she wasn't getting away from him! He grabbed the first thing he saw. His lasso. He tossed it over Hannah's head.

She uttered a cry of surprise as he pulled the rope tight, pinning her arms to her sides. Her breasts were imprisoned too, the rope making their lush cleavage even more impressive. She struggled, and it was sheer delight watching her strong body as it twisted and turned. But Mitch had held onto tougher critters than his sweet Hannah.

He knew he had to have her. Everything about her seemed familiar and so very right—her smell most of all. For some reason, the scent of her aroused pussy brought to mind hot days on his favorite saddle, with Hi Ciarra galloping fast beneath him.

"Let me go!" she cried, tossing her head just like a wild filly.

"Nope." Mitch shook his head. He cleared his throat. "I ain't letting you go, little missy, until you say yes to my proposal." Seeing her naked body held by his rope made his cock stir with interest. When his mammoth meat moved, her eyes fastened onto it, and Mitch watched her nipples harden. His groin flooded with desire, and his cock stood up at attention, throbbing with renewed desire. Just the memory of slipping into her tight pussy was making him lose his train of thought. The curls around her sweet pussy had been black as night—brunette? He wanted to ask her, and he wanted to ask her if she'd noticed his tattoo, but first he needed her to agree to marry him.

Hannah tried to get free, but he tugged on the rope, spinning her into his arms.

"Mitch!" she said breathlessly. Her eyes were very bright and now a smile tugged at her full lips. "Don't I get to think about it for a little while?"

"Nope." He grinned and then quickly slipped the rope between her legs. Now it pinned her arms to her sides and ran between her thighs. He pulled on it slowly, and watched her eyes widen as the rope came to rest against her cunt. He tugged a bit more, and her mouth grew round.

"Oh!" she breathed. Her eyes glazed and she opened her legs. Now he saw the rope between her labia. He pulled it even tighter, and she gave a little mew.

"Say yes," he said. His cock throbbed hard, letting him know just exactly what it thought of this game. He reached down and adjusted the rope, so that it fit right between the crack of her luscious ass—her labia hugged the rope now too. Mitch knelt so that he could see better.

Hannah spread her legs wider. Mitch tugged the rope, watching as the rough hemp touched her sensitive flesh. Her clit stood up, a shiny pink nub, and as he watched, Hannah arched her back and rubbed her clit against the rope.

"More!" she begged.

Mitch pushed her back onto the soft pile of hay, careful not to let the hemp harm her. "Please Mitch," she cried. "More!"

"Not until you agree," he said. He knelt between her legs and kissed her pussy. His tongue sought her clit, and he tasted the saltiness of his lasso. The fibers felt hard against his tongue, but her flesh was sweet and soft. He tongued her clit, and eased his finger beneath the rope into her cunt. He found her hole open and ready for him, wet and swollen.

He almost lost it there, and he had to close his eyes a second to get a hold of himself. His cock ached with terrible need. He felt it building in his loins. In a minute he would explode all over her belly and thighs.

"Yes!" Hannah cried, as his finger slid into her cunt and his tongue twirled around her clit. "Yes, please Mitch, yes. I'm gonna marry you if it's the last thing I do, but please…please fuck me right this minute!"

Hannah

Hannah couldn't believe things could get more crazy, more exciting. First her dream come true—sex with The

Phallus from Dallas, then a proposal. Never had she experienced anything like sex with Mitch or the hemp against her cleft with the little velvety abrasive pieces of rope fiber like pubic hair rubbing, teasing, until she creamed herself. Then Mitch had tenderly moved the rope aside and his large fingers took its place, so careful to deliver maximum pleasure, like precision instruments, knowing where to strum and stroke, playing her till she thought she would sing out her orgasm.

And just when she thought she couldn't take anymore, Mitch's tongue found the center of her sexual sundae and licked her cream like he couldn't get enough. Hannah tried not to thrash underneath his tongue. He was so close to hitting her love button and sending her to the big 'O' corral but she wanted him inside her when she peaked.

"Now…Mitch. Please! Put that big schlong of my dreams inside me and brand me as your own." Hannah caught her breath as Mitch's tongue withdrew from her cunt and covered her lips. She tasted her own love juices and found she liked the musky, acrid taste.

She gave Mitch a reassuring kiss then pulled her head away and looked down their bodies. "I want to watch you enter me, Mitch. Bit by bit, inch by inch. No matter how I beg, give it to me slow and easy. Then when you can't stand it any longer, give me all you've got. Make me quake like an aspen in a hard-blowing March wind." Hannah watched as his dick parted her slick glistening lips. The tip slowly undulated inside, wedging itself stubbornly.

"You want some more, pretty Hannah?" Mitch rasped. "Talk dirty to me. Tell me what you want."

"I want two more inches of your delicious prick, filling me slowly till my juices flow, covering the head. Give me that much, my big stud." Two more inches went into her with a sucking noise as air was replaced by cock and Hannah's own juices smoothed the way. The slick passage was stretched and Hannah could not help but writhe as she felt the expanding and welcomed his cock home to her moist, accommodating cave with a sigh of anticipated bliss. She felt like a pig in a puddle, about to dive in deep.

"Now give me four inches and take back one, then give me three more." Hannah hoped Mitch could add and subtract to keep her in maximum overdrive of sexual pleasure. He sank in four inches of skin then withdrew before plunging in to the hilt.

Hannah gasped. "That's not..." But she couldn't finish her sentence because Mitch reared back and plunged in again, all the way, driving the air from Hannah's lungs and pussy at the same time. She was filled one-hundred percent with pure all-American cowboy cock and it felt as incredible as skinny-dipping in the dead of winter. All the blood rushed to her cunt and she could feel every nuance, every ridge of the straining member that burrowed inside her.

Mitch gave her all he had and kept going, till Hannah's head spun and her vagina contracted and expanded, milking Mitch's cock. With a roar that perfectly emulated a bull, Mitch shot his load. When Hannah felt hot cum shoot inside her, it set off a chain reaction. The feel of torrid jism spreading through her brought her to an orgasm that curled her toes and brought her heels up under Mitch's butt as she rode him like a bucking bronc. Their mutual cries echoed through the barn and from somewhere outside a lonesome bull answered the primitive cries.

They collapsed, still entwined, gasping for breath. Mitch pulled out and plopped his glistening rod onto Hannah's belly. Hannah stared down at the huge phallus like it was her own personal lollipop. "Ah, I have never seen a more beautiful sight!" She patted the still erect dong affectionately.

Hannah caught sight of something written just above her gorgeous cock. Feeling territorial, she tried to get a closer look. "What's that?" she demanded. It looked like writing but it couldn't be...could it? A stab of jealousy pricked her heart. Had there been someone else in Mitch's life? Who else would write a note on the hard, flat slats of his lower belly muscles?

"I have to hit the lights to show you, darlin'." Mitch got up and, naked, padded to the light switch.

Hannah forgot her jealousy and stared admiringly. She was so entranced with his magnificent physique and the afterglow of the hottest sex she had ever experienced that she wasn't paying attention as Mitch hit the switch and plunged the barn into darkness.

Then suddenly an eerie incandescent green glow came from out of the dark and Hannah saw what she had dreamed of all her adult life.

The Phallus from Dallas was coming right at her and it was all hers…gloriously hers.

Epilogue

Mitch

Hi Ciarra tossed her head.

"Whoa… Easy, baby." Mitch held out his hand and said, "C'mon Mrs. Winston, darlin', let's go for a ride."

Hannah brushed her hair out of her sparkling eyes. She'd let it go back to its original color, dark brown with coppery highlights. "I still can't believe I'm Mrs. Mitch Winston."

"Well, honey-pie Hannah, you'll have to get used to it, 'cause your gonna be Mrs. Winston for a long time," Mitch drawled, pride in his voice. He grinned at his bride. The wedding had been a rowdy, wild, whirlwind of country music, a big barbeque and square dancing. The farm still sported signs of the party—some beer bottles lay in a patch of black-eyed susans. He and Hannah hadn't had time to clean it all up yet. But there was plenty of time. And right now, the heat was wilting the leaves on the trees.

Hannah batted her eyelashes at him. "So, handsome cowboy, where are we going?"

"How about to the creek for a swim?" Mitch asked.

He settled Hannah on Hi Ciarra's back in front of him and clicked his tongue. The horse moved at an easy canter, and the rocking-horse gait pressed Hannah close to Mitch's britches. In a minute, the inevitable happened. His cock grew so hard it hurt to ride.

"Sorry, hon." Mitch pulled back on the reins, and Hi Ciarra slid to a stop. "I'm about to burst outta my jeans," he said apologetically.

Hannah dismounted. "Get down," she said.

Mitch thought he knew what she was getting at, and he started to grin. His grin widened when, after a quick glance around the deserted arroyo, Hannah peeled off her jeans and shirt. She stood naked, and raised her eyebrows. "What are you waiting for?" she asked archly.

He quickly unbuttoned his pants and pushed them off. But Hannah pointed to Hi Ciarra and said, "Get back on, cowboy."

"Huh?" He did as she asked though, carefully setting his bare ass on the sheepskin riding blanket cinched over Hi Ciarra's back in place of a saddle so they both could ride.

"Help me up now," Hannah said, giving him her hand.

"Wrong hand," he said, then stared as Hannah clambered up and sat facing him. Her face was split in a grin. She leaned back a bit, and he caught sight of her delicious pussy. Her eyes were fixed on him, though.

"What a hard-on," she purred, and she scooted her butt back towards the mare's neck, hunched over, and slid her lips over his cock.

"Whoa!" cried Mitch. He moved back a-ways, careful not to rile Hi Ciarra, who didn't like weight on her croup. But the mare was being mighty accommodating today, and only twitched her ears a little. Hannah's mouth was wet and warm, making him think of something else. He reached around and slid his hand between her legs. She rubbed right up against him, purring like a cat, her throat vibrating his cock. His fingers slipped and slid over her desire-greased slit. She rubbed harder and her clit tickled the palm of his hand while his fingers sank into her ready cunt.

He was so hard it hurt. "Lordy, woman," he gasped. "I'm as hard as a hickory branch."

The words were hardly out of his mouth before she hitched herself up and settled herself on his cock.

"Easy, cowboy," she whispered. Her flesh stretched, letting him enter her bit by bit. She held him tightly around his shoulders, her breasts brushing against his chest. Her nipples were so hard they felt like pebbles. He wanted to grab them and suck on them, but he didn't want to let go of the mare's reins. With his free hand, he clasped Hannah's ass, holding her steady. Hi Ciarra snorted and started walking towards the creek.

"Oh Lordy," he groaned. He hardly dared move. Hi Ciarra's gait jarred Hannah farther onto his aching cock. Her cunt slid down with each hoofbeat. Down, slowly easing down... Then the horse broke into a trot, and he plunged deep.

"Oh Mitch!" Hannah cried. Her voice broke and she ended the cry in a shrill scream. "Oh yes!" Her whole body shuddered against him. The trot was getting bouncy and Hannah bounced along with it, slamming onto his dick with each quick step. Mitch felt himself losing control.

"Giddy up there," Mitch said. He kicked Hi Ciarra into a canter. The up and down bumping turned into a gentle back and forth movement. Now he could control himself better. He watched his cock sinking into Hannah's cunt, sliding in and out in an even rhythm. The sheepskin blanket softly stroked his ass and thighs, while Hannah moaned and bucked against him. Juice spurted from her cunt—she was so aroused he could feel her muscles bunching and tensing.

His free hand slid lower on her butt, and he put his hand between her ass and the saddle blanket. He felt his cock thrusting into her. It was incredible. He was plunging in and out—all the way in. He still couldn't believe it.

Sinking into her tight, slickly buttered cunt made his heart pound in his ears. Black spots danced before his eyes and his legs and arms twitched. His cock started jerking, and with each jerk his seed spurted out in a hot, steady stream. His orgasm grabbed him and squeezed him as tight as Hannah's pussy, which contracted like an iron fist when Hannah came. He pumped as long as he could, trying to make it last. And when it was done, he wondered if he had any liquid left in his entire body.

Hi Ciarra came to a stop at the water's edge. Mitch needed a minute to catch his breath. His body felt as loose as pulled taffy. Hannah slumped against him, her arms flung around his shoulders, her head resting on his chest. Her lips moved, tickling his left nipple.

"What was that, sugar?" Mitch asked, when he could speak.

"I said, 'I love you, Mitch, my darling Phallus from Dallas'."

"Me too, Hannah, my love. That said, how 'bout you race me to the other side of the creek?" he teased.

She raised her face to his and grinned. "And the winner gets to tie up the loser with your lasso."

"Whatever you want. We have a democratic marriage." Mitch laughed.

Hannah smiled innocently, then slid off the mare and yelled, "On your mark, get set, go!" She streaked off into the creek, splashing Mitch liberally.

Mitch patted Hi Ciarra's neck. "I never said *I* was doing the running. Go get her, girl!" Encouraged, the mare took off after Hannah, like the trained cow horse she was. She would round Hannah up just like an errant calf.

Hannah

Hannah was intent on keeping her speed and balance in the deepening water. She splashed noisily into the middle of the creek. Abruptly Hannah realized all the splashing wasn't coming from her. The sound of raspy breath was all the warning she received before she found herself knocked flat, face down in the water, fighting to come up for air and sputtering with rage.

131

"Mitch Winston! You son of a bitch! You ran me down like a cow! I have a mind to—" She rubbed the water out of her eyes and stared, finding herself face to face with the sleek hide of Mitch's sorrel mare. She pushed the horse aside and got to her feet. Mitch sat astride the horse, leaning over her with a worried frown.

Mitch's face split in a grin and a note of pride crept into his voice. "I'm sorry, honey. I didn't realize Ciarra would take it to heart and knock you down like that. But damn, she was impressive, wasn't she?"

"Yeah, we'll see how impressive she is on cold winter nights, because you ain't snuggling up with me anymore!" Hannah glared at Mitch, daring him to take one step closer on the mare.

But Hannah wasn't prepared for the speed in which Mitch dismounted, landing next to her. He gave her no choice in the matter as he swept her up in his arms and carried her to the grassy bank. "You know what I think?" Mitch's hot breath seared Hannah's ear.

"What?" Hannah tried to still sound angry, but her voice came out breathless.

Mitch continued, "I think you need to be rode, and rode hard from behind, till you can't take any more and collapse with my big cock still buried inside you."

Hannah's eyes widened in terror. "Mitch, I can't take that big thing in my booty! It'll tear me apart!"

"Not that way, sweetheart. I'm going to pump into your love canal from behind and fill you with my jism. You seem to doubt my ability to get back in your good graces so I think I will apologize in my own way." He set Hannah down on the embankment. "Get on your knees, Mrs. Winston. Your husband wants to say he's sorry."

Hannah was about to argue. Would penetration from behind with that big cock hurt? But she trusted Mitch and he wouldn't hurt her...at least not in a bad way. Mitch settled the issue by grabbing his rope and smiling impishly. Her wrists were loosely bound before she could protest and she was gently forced to her hands and knees. She saw Mitch's shadow rising up behind her and the stiff rod of his magnificent phallus approaching. She felt her butt cheeks being creased as the big serpent passed by and approached its destination. Hannah's cunt lips split open as the massive head slid into her at an angle. The rest slowly followed until it met resistance.

"Relax, sweet thang," Mitch drawled.

Hannah responded to his soothing words and instantly felt the cock inside her bypassing her resistant cunt muscles and burrowing deeper until it struck bottom. Mitch drew back and lunged forward. The friction against Hannah's ass cheeks was incredible but the kicker was the way Mitch rubbed at her clit. Back and forth. To and fro. Slow and fast. Like hot fudge sliding over ice cold ice cream. Hannah thought she would melt out from under Mitch but to her credit she backed up, encouraging Mitch to bring it on…

The setting sun made the sky glow orange and set their bodies on fire. Their dark shadows on the bank mimicked him riding her. Their reflection in the water's edge showed him fucking her like a bull, thrusting to the hilt, his balls slapping against her thighs. His breath rasped in her ears…or was that her own breath? Hannah could not tell the difference between the two and panted out loud, "Mitch, before you, there was never a man who could make me feel this way. I love the way you fill me totally, branding me with your hot iron. I want to feel your cum shoot inside me. I want your taste on my lips every night before we go to sleep. Promise me that, will you?"

Mitch's voice was husky and low, "Yeah, baby. I promise. Just as I swear to love you till the day we die. You're my woman Hannah, forever and always."

Hannah's joy in the words doubled as she felt Mitch's lips on the back of her neck, sucking gently, then his shaft withdrew and plunged, punctuating his declaration. Without warning Hannah felt the spiraling of an orgasm and cried out as Mitch shortened his strokes and hit her clit with quick rubbing flicks that made her cream over his embedded shaft. Mitch roared to his own orgasm but kept pumping.

Hannah's breath expelled in short gasps as she came again and her knees shook unsteadily. But The Phallus from Dallas showed no mercy as he bucked against his quaking wife, giving her the ride of her life as the sunset turned their entwined bodies to gold.

Also by Samantha Winston

ഌ

A Grand Passion
Asteroid 6969: Tiger Gold
Cajun Nights *(anthology)*
Darla's Valentine
Diamina
Fairnight: Elf Song
Fairnight: Llewellyn's Song
Fairnight: Merlin's Song
Gladys Hawke
My Fair Pixie
Once Upon a Prince
Renegade Aquarius
Taming the King
The Argentine Lover
The Frog Prince from Planet Marecage
Storm Warnings *(anthology)*

Also by Ciarra Sims

ഌ

Felidae
Walk on the Wild Side

About the Author

ଙ

Samantha Winston is the pen name for Jennifer Macaire, an American freelance writer/illustrator. She was born in Kingston, NY and lived in Samoa, California and the Virgin Islands before moving to France. She attended Parsons school of design for fine art, and Palm Beach Junior College for art and English literature. She worked for five years as a model for Elite. Married to a professional polo player, she has three children.

After settling in France, she started writing full time and published short stories in such magazines as Polo Magazine, PKA's Advocate, The Bear Deluxe, Nuketown, The Eclipse, Anotherealm, Linnaean Street, Inkspin, Literary Potpourri, Mind Caviar and the Vestal Review. One of her short stories was nominated for the Pushcart Prize. In June 2002 she won the 3am/Harper Collins flash fiction contest for her story 'There are Geckos'.

Ciarra Sims is a native of southern Cal. where she lives with her dogs, cats, and horses. She enjoys writing gothic horror, Regencies, westerns and contemporaries; but is game to try any new genre, whenever the notion pops into her head. She believes a person is only limited by their imagination and prides herself in following the beat of a different drummer.

Samantha and Ciarra welcome comments from readers. You can find their websites and email addresses on their author bio pages at www.ellorascave.com.

Tell Us What You Think

We appreciate hearing reader opinions about our books. You can email us at Comments@EllorasCave.com.

1-800-SEX4YOU
Chris Tanglen & Michele Bardsley

જી

Chapter One
Arissa

ಎ

"I can't do this." I looked in the bathroom mirror and assessed my new purchase from *Madame Persia's House of Erotica*. I had to admit that the black bustier made the most of what little boobage I owned. The sheer black hose felt good against my freshly shaved legs, too. The scrap of black lace that passed for underwear hid the thin line of pubic hair left from my painful and tear-inducing Brazilian bikini wax two days earlier.

My best friend, Drae, peeked over my shoulder. "Arissa Montague," she intoned. "Sex Goddess."

"I cut my hair for this emotionless sexual encounter," I said, shaking my head. My new short tresses resettled into the sleek new 'do, a wash-and-wear and gel-and-blow-dry specialty that cost me two hundred bucks. "I'm an idiot. I don't spend that much money on my clothes."

"It shows," said Drae, who threw a glance at the stack of sweats and T-shirts on my bed that had yet to make it into my closet. "But you're worth an expensive haircut and fancy lingerie and hot sex with a stud who will put ol' Jeremy to shame."

Our eyes met in the mirror. My fiancé had dumped me six months ago in a very public scene at our mutual workplace, Mortenson's Public Relations. Drae worked in the same building for a collection agency and had arrived to take me to lunch at the same time Jeremy arrived with his whore, our lovely lobby receptionist, to announce the end of our engagement. The receptionist was a sweet young thing who fucked anything that walked and her little poisoned claws were still embedded in the man. And, oh yeah, my boss, Derek Mortenson, also known as the biggest asshole in the world, witnessed my humiliation too. He was a dark, moody man who never smiled, always worked and probably had hot sex all the time. Especially on that big cherry wood desk...*oh baby*. He was big, tall, broad-shouldered and muscled. I wondered what he looked like naked. His big hands would cover my breasts, knead them, pinch the turgid points...

"Earth to Arissa."

I blinked. My breathing had shallowed and my eyes had glazed. I cleared my throat and looked away from my turned-on mirror image and Drae's crafty smile. She probably thought I was getting all hot and horny for the upcoming encounter.

"Life sucks." I exited the bathroom and picked up the slinky, strapless black dress. I'd bought matching black shoes with three-inch heels. "If these aren't fuck-me pumps, I don't know what are." I shimmied into the dress and put on the heels. Then I sat on the bed, my body trembling, tears threatening to ruin my carefully applied makeup. I was still pissed off at my rotten ex-fiancé and still felt vulnerable to any man, even one who just wanted a sexual playmate. "I'm a desperate, sex-crazed woman. I am paying a service so I can boink with a stranger."

"Yeah, you're pathetic," agreed Drae in a cheerful voice. "Put on your earrings."

I stuck the tiny diamonds into my ears and twisted on the backs. Drae spritzed me with expensive perfume then stood back to look at the end result of a month's planning.

That's right. *A month*. Drae found 1-800-SEX-4YOU. It was her last weapon in the Get-Arissa-Laid-So-She'll-Stop-Whining plan. Jeremy's desertion put me into a depression that had me on the couch with a stockpile of coffee ice cream. I overdosed on romantic-comedy movies, too.

Drae put up with this behavior for a couple of weeks—a record for her. She's short on sympathy, preferring action to moping. Me, I'm a moper. I've spent the last six months going out to dance clubs, bars, parties and the occasional blind date in the hopes Drae would tire of her efforts. She's got a short attention span too, but nothing, and I mean *nothing*, distracted her from The Cause.

If having sex with a stranger meant she'd leave me alone long enough to sneak a pint of mocha fudge ice cream, I'd do it.

"It's safe. You viewed the facility. You've been tested physically, emotionally and mentally. They have your sixth grade school records, for Pete's sake." Drae grinned. "This is the best way for you to get into the game again, love. Treat yourself to hot, hot, hot sex and re-enter the world of the living."

"I really can't do this," I said, thinking of Derek again. He was a cold man. A brilliant man. An emotional black hole. Would he consider a passionate one-night stand? He was a guy, after all. Maybe if I arrived in my current outfit and splayed myself on the desk, he'd fuck me until I couldn't remember my name.

Yeah, right.

"You're in charge, Drae," I said. "Watch my babies. I'll be back in the morning."

"I'll watch your cats," she grumbled. She pretended not to like Mou Mou, Sallie and Talina, but she loved the rascals. The cats didn't really need a babysitter but Drae, for all her tending of my love life, didn't have a relationship in sight. Maybe I should badger her to try 1-800-SEX-4YOU.

The idea had merit.

* * * * *

"I'm nervous," I admitted to the cool blonde. I'm blonde too, but not cool. More like too-much-sunshine blonde. Her secretive smile did nothing to reassure me. Instead she crooked a finger, sashayed from behind the desk and gestured for me to follow. I didn't give my name or any information. I was annoyed that she knew who I was and what I was here for without me saying a word. "Uh...you're not confusing me with anyone, right?"

"Arissa Montague. Age twenty-seven. Measurements thirty–twenty-four–thirty. Loves animals. Works for Mortensen's Public Relations. Recently ended engagement." She stopped at one of the white-paneled doors, opened it and pointed with her elegant arm. "You received three As, two Bs, and one D in the sixth grade."

"That's scary."

Her smile warmed. "You have no idea."

I entered the room and the woman followed. "Your partner will arrive shortly. You both requested anonymity. In order to ensure those requests, we ask that you wear the silk half-hood. It will cover the top half of your head, allowing your lips to remain free." She pointed to the two silk purple hoods hanging on hooks near the door.

So much for the freakin' $200 haircut and va-va-voom makeup. All my partner would see is the ends of my hair and my lips. "He'll wear one, too?"

"Only one of you needs to wear the half-hood at a time." Lit candles were everywhere, on the nightstands, the floor and the tables in the sitting area. It was huge! The mattress looked soft, comfortable under the white cotton fitted sheet. Pillows of all sorts and sizes heaped against the headboard; a mass of folded blankets covered the other end of the bed.

"Toys are in the drawers of the nightstands. We've provided protection, too, if you need it. When you're ready for a break, simply ring the bell and your personal butler will bring an assortment of goodies." She finished checking the preparations then rounded the bed to stand in front of me. "Butterflies in your stomach are good." She pressed slender fingers against my stomach then trailed up to circle my left breast. My nipple hardened at her light caress.

"I'm not a lesbian."

She laughed, circled my right breast with the same soft, seductive touch and the damned nipple hardened. Didn't my body know the difference between a woman's seduction and a man's?

"I'm not a lesbian, either," she said as she lowered her head to kiss the dimple at my throat. Her soft lips moved up my throat to my earlobe. She nibbled around the diamond, her tongue flicking to touch the inner shell of my ear. I stood still, trying to assimilate what I was allowing to happen.

Maybe I *was* a lesbian.

Her hands found my breasts and kneaded them through the bustier. The nipples tightened into hard buds and scraped against the lacy material. I couldn't stop the moan from escaping my lips.

More embarrassing than my reluctant moan was my pussy getting wet.

As if she knew, one of her hands reached under my dress and slipped into my panties.

"Hmmm. Good girl." She moved away, took a hood from one of the hooks and returned. "Ready?"

"Uh…" Did she think she was going to fuck me? Oh hell no. "I requested a man."

She laughed again. "Arissa, you worry too much. I'm not going to seduce you. I was trying to…relax you." Her grin was wicked. "The client who matched your profile is a longtime customer. He knows the rules of engagement in our little playground. You will be pleased."

The next thing I knew, the hood came down over my head, covering my eyes, and I felt it tighten at the back where she tied it.

"I'll take your purse to our safe," she said, tugging the strap from my shoulder. I released it.

She led me to the bed. I sat on it, knees together, heart pounding, and waited. I heard the door click shut.

This hood business was tantalizing. And fearsome. My body felt tingly from the non-lesbian's touches and I wondered when Prince Charming In Bed would arrive. My hand slid between my thighs, up my dress and into my panties to stroke the clit.

Oh yeah.

Whoa. I didn't pay for a fancy place to masturbate. I paid for a full night of amazing sex with a guy...a guy I hoped was like Derek. Okay, I know I said he was an asshole. It seems like all the sexy men are assholes.

And women like me, who can't even hold on to their fiancés, are prime targets for men like Derek. Cheap dates. Easy lays. Forgettable faces. At least here, in this environment, the using for pleasure was equal. There wasn't any emotional baggage.

What the—?

It wasn't so much that I heard a door open but that I felt a tremor in the air, like something had disturbed the tiny atoms and they were scrambling to rearrange themselves.

"Hello."

A spike of fear dug into my guts. *What the hell am I doing?* I didn't know this guy from Adam. Was I really going to open my legs for Joe Schmoe? I mean, geez, I was so overwrought with Jeremy's betrayal, I was going to have anonymous sex. What would that prove?

That orgasms are fun.

"I...uh. Maybe this was a mistake. I'm thinking I need therapy." I cleared my throat. "Real therapy. Not, ah, sex therapy." I laughed but it turned into a cough.

"I see."

Not a big talker, this guy. I chewed on my bottom lip, trying to decide what to do next.

"Perhaps you would like to take off your dress." His voice was low, soothing, edged with desire. "The hose must come off, too, because I want to feel your soft skin on me, the way your thighs feel against mine when I take you. Hmmm…but the heels…those stay on your feet."

My heart jumped, somersaulted and returned to beating—fast. Maybe I could stay. For a minute or two. It wouldn't hurt to hear the guy out, after all.

"What's under that dress?" he asked.

God, he had a great voice. Deep, seductive and oh-so-smooth. If his body matched his voice…I was a goner.

"Why don't you find out?"

I don't know where I got the courage to utter the words but when I heard his sharp intake of breath, female satisfaction purred through me. Then I felt one finger trail across my shoulders.

"No zippers. No buttons. No ties."

The finger danced down my spine then a firm male hand splayed there and pushed gently. I rose. I couldn't see a damned thing, so I tottered but he steadied me. I stood there for an endless moment, wondering where he was, what he would do.

I felt the edge of my dress lift then the warmth of his hand against my flesh. His fingers felt smooth and strong. I sighed in pleasure as his hand slid up my thigh to cup my buttock. He kneaded the flesh, squeezing it gently, before gliding to the small of my back. The dress lifted higher, the silky material sliding along my sensitized skin. I felt good. Really good. But my doubts wouldn't go away. I bit my lip.

"You do that when you're unsure."

I froze. "How do you know that?" Just how much lip-biting had he witnessed in the five minutes he'd been in the room? Then a horrible thought crossed my mind. "Do you know me? Oh my God. Do I know you?"

Was that a muttered curse under his breath? I couldn't be sure. Silence as thick and heavy as the blankets waiting for us on the bed descended. Did I know him? Worse, did he know me? Even with the hood?

"It is a general trait of women," he finally said. "I didn't mean to frighten you."

"You didn't frighten me," I lied. "It's just...I'm doing this so I wouldn't have to get involved with someone I know."

"Forgive me, but you don't appear to be someone who has sex for the hell of it."

"How do you know?"

"Women who come here do not need therapy, sexual or otherwise." I could almost feel his arrogant grin. "They want no-strings fucking."

"That's what I want."

"Somebody hurt you and you don't want to risk love again."

Anger fired through me, killing the tendrils of desire clinging from his previous touches. "I didn't know the package included armchair psychology. Now, do you want to have hot, hard sex or not?"

"Since the moment I saw you," he replied.

Just like that, my anger disappeared and the weird pleasure-fear he invoked replaced its heat.

Before I could form another coherent thought, he lifted the dress over my head. I heard a soft *slish* as it hit the thickly carpeted floor. I felt the curve of his lips against my ear then he whispered, "Are you ready for the best fuck of your life?"

Chapter Two
Derek

෨

Before I introduce myself, let's discuss that whole non-lesbian bit.

I wasn't around for the first part of that chapter, so I was enjoying the read and learning some new things but it really threw me when the cool blonde, whose name is Vivian, started fondling Arissa. Not that I'm opposed to such activities by any stretch of the imagination but I couldn't help but think *C'mon now, why would this lady just start pawing at her*? Is it just a woman thing? I can tell you that if I were preparing myself for sex with a hot lady and some guy took it upon himself to manipulate my testicles, he'd be dealing with the completely heterosexual sensation of my foot up his ass.

But, okay, though I thought that it sounded kind of farfetched, I was getting into the whole erect nipples description. Wet pussy? Sounds good to me. In fact, I was all ready for them to break out the toys and leap onto the bed, when the cool blonde said that this was to "relax" her.

Now, let's think about this for a moment. If you're trying to relax someone, do you really think that making her confront her latent bisexuality is the way to do it? I mean, if the aforementioned hypothetical guy were manipulating my testicles and I developed a hearty erection, I'd be anything *but* relaxed. It just doesn't make any sense. Do you really think that this cool blonde gets away with fondling all of the customers? Don't you think that maybe, at some point, one of the customers would fill out a comment card that said, "Nice furnishings, good sex, but I wasn't real keen on the cool blonde grabbing my tits."

So I made a couple of phone calls and found out what happened. Vivian noticed that Arissa's shoulder strap was a bit crooked and politely reached over to fix it for her. Arissa turned suddenly and her breast brushed against Vivian's arm. That was it. I'm not saying that Arissa didn't acquire perky nipples or a dampening of her nether regions as a result of this contact but I am saying that the whole hand-in-the-panties thing didn't happen.

Okay, to be fair, I've already admitted that I wasn't there. For all I know, Vivian dropped to her knees and slid Arissa's panties down to her ankles. Her moist, sensuous tongue danced circles around Arissa's sensitive clitoris and sent waves of excruciating ecstasy pulsating through her glorious femininity. But if you look at the credibility factor here, I'm just saying that it's much more likely that Vivian's story (accidental arm against boob) is the truth and Arissa's story (emerging bisexuality used as relaxation technique) is a severe exaggeration.

Still, it was a nice little moment.

I don't want you to think that my primary goal is to point out all of the errors in Arissa's narrative but I'd also like to briefly mention her annoyance that the hood would hide her $200 haircut. I'm sorry, but the hood thing was mentioned in the pamphlet. If she didn't take the time to read the documentation, it's really nobody's fault but her own. Maybe if she would read things more carefully at work, I wouldn't always have to *be* the "biggest asshole in the world".

Yes, I'm Derek Mortenson, Arissa's boss. But you already figured that out.

I'd been a regular client of 1-800-SEX-4YOU for the past three years. I'm what you would call a workaholic...I put in seventy, eighty hours a week easily. Not because I have to, but because my public relations company is my life. I'd started out ten years ago with one client, a country singer who couldn't sing, play a musical instrument, or wear a cowboy hat because it made his scalp itch. Well, let me tell you, I put in the hours. I worked tirelessly, late into the evenings and all day every weekend, to get this guy some press. No matter what it took, no matter how much blood, sweat and tears I had to bleed, perspire and cry, I was going to make sure that everybody in Las Vegas knew his name.

I forget his name now, though. None of my hard work did a damn thing. I mean, let's be realistic, the jackass wouldn't even wear a cowboy hat. I'm not a magician, for crying out loud.

But my next client, a ventriloquist, had a bit more talent. Not a lot, mind you, but there was a smidgen hidden away somewhere in there. And this time, the whole city of Las Vegas *did* know his name. Of course, that's because he was busted in a casino for engaging in unnatural relations with his dummy, but before that shameful scandal he'd been building some name recognition as a direct result of my efforts. Really.

My third client was another singer, this one a… You know, this is becoming too difficult to talk about. I'm not supposed to be reliving the string of disasters in my professional life. Let's just flash forward to ten years later, when Mortenson's Public Relations is one of the most successful firms in Las Vegas and I'm putting in seventy to eighty hours a week because I want to.

This didn't leave me with time for a romantic relationship but that was fine. I'd had girlfriends in the past and they always wanted me to spend less time at the office. I didn't want to spend less time at the office. I liked the office. The office was my home. And I definitely didn't want to get married and have kids; so really, a girlfriend for me was just somebody to have sex with.

Okay, okay, I realize that a statement like that comes dangerously close to justifying Arissa's "asshole" assessment but that's just the way it was. I loved my freedom. I loved being able to put in long hours at work without apologizing for it and I loved being able to select which television show I watched when I got home. I had enormous amounts of responsibility at my business and I relished having no responsibility to anybody but myself when I was home.

That said…I also love sex.

Three years ago, I discovered 1-800-SEX-4YOU.

This service wasn't prostitution. Both partners were paying for it. It was an anonymous sexual encounter with none of the danger, emotional or physical. For a guy like me, it was absolutely the greatest idea *ever*.

It was also expensive as hell but hey, I could afford it.

I quickly became a regular patron, sometimes visiting as often as once a week. It was fantastic. I grew friendly with the staff and became a Preferred Member with the card and everything. The secretaries weren't supposed to share any private details about the encounters but, before too long, they were happy to let me know about any feedback they'd received. I don't want to sound like a raging egomaniac here but there were plenty of times where a grinning secretary would inform me that a female client had expressed her *extreme* satisfaction with the experience.

Six months ago, they let me start picking my women.

I don't wish to in any way indicate that 1-800-SEX-4YOU compromised the anonymity of their clients, male or female. I never saw the names or contact information. I did, however, get to see the interview videos, which were conducted in a darkened room.

When I saw Arissa's video, I couldn't see her face but I knew damn well that it was her.

And I got an immediate erection.

Arissa Montague has a low self-image but she's gorgeous. I wanted to make love to her since the day I hired her. Of course, if there's anything less desirable than a romantic relationship, it's an interoffice romantic relationship. There was no way in hell I was going to bed one of my employees. Not a chance. She was engaged to that prick Jeremy, so it wasn't an option anyway. To be completely honest, I almost didn't hire her because I thought the temptation would be too great, that she would distract me from my work. However, she was the most qualified candidate for the position and I wasn't about to admit that I couldn't handle having an attractive woman in the office. That would just be pathetic.

She worked out fine. Maybe not as attentive to details as I'd like, but certainly hard-working. I do have to admit that while I strive to be all business at work, with her I was probably even more so. Colder. Meaner. More of the emotional black hole that she mentioned.

But let me say this. If she *had* arrived at work in her current outfit and splayed herself on my desk, it would have been very, very, very difficult to resist the temptation to fuck her until she couldn't remember her name.

One of the worst days of my life was when that prick Jeremy dumped Arissa at work. Her devastated expression was so painful to watch that I had to return to my office and distract myself with fantasies involving that prick Jeremy and a plethora of spiked objects. I wanted to just go out there and give her a big hug, but again, I'm a professional. I don't show emotion at work. Emotion is what lets people take advantage of you, and *nobody* takes advantage of me.

Yeah, I wanted her but I couldn't have her. And if I couldn't have her, I wanted her to be wildly, blissfully happy. So watching the spark go out of her eyes and stay gone for the next six months was as painful as watching that dumb-ass no-cowboy-hat-wearing country singer perform for the first time.

When I watched the video, my intellect said "No". My penis said "Hell yeah…a million times, hell yeah!"

This was my chance to have sex with the woman I'd wanted for more than a year.

Anonymously.

The thing is, sexual anonymity is tough to pull off. Let's face it, the silk half-hoods make both parties feel better and they'd probably keep you from recognizing the person if you passed them on the street but if you already knew this person, if you worked with them five days a week, you'd recognize them.

Not to mention the voice problem. Early on, when I was paranoid about being recognized, I developed my "anonymous sex" voice. Lower, more sensual, more emotional than my "work" voice and, by now, using it was effortless. So if I could get her to keep the hood on the entire time, she probably wouldn't realize that it was me.

Unless, of course, in the throes of passion I screamed out her name. Always a concern.

Requesting Arissa as my partner was a bad idea. I knew it was a bad idea. I was a man who'd spent his entire life striving to avoid bad ideas in any possible incarnation. A man who never let emotion or libido get in the way of raw intellect and yet I did it. I asked them to set me up with Arissa and justified it to myself by pretending that I'd been mistaken and that it wasn't really her in the video. I'd just been wrong about the voice, the telltale hesitations, the nervous little giggle.

When I walked into the bedroom, it was definitely her.

And I was instantly hard.

Arissa didn't get the conversation quite right in her description but she did convey the basic gist of it. Yes, I did slip up with the "you do that when you're unsure" comment. In fact, it made me so nervous that I almost called the encounter off right then and there.

But she looked *so* incredibly good.

I had to have her. Screw the risk.

"Are you ready for the best fuck of your life?"

She giggled.

It was one hell of a sexy giggle but still, it was a giggle.

"What?" I asked, still whispering into her ear.

"Nothing."

"No, really."

She giggled again and put a hand over her mouth. "Sorry," she said a moment later. "I still can't believe I'm doing this. This is so unlike me."

"It's all right. You can relax."

"I'm relaxing." She took a deep breath and slowly exhaled. "Okay. I'm fine. Yes, yes, I'm very much ready for the greatest fuck of my life."

I stepped away from her and just stood there, staring at her. The black lace bra and panties she wore had to be brand new, purchased especially for this occasion. I'd have to let her keep them on for a while.

Her body was *incredible*. No, it wasn't a silicone-implant-enhanced-swimsuit-model body but it was the body of a *real* woman. The excited nipples of her small breasts were clearly visible through her bra and the various imperfections—a mole here, a stretch mark there—made her look even more incredible in my eyes.

"What are you doing?" she asked, nervously.

"Just taking in the beauty before me."

"Why? Is there somebody else in the room?"

"You're far too willing to insult yourself. I want you to repeat after me: *I am a beautiful woman.*"

"You've got a pretty low voice for a beautiful woman."

"This is no joking matter. I want to hear you say it."

"I am a reasonably attractive woman on my rare good days."

"Say it."

"I'm a beautiful woman."

"Now say it like you mean it."

"We're drifting away from the whole point of this visit again. Am I here for a cheerleading session or hot sex?"

"Very well." I should've known that she'd be a pain in the ass.

"You sound disappointed. Look, I appreciate the whole building-my-morale thing but I'm here to fuck. Well, and to have some great foreplay. Lots of it, if possible. Anyway, foreplay and fucking. That's my mission."

I almost laughed in spite of myself. I wasn't sure I'd ever been in a situation where the *woman* was the one anxious to eschew conversation in favor of fornication.

"You have a fantastic body," I said.

"Now that's the kind of talking I want to hear."

I approached her and put my hands on her waist. I inhaled deeply. She was wearing different perfume than what she wore to work. She'd probably purchased it especially for this occasion as well. I'd switched from my regular brand of cologne, just to be safe, too.

I slid my hands up her sides, then down over her belly. I leaned in and began to kiss her shoulders.

She put her arm around my back. "Ooh, soft."

I was wearing a fluffy white robe that 1-800-SEX-4YOU had provided. I liked their robes so much that I'd bought one to wear at home, monogrammed with my initials.

Underneath the robe, I was wearing my finest pair of silk boxer shorts and nothing else.

As I kissed a path up her neck, her hand moved from my back to my waist and then lower. "Ooh, not so soft," she said.

I chuckled.

Then I froze, wondering if she'd recognize my laugh. I quickly realized that the idea was ridiculous, since she'd never heard my laugh. Dark, moody man who never smiled, remember?

Her hand continued to caress my penis through the silk. Soon, her other hand joined in the fun, making me squirm with pleasure.

I nibbled on her right ear, making Arissa squirm as well. Her hands moved away from my erection, which I thought was rather heartless, but then slid around my waist and cupped my ass.

She gave it a tight squeeze.

"I can't wait to see this," she said.

I grimaced a bit. I hadn't quite figured out what to do if she insisted on trading places as the official hood-wearer. Maybe hide the lower half of my face in the blankets or something. I'd worry about that later.

I kissed her on the lips, gently.

She responded, not quite as gently.

Then something snapped. We simultaneously *dove* into each other, kissing with furious passion, our bodies pressed together and our hands roaming. I slid my tongue into her mouth and she sucked on it as if it were a cock.

She was kissing me with such vigor that I was starting to find it difficult to breathe…not that I was going to let myself be out-kissed by admitting it. I kissed back harder, eliciting a loud moan from her.

Without breaking the kiss, she threw open my robe and pushed it off my shoulders. It slid to the floor and she pressed herself more firmly against me, her pelvis tight against my cock. I wanted to just rip off her panties, throw her against the bed and fuck her from behind until we both screamed for mercy but I withstood the urge.

Instead, I was the one who broke the kiss. I scooped her up in my arms, startling her, and put her on the bed.

I set her down on the mattress. She immediately stretched her arms out over her head and arched her back like a cat. I have more than adequate control over such things but for a second I thought I was going to come right then and there.

I climbed on the bed with her.

"Are you comfortable?" I asked.

"Oh yes."

"Good." I slid my hand over one knee while I kissed the other. Her skin was soft and smooth and smelled like roses. I kissed a slow, lingering path up her leg, skipped her panties for the moment and then kissed my way up her stomach. She sighed happily the entire time.

I kissed one of her lovely breasts through the bra, starting at the underside and moving in a slow spiral until I reached the nipple. It was hard beneath my lips. I caressed her other breast with my hand, my thumb tracing the edge of the fabric.

She gently moved her leg, sliding it against my cock.

These boxers were becoming *very* uncomfortable.

I stripped out of them and tossed them onto the floor.

"Are you naked?" she asked.

I scooted into position and placed her hand on my penis. She began to slowly stroke it.

"I can't wait to see it," she said. "Maybe you should wear the hood."

"Oh, no, no," I replied. "You need your pleasure first."

I really had no idea how I was going to pull this anonymity thing off but I forced it out of my mind for the time being. My goal was to make Arissa so dizzy with ecstasy that she wouldn't care if she *ever* took off the hood.

"Sit up," I told her.

"What'll you do if I don't?"

"I think there may be a paddle in that drawer. I could roll you over and administer a spanking."

"You could spank me with your tongue." She sat up. I reached my arms around her and unfastened her bra.

I pulled it off and gazed at her bare breasts. Small, yes, but beautifully shaped, with a visible tan line. There's something about a visible tan line that I've always adored. Maybe it just enhances the feeling that I'm seeing something forbidden.

I touched the forbidden somethings.

We kissed again, deeply, as I caressed her breasts and ran my thumbs over the nipples. She moaned. Still kissing her, I eased her back down onto the bed.

I took her left nipple in my mouth and suckled it, causing her to gasp and run her hand through my hair. I continued to gently suck it as she writhed on the bed, biting her lip in a gesture that did *not* appear to mean that she was unsure about anything.

I switched to the other breast, giving it the same attention.

"Oh, that's good…that's so good," she moaned. "This is just what I needed."

I pinched the nipple between my lips, not too hard, and she let out an incredibly sexy whimper.

I alternated back and forth between her breasts, sucking one while fondling the other. Beads of sweat had formed on her neck when she pushed me away and sat up.

"I want you," she said. "I want to do the same to you."

She pushed me onto my back, rougher than I would have anticipated, and began to kiss all over my chest. Wet, hot kisses were accompanied by her hands sliding across my flesh, as well as more than a few love bites.

Arissa was getting herself worked up to become quite the little hellcat.

This was not a side of her I would've ever expected to see.

Her lips found one of my nipples and her tongue flicked rapidly across it. I have to admit, I've never really been comfortable with that kind of attention. I'm not sure why…maybe there's some social standard out there saying that a *real* man shouldn't enjoy having his non-functional nipples licked.

That said, this was *sensational*. In fact, I let out a whimper of my own and I'm pretty fucking sure that I have never, ever let out a whimper in a sexual situation.

She took my whimper as a good sign and began to suck.

I clenched my hands into fists and just let myself savor the sensation.

After about a minute, she switched to the other nipple, starting off with a soft bite.

I whimpered again.

I could tell that I was quickly losing control of the situation, which was not a good thing. In fact, Arissa was getting so worked up that I was scared she might thrash her head around and send the hood sailing across the room. Not a good thing either.

I moved back a couple of inches, so my nipple came free of her mouth. "On your back," I said.

"No."

"Don't make me break out the paddle."

"Don't make me break out the cat o'nine tails."

The scary thing was that 1-800-SEX-4YOU *did* have a cat-o-nine-tails on the premises. Not in this room, fortunately.

"Do as I say," I said, following it up with a comical growl. We wrestled playfully for a few moments and she ended up on her back as desired.

"I guess you're the boss tonight," she said, her voice almost a purr.

"That's absolutely right."

"Well, boss, may I make a request?"

"Of course."

"May I make a really graphic request?"

"You certainly may."

She very, very slowly spread her legs. My breathing quickened as I stared at her thin black lace panties, which had shifted enough to show that if she wasn't clean-shaven, she was darn close.

"I'd like to formally request that you lick my pussy."

158

Chapter Three
Arissa

ॐ

At this point in the evening, I still had no idea who my mystery man was but I know who he is *now* and I can tell you that his account is inaccurate. I don't care what that blonde bimbo reported to Gorgeous Guy, Vivian wasn't adjusting my bra strap. Okay, *maybe* I have latent lesbian desires and that's why I didn't protest overmuch. But I know when someone intentionally grabs my boob and when that same someone accidentally brushes against it. Big difference, believe me.

Like I said, I was blissfully unaware of my lover's identity. I was relieved that I didn't know the guy—or even if I did, God forbid—I wouldn't tell anyone I paid a sex service to hook me up with him. I mean, really, what kind of lazy commitment-phobic loser uses a service to find willing partners? Oh well. It made me glad we had to sign confidentiality agreements.

So anyway, the part about him thinking my body was incredible...hey, the guy can't be all bad. And yes, he wasted too many good fuck-me minutes with the whole cheerleading routine. Just because Jeremy criticized my thighs and hips and breasts when we made love doesn't mean I'm sensitive about how I look. I don't lack self-esteem. Entirely. So what if my boobs needed a boost and my hips weren't those of an eighteen-year-old?

Let's not go there.

I appreciated the guy's efforts because, well, it was sexy as hell for him to try to reassure me. Thinking back on it, I know I sounded prickly but I guess I felt uncomfortable with his kindness. I sound cold but I didn't want to feel anything except passion. I didn't walk into that room wanting a romantic, emotional evening. I was thinking more along the lines of down and dirty nonstop fucking.

Maybe it was a stupid way to finally rid myself of Jeremy but I was so tired of him and his bimbo flaunting their relationship at work. They played kissy face to a nauseating degree. It was like they waited for me to appear then— *boom!* Tongue wars. Hadn't I let Jeremy hurt me enough? It was as if he needed to drive home the point that he thought—and told me too often—that I was frigid. If he hated our bedroom antics so much why did he ask me to marry him? Why did he say he loved me the night before he dumped me? Why do I give a shit anymore?

Forget this potholed trip down memory lane. Let's get back to Gorgeous Guy's account of our evening....

I'd love to tell you the details of how my mystery man licked my pussy but first I must address the giggling issue. I. Do. Not. Giggle. I will admit that my mind was trapped in a sensual fog and most of my senses were...um, distracted but I have never giggled, not even the time I drank half a pint of bourbon and danced topless on a pool table. It was a frat party in college and I was twenty-two. My last memory of that night was crooning "Home on the Range" while my boyfriend tried to reattach my bra—an especially difficult task considering I was shimmying during his valiant attempt.

Just for the record, I did not formally request that the man lick my pussy; I *demanded* it. He obeyed without a whimper. In fact, I think he moaned, groaned and proceeded to strenuously lick, suck and moan some more. But that's just the overview. Here are the details...

He lowered his head and I felt his breath on the side of my right thigh. One fingertip traced my opposite thigh, from knee to stomach. Hot breath on one side. Slow finger trails on the other. Hot breath. Slow trails. Hot. Slow.

Then he switched sides.

Squirming? Me? No. I was writhing, thank you very much.

His hands coasted under my thighs; he pushed my legs up and back so my knees were near my breasts and my fuck-me heels dangled right above his head. At least I assumed so because I still wore the damned and downright annoying hood. I was starting to dislike the lack of visuals but the sensuous stimulation...that was worth the price of being temporarily blind.

I hoped to God one of my shoes didn't fall off and poke him in the eye. Not when...*holy frijoles!* Did he just do what I think he did? And I was worried about poking him in the eye when his finger just poked—whoa.

What was he doing now?

He shifted my panties to the side then I felt his tongue flicked the tiny bit of flesh between my vaginal opening and anus and I nearly fell off the bed. Not that it was sexy or intense or unexpected...oh wait. Yeah. It *was* sexy, intense and unexpected.

But his warm, wet tongue had only begun its journey. He slid around the opening to my pussy. He dipped inside and swirled then moved to the inner lips, wet and wanting, sweeping up and down, working toward my clit. My breath quickened. *Oh please...well, damn.* I attempted to maneuver my cunt closer to his mouth but he moved his head down, away from the hard little nub that needed his attention. He kissed, suckled, licked and neared Ground Zero only to zip down again.

I didn't know if I wanted to die from frustration or from pleasure overload. "Hold your thighs," he rasped.

Oh, good. He sounded as turned on as I was. It took a few seconds to untangle my hand from the covers I'd been mercilessly twisting but I managed to slip my hands under my knees and hold my trembling thighs.

I'm not sure how he managed to rip off my panties, because they were expensive, good silk and should've shown more fortitude but the next thing I knew the scrap of lace covering my nether regions was a distant memory.

His indrawn breath was very satisfactory. "You have a beautiful pussy."

He kissed the tiny strip of hair, then I felt his fingers on the edges of my pussy lips. He spread the flesh and rained tiny kisses along the slick folds. His tongue took long, sweet strokes but still missed Ground Zero, damn it. One finger, then two slid into me, then, thank heavens, his hot mouth encircled my clit and he suckled the poor neglected nub; at the same time he moved his fingers slightly up and pushed.

I came so hard, I swear to God I levitated. I screamed so loud, they heard me in fuckin' Miami. I didn't see stars. I saw planets. Wave after wave of pleasure assaulted me.

When I finally floated back to Earth and released my shaking legs, which collapsed as if they were made of gelatin, the so-called Boss crawled between my legs and moved around until I didn't know which parts were where. His breathing was harsh and I'd like to think that was a good sign.

With lots of feeling around with my hands, I figured out that he sat above me, his strong thighs near my shoulders, but for what possible reason... The ridge of his penis caressed my lower lip. Oh. I got it. I flicked my tongue across the hard flesh but not being able to see was a real bitch. I stroked up his thighs until I felt the long thick shaft—dear Lord, how big was it?—and grabbed the base and leaned forward to lick the top. *Lollipop. Lollipop. Oh la-la-lollipop...*

I swirled my tongue around the tip, thinking I would torture him the way he'd tortured me but I lost patience with the Torture-Me-Slow game. I wanted that yummy cock in my mouth.

Too bad I was getting a crick in my neck.

"Can you roll over and guide me to your...er, stick shift?"

"You mean my throbbing salami of man meat?"

Okay, he didn't really say that. But I did use the unfortunate term "stick shift" and he laughed so hard the bed shook. Can I help it if my mouth chickened out? I really meant to say penis, or cock, or throbbing man meat but I didn't. Yeah, I know we were as intimate as two people — well as one person with a hood and one without — could get but I still felt shy.

Suddenly, I was really grateful for the hood, because he'd never see my face and, more importantly, I'd never see his face. I could do whatever I wanted — indulge my wildest fantasies — and even if I bumped into this guy on the street, I'd never know he was the one who'd fucked me. Well, that's what I thought at the time. It was a comforting thought, too.

Shyness conquered, I grabbed his thighs and pushed. It was like trying to move marble pillars. "Do you want a blowjob or not?"

He moved fast and he took me with him. Next thing I knew, I was face first in his manhood, his ball sac grazing my lips. I ran my tongue around those humongous things and sucked one gently into my mouth. It was like trying to swallow a large egg. If his family jewels were this big, his scepter was huge.

I found the base of his cock and licked up, up, up...my goodness...and up, finding the sensitive ridge and swirling my tongue around it before taking the tip into my mouth. I sucked gently but didn't go down. Not yet.

I wanted to see him, to see his equipment. I wanted to pleasure him the way he had pleasured me. I'd been wearing the half-hood long enough. It was his turn.

I rose to my knees and looked in what I hoped was his direction. "You know, I think this would work better if I could see what I was doing."

"You're doing fantastic." His voice sounded hoarse and strained.

Huh. I guess I was doing fantastic. Yay for me! But he wasn't getting out of the half-hood experience. "Didn't you read the brochure? We both have to wear the hoods. Fair's fair."

"I have another idea."

"You can have another idea later, boss man. I want to see you and your luscious cock. I admit that *feeling* you has been a lot of fun but there's something to be said for visual effects."

"What if — what if…we both went without the hoods?"

"What?" Was he insane? If I saw him, the fantasy would be over. I wouldn't be in bed with a handsome stranger…I'd start to feel like I was making love, that I was forming a relationship…and I already knew how bad I sucked at those.

"No." I abandoned his cock and rolled onto my back. "It's better if we don't see each other's faces. We're only together for tonight — just for this *one* night. I came here for hot, frequent sex. It can't be any more than that."

"You're afraid."

I snorted. "Yeah, right. I didn't know I was going to get stuck with Mr. Sensitive. What are you? A psychologist? A sexologist? A fuckin' psychic?"

I heard his sharp, indrawn breath and grimaced. How did I go from wanton woman to whiny bitch? I rolled onto my side and reached for him. My hand smacked into his muscled stomach. Ow. I trailed my fingers over his hip. "I'm sorry."

His hand covered mine and stilled my movements. "I'll wear the hood." He brought my fingers to his mouth and kissed the tips. "But you'll play my game, sweetheart. By my rules."

Chapter Four
Derek

&

Fine. I'll let the non-lesbian thing drop.

I will say, for the record, that Arissa's description of events from her request to lick her pussy to playing the game by my rules was surprisingly accurate, especially the part about the size of my penis.

At this point, I was thinking only one thing—*Shit!* And I was thinking it over and over and over.

What the hell was I going to do? I wasn't Batman; the half-hood might provide a standard amount of anonymity but it wasn't going to stop her from recognizing her boss. More disturbing was the fact that, without thinking, I'd suggested that we both go without hoods.

Why?

Was I falling in love with her?

Did I *want* her to know it was me?

Was I fucking nuts?

Okay, I could figure this out. I got off the bed, grabbed my own half-hood from the hook and climbed back on the mattress. I put on the hood, casting myself into a nerve-racking darkness, and reclined on the bed. I fumbled around for a small pillow and held it to my face.

"Very well," I said. "You may remove the hood."

I heard her fuss around for a minute, muttering "goddamn it" a couple of times then a loud, annoyed "ouch" before the half-hood landed on my stomach. I tossed it to the floor, pleased by Arissa's sharp intake of breath that I hoped was a direct result of gazing upon my erection. "What's with the pillow?" she asked.

"A precaution. I can be extremely loud. We wouldn't want to disturb the neighbors."

"I hate to break this to you but, if they're gonna be disturbed, I've already done it. Anyway, they said not to worry about it. Good soundproofing, I guess."

"Yes, well, I always enjoy moaning into a pillow. Call it a quirk."

"Okay, it's a quirk."

"Can you see what you wish to see?"

"Oh, *yeah*."

Her fingers encircled my cock. It felt absolutely incredible but I was so nervous about being the blind party that I couldn't fully....

When her tongue arrived on the scene, the nervousness vanished. She couldn't see me. It was fine. Time to relax and enjoy.

She only got in a few quick licks before she took my penis into her mouth. I moaned into the pillow. I couldn't believe it. Blowjobs typically work out pretty well for me but this...this was more than I'd ever expected. Her tongue swirled over the shaft of my cock while her lips slowly moved up and down, taking me in deep. I would've loved nothing more than to watch this.

Still, I had my imagination. *I could see the hungry look in her eyes as she sucked on me. The freshly applied nail polish on her fingers as they slid over my cock at an even pace with her mouth.*

"Oh, God..." I moaned, letting the pillow fall away.

Pick up the pillow, dipshit.

I wasn't sure if I'd *ever* been this hard. It was almost scary.

I placed my hand over my face and let the sensations wash over me. What was she doing that made this so unbelievably, unbearably pleasurable? Had she swallowed a miniature vacuum cleaner recently? Because I swore that this was the best blowjob I'd ever received in an entire lifetime of receiving blowjobs on a fairly regular basis and I couldn't figure out what made it so incredibly—

Then I figured it out.

It was an emotional thing. I absolutely adored her.

The blowjob was so fucking good because Arissa was the one giving it to me.

I mentally said "shit" a few dozen more times, although I continued to enjoy the pleasure her mouth was bringing.

I wanted to roll her onto her back and make love to her until she screamed my name.

Not gonna happen.

I wanted to be inside her *so* badly.

If I got her on her hands and knees and took her from behind, she wouldn't see my face.

No. I couldn't do it. Because suddenly the emotional black hole was feeling one hell of an emotion—guilt.

Arissa believed that she was with a stranger. And here I was, letting her believe that, violating her trust. How could I talk to her at work, knowing I'd fucked her senseless without her realizing it was me? Or, worse, what if I accidentally gave it away after the fact? This was unquestionably the type of behavior you'd expect from the world's biggest asshole.

This was wrong, it was stupid and it was time to end it.

"I can't do this," I said.

Arissa pulled her mouth away from my cock. "What?"

"I can't. I just…I just can't."

"What happened?" I could imagine the hurt in her eyes. "Was I doing something wrong?"

"No, it's not you, I promise. It's me."

I heard her sigh. "Like I haven't heard that one before."

"It's okay, you'll get your money back." 1-800-SEX-4YOU obviously couldn't guarantee against second thoughts or sexual dysfunction, so if the encounter went badly or didn't happen at all, one of the parties was entitled to a refund.

"Yeah, well, that makes me feel all better. Shit. Am I gonna get a refund for this fucking $200 haircut?"

"Arissa, I'm sorry."

"Fine. You're sorry. That's just wonderful. Maybe this stupid place has an emergency backup dick or something."

I couldn't breathe. It hadn't registered for her that I'd called her "Arissa".

I hadn't done it on purpose. At least my conscious mind hadn't.

"You know, I got this fucking bikini wax that hurt so much that I thought they'd ripped off the top six or seven layers of skin. Then I spent way too much money on a new sexy outfit and that haircut that I couldn't even enjoy because it was squished underneath that itchy mask-thing, not to mention the whole blow to my ego for having paid for sex in the first place... I mean, shit, I can't even get laid if I pay for it! What am I supposed to do now, knowing that even a guy who is so horny that he'd cough up big bucks for this kind of service isn't interested in fucking me? That's not gonna be an easy thing to get over. I'm not sure it can even be done. Did you just call me Arissa?"

I nodded.

I'm sure her eyes widened but I couldn't see them. *"Holy fucking shit!"*

I removed the mask. She was staring at me, mouth moving quickly and wordlessly, hands trembling.

"I'm sorry," I insisted.

Arissa suddenly seemed to realize that she was naked and put her hand over her pussy. "What the *hell* are you doing here?"

"I'm a client."

"And we just ended up together?"

"Yes." I frowned and shook my head. "Well, no. I made special arrangements."

"They let you do that? Oh, I'm gonna sue these motherfuckers." Arissa got off the bed and picked up her dress. "I'm gonna sue them for every cent they've got. I'm gonna shut this place down. I may be humiliated but I'm gonna be humiliated with a shitload of money!"

"Can we talk about this?" I asked.

"I'm thinking no."

"Because if they *had* matched us together, it couldn't have been more perfect."

She glared at me while she put on the robe. "Fuck you. And I quit."

"I'm sorry, it wasn't some long-term scheme or anything. You're just completely irresistible to me and, when I saw your video and recognized your voice, I did something really idiotic. I just wanted you so badly."

Arissa appeared to soften. "Since when am I irresistible to you?"

"Since always, I guess. Look, I know what you think of me but it's really not true. Yes, I play the big, coldhearted boss, but only at work. Outside of work I'm the kind of guy who could fall in love with you."

She bit her lower lip. "You fell in love with me?"

"I've wanted you for a long time but there was nothing I could do about it. Even after Jeremy broke up with you, you were still my employee. I just wish that I could take all of this back and start over. I'm sorry. Please don't quit."

She stared at me for a long time, looking into my eyes.

Having her see me this weak wasn't painful at all. The thought of losing her was pure agony.

"How would you start over?" she asked.

"I'd ask you on a date."

"Where?"

"I know this great Italian place a few blocks from work. The second-best lasagna in town. Do you like lasagna?"

"I love lasagna."

"Would you like to go out for lasagna sometime?"

"When?"

I hesitated. "Tomorrow night?"

She stared at me for another very, very long moment. An endless, torturous moment.

"I already have plans."

"Oh."

She smiled. "How about the night after?"

"That'd be great."

"You don't have to check your planner?"

"I'll clear my schedule."

I was almost ready to burst into tears. I didn't, though. We emotional black holes avoid that kind of mushy stuff.

"I think that 1-800-SEX-4YOU would've made a pretty good match, too," Arissa admitted.

"Well, you never know. They might've hooked us up anyway."

"Maybe. And it *was* a good orgasm."

"I'm glad you liked it."

Her eyes shifted to my still-hard cock. "It seems a shame to waste that."

"You think?"

She cleared her throat. "You know, I paid for an anonymous sexual encounter but having sex with somebody you know is so much more fun. Look, I'm going to reserve the right to get mad at you later and to bring up your idiocy at irrelevant moments during future arguments and to use it as a bargaining chip to get my way. But for now, we've paid for this nice room, we're both really horny, the night is still young…why not pick up where we left off?"

Chapter Five
Arissa and Derek

ॐ

When Derek unmasked his face, I almost had a fuckin' heart attack. My desk fantasy aside, I'd always felt an attraction to him, admiration for his work ethic and now, his sense of justice. Not long after he dumped me, Jeremy, former PR star of the agency, had gotten stuck with the cowboy-without-a-clue client, not to mention that weird guy with a thing for painted wood. It was Derek's way of saying he cared about me — without saying it. Oh, that man and I were going to have a loooong talk over lasagna.

Back to my almost heart attack... My first thought was that he'd wanted to humiliate me somehow or maybe this had been his very sick way to terminate our work arrangement. The idea that he cared about me, that he wanted me so much he risked this encounter... Okay, I'll admit it — I was stunned. *He cared about me.* He meant it, too, because the one thing I knew for sure about Derek Mortensen was that he never said or did anything he didn't mean.

That's why I shucked off the robe and my heels and climbed into bed. Derek, despite our argument, was still hard as a steel pole and damn, he looked good. Emotional black hole? No way. Not anymore.

I slithered onto that beautiful, long, thick cock and rode it hard.

* * * * *

I don't mean to keep correcting Arissa's contributions but I do want to mention that she omitted the condom. The fastest damn condom I've ever put on in my entire life and I'd barely finished unrolling it all the way before she slid down onto me. Within seconds she was bouncing hard, head back, eyes closed.

Me, I kept my eyes open. There are few sights better than the great view afforded by this position and *none* better than watching Arissa thrashing in passion. I watched her and groaned with pleasure and wondered how the hell I'd been able to keep my hands off her all this time.

* * * * *

And he *should* have been wondering how the hell he'd been able to keep his hands off me all this time. His hands belonged exactly where they were at that very moment — kneading my breasts, pinching my nipples until I moaned.

Of course, I was already moaning because of his cock. It felt good inside me, filled me completely, made my cunt tingle with pleasure. And I was wetter than I'd ever been for any man and it *wasn't* by a narrow margin.

I kept bouncing on his penis, moaning, whimpering, gasping for breath and probably making plenty of other noises that I wasn't even aware of. I picked up my pace, fucking him harder. He groaned even louder but as I stared into his eyes I could see that he was going to have absolutely no problem making this experience last for a long, long time.

* * * * *

Shit! She was gonna make me come!

Premature ejaculation had not been a problem for me since the early days of my sexual experience. I'm not saying that I can time an orgasm to the desired millisecond but I can usually keep an erection going for as long as necessary. Except that as Arissa fucked me hard, putting a hell of a lot of passion into it, I started to feel that familiar sensation that I *really* didn't want to feel this early.

I thought about baseball.

I thought about baseball played very poorly.

Arissa howled and made a couple of other interesting noises as we fucked.

I thought about an extremely unattractive umpire making a terrible call.

The sensation began to fade.

Thank God, I'd made it over the wave. Now back in action, I proceeded to thrust upward, fucking her as hard as she was fucking me.

* * * * *

When Derek put his hands on my hips and matched his thrusts to mine, I think I said something like, "Ohmigodthatfeelssofuckingooddoitsomoreooh." But I'm not sure. It might have just been a really long moan.

We were fucking each other hard and fast, our pants and moans mingling. We were sweating, too—that kind of really-great-sex sweat that pearls on the skin when a couple go at each other like wild animals.

Derek's cock plunged into my cunt with such expert precision. Did he know about the G-spot? Oh yeah! Pleasure curled through me. Oh God. I was going to come and I didn't want to. Not yet.

I thought about shopping on non-sale weekends.

I thought about mark-ups at Neiman Marcus.

Derek groaned, his eyes closed, and his fingers dug into my flesh as his cock pumped inside me.

I thought about that bitch salesperson who told me I wasn't a size 3.

The sensation began to fade.

Thank God. I didn't want to end this experience with Derek. We had so much more to give each other, to show each other. But right now, at that moment, I wanted nothing more than to feel him inside me, pleasuring me. I hope that I was pleasuring him, too. I wanted him to realize this was more than just sex between two compatible partners. This was the beginning of some really wonderful…something close to love.

* * * * *

She was *so* wet and *so* hot inside and I continued watching our connected bodies as she rode me. By now her breasts were sweat-soaked and slippery to the touch, which made them feel even better than before, if such a thing was possible.

Though we did not carry on an actual conversation while we fucked, we communicated using our incoherent sex-speak, which I believe can be translated approximately as follows:

ME: My, this is certainly a most delightful sensation I am experiencing.

HER: Indeed it is. My genitalia feel superb. I hope that your own personal genitalia feel equally superb.

ME: Yes, I can assure you that it does. Thank you.

HER: No problem.

We kept it up for another five, six or maybe eighteen minutes but probably closer to five, then Arissa stopped. This wasn't good. She wasn't supposed to stop. Stopping was bad.

But instead she readjusted her position, so that she could lean down on top of me. Her breasts slid against my chest and I reached around to cup her fine buttocks as she gave me a deep, passionate kiss.

My whole body tingled. And I wasn't the kind of guy whose body tingled.

I closed my eyes as our kiss lingered.

* * * * *

Derek tasted like mints…and sex. Don't ask me what "sex" tastes like. It's tangy-sweet, I guess. The kiss turned me on even more, if that was possible. My heart pounded, partly from the rousing "exercise" and partly from excitement. We kissed for a long time, our tongues intertwining, our lips getting slick and swollen as we dove for each other again and again.

He squeezed my buttocks, his hands stroking up my back until his fingers tangled in my hair. He nipped my bottom lip then trailed his tongue along my jaw, licking the sweat on my neck.

He returned to my mouth and assaulted my lips, slipping his tongue inside to duel with mine. He lifted his head, his grin wicked, and said, "You taste like sex."

I laughed but the sound vibrating in my throat was more like a purr. He wrapped his arms around me and flipped me onto my back. He managed to keep his cock inside me, too.

Seconds later he withdrew, damn it, and sat up, his knees on either side of my thighs. His condom-wrapped cock, slick with my juices, jutted proudly among the black curls. I licked my lips. God, I loved his cock. I couldn't wait to taste it again.

"I bet you didn't notice all the fine qualities of this bed," he said.

"It's got you in it."

"And you."

"That's all I need to know." I reached for him but he leaned forward and captured my wrists.

"Stretch out your arms."

Not exactly a romantic phrase. And we were so good at the mushy talk, too. He scooted forward until his knees almost made friends with my armpits and that awesome penis was a mere inch from my mouth. He reached up to the posts on either side of the elaborate headboard. Two red silk sashes drifted down. He carefully wrapped my right wrist, then my left. "Too tight?"

"No." I experimented with the sashes. There was enough room to move my arms, but not enough to reach Derek. My breath hitched at this new twist in the game. I can't remember ever being this adventurous in bed before. In fact, I had no idea what a boring sex life I had before this night.

It was a little frightening, too, being bound, even just partially. I know that if I asked to be let go, Derek would oblige. But it was sexy to offer my body to him this way. He was free to roam, to taste, to touch and yet I was denied the same pleasures—unless he allowed 'em.

He wiggled down until he sat across my thighs, teasing me yet again with the sight of his cock. "I want to feel you inside me again," I said.

"You will." He smiled. "But not yet."

* * * * *

I've always felt that sex tastes like blueberries but I'm a bit weird.

Okay, I'm going to admit that the whole bondage thing was a spur-of-the-moment decision. Not that sexual encounters should be planned out in detail beforehand. I mean, who wants to say, "First we'll do some missionary-style fornication for three-and-a-half-minutes, after which we'll switch to a good six minutes of doggy-style, followed by an orgasm for at least one of us…" But I really hadn't intended to make tying Arissa up part of our sex play.

Mostly because I was her boss and for the very first time we were together on equal terms. But what can I say? The urge to put those silk scarves to use struck me, I acted upon it and suddenly I had a sexy naked lady tied to the bed. It wasn't what I'd planned but it worked.

I looked at that glistening pussy and wanted almost nothing more than to swirl my tongue over it once again. I say "almost" because that pussy had, of course, just been penetrated by a lubricated condom and so it was not the most appealing destination for my tongue.

But that was okay. We had toys.

I climbed off the bed and opened the dresser drawer.

"So many to choose from," I said, rustling through the contents. "What to pick, what to pick, what to pick...?"

"Hurry," Arissa whispered.

"Oh, now, you wouldn't want me to make a hasty decision, would you? This is a matter that requires time and thought. Hmmmm...hmmmm... hmmmm..."

"Don't make me hurt you," Arissa warned.

"I wouldn't want that," I told her, making my selection. I climbed back onto the bed and turned on the vibrator. It was a standard toy choice, I'll admit, and it wasn't male-shaped or anything like that but, as I pressed the tip against her wet pussy, I had a feeling that she wasn't going to be filing any complaints.

* * * * *

The vibrator touched my clit, its gentle movements causing all kinds of pleasurable havoc. I wrapped my hands around the scarves and held on for dear life as Derek tormented me with the toy of his choice.

I moaned when he slid the device between my pussy lips and traced a long, slow line to the entrance of my cunt. Then that unmerciful man pushed a button that increased the vibrations and slowly slipped the vibrator in and out of me.

I arched, my hips moving in a rhythm that was shameful. But I didn't care. It felt so good....too good. Pleasure rolled over me, threatening to burst into an orgasm that might very well make me pass out.

Thinking about Neiman Marcus, mark-ups or no-sale weekends was not going to stop it this time.

"Wait," I cried.

He removed the toy. I was sweaty again. My heart tha-thumped and my thighs trembled. I felt the pulsations in my pussy, the prelude to the big quake, and slammed my knees together.

"Something wrong?"

"No," I said. "You keep doing that and I'm going to come."

His left brow arched. "I thought that was the point."

I thought about this for all of a second. I let my legs fall apart and offered my pussy. "You're right. Get to work."

"Oh no." He wagged a finger. "You had your chance."

Damn he was lucky my arms were tied because I could have gladly strangled him. Or maybe I would've just jumped his bones and ridden his cock again until we both had mind-shattering, body-numbing orgasms.

It would serve him right, too.

* * * * *

If she wanted to come, by golly Arissa was going to come.

And not from the vibrator.

I quickly untied her hands. It was the briefest bondage experience I'd ever had, but oh, well. She immediately sat up and threw her arms around me, rewarding me for her newfound freedom with a great big kiss.

We continued that great big kiss for quite a while, tongues sliding over each other, hands roaming.

Then we pulled away and I patted her leg. "Time to fuck again," I announced.

"Works for me!" Arissa plopped on her back and spread her legs wide.

"Oh, no, no, no, no," I said with a mischievous grin. "I want you to come on your hands and knees."

"You don't mean…" Arissa let out a mock gasp of shock, "…*doggy style*?"

"Woof, woof."

Arissa obligingly rolled onto her tummy. I placed my hands on her hips and lifted her into the proper position, giving myself an absolutely sensational view of her absolutely sensational ass. I pressed my erection against her still-wet entrance and pulled her toward me.

She let out a squeal.

There was no reason to take things slowly. I rammed into her as hard as I could. This was a position for serious, hardcore fucking and I was going to make the most of it. I thrust into her over and over, picturing the way her breasts were rocking back and forth.

"Ooh…ooh…" Arissa cried.

I gripped her even more tightly and fucked her even harder. My waist slapped against her ass, all accompanied by those incoherent sex sounds Arissa was making.

And then she spoke quite clearly: "I'm gonna come!"

* * * * *

Why Derek thinks a low, sexy moan is a squeal, I'll never know. I don't giggle. And I don't squeal.

I didn't have time to be disappointed about the removal of the scarves. Derek was…crazed. So was I. I wanted to taste him, touch him, God…just feel him all over me.

When I flipped onto my stomach, I didn't have time to get settled. Derek grabbed my hips, pulled me back and plunged into me. That delicious, hard cock filled me.

Derek was groaning and panting and so was I. My hands fisted the sheets. My breasts swayed, my nipples hard with excitement, and my entire body felt like liquid heat. I loved being fucked like this…oh God. I had been at the edge too many times. My pussy had had enough teasing. Ripples of pleasure caused my cunt to pulsate. And I knew… "I'm gonna come!"

The orgasm rolled over me, taking with it my ability to think, to breathe. I screamed, at least, I tried to. I didn't have a voice anymore. I just had this incredible feeling of bliss that left sparkly trails of lust and joy.

* * * * *

As I listened to Arissa come, I knew that my own orgasm was on its way. I just needed to hold off for a few more moments... I wanted to fully enjoy her orgasm before I was distracted by my own.

She thrashed so hard that I thought for a second that she was going to yank herself away from my cock. I held her hips even more tightly to make sure that didn't happen.

It took her a long time to calm down.

I loved every second of it.

When she finally settled, I resumed the process of fucking her, using long, deep strokes. I wasn't going to last much longer, which was perfectly fine with me. I'd only delivered a few strokes before I hit the point of no return.

I came so hard that I thought I might go permanently cross-eyed.

I'd been with a lot of women and I'd never had an orgasm this intense. Even with the soundproofed walls and lack of neighbors, I wondered if 1-800-SEX-4YOU was going to be hit with a noise complaint.

I don't even know how long it took for my orgasm to subside. When it finally did, I collapsed onto the mattress, gasping for breath. Arissa lay down next to me, snuggling against my chest.

* * * * *

I felt deeply, utterly, overwhelmingly...complete. I wrapped my arms around Derek and put my head on his chest. His heartbeat was still frantic. Apparently, we both needed some time to recover from the incredible sex-o-rama. I knew that very soon I would want to play some more but right now it felt good just to cuddle. Derek and I had all night to do the mattress mambo. He was definitely getting the scarves wrapped around his wrists.

Despite his earlier confession, I wondered if he really did care about me. Did he want more from me than sex? Damned good sex, but still…a girl needs emotional commitment. Did he want a relationship?

"After tonight—" I cleared my throat. "Um…after tonight, I think—"

He sat up, taking me with him, and grabbed my arms. "Don't tell me you've decided not to see me after tonight! I see you every day in the office. I'll know what you look like under your clothes. I'll spend all day imagining you out of them. My business will fail because no work will get done. I'll daydream the hours away, thinking about your breasts and your ass and the way you squeal."

I blinked. What was Derek saying? Either he wanted to see me outside of this bedroom or he was firing me. I opened my mouth to get clarification, but could only manage, "I don't squeal."

* * * * *

"Yes," I said calmly, "you do squeal."

"I'm pretty sure I don't."

"You would be wrong."

Arissa smiled but I could see that she was nervous. "You're not firing me, are you?"

"Nope."

"Do I get a promotion?"

"Nope."

"Aw."

I stopped clutching her shoulders and grasped her hands. "Arissa, I want us to be together. We'll just...well, we'll admit to everybody that we're seriously dating. I mean, *seriously*. As in, no other guy gets to touch you, ever. If you're okay with that idea, of course."

"*Very* okay."

"I mean, it'll be weird and stuff for a while and there'll be gossip galore and we probably shouldn't fuck like wild animals on my desk during business hours but, aside from that, I really think we can make this work. That is, assuming that you don't mind being publicly linked with an emotional black hole asshole boss."

"I think I can handle that," Arissa said.

"Good. Me too."

And I meant it.

* * * * *

Derek liked me—a lot. He was willing to commit to a monogamous relationship and that says, "You're mine." I have to admit, I liked him, too. If I wasn't being so cautious about men, I might admit that I could fall in love with this guy. So what if he wrongly believed that I squealed and giggled? We could work out those little details.

I slid onto his lap and wrapped my arms around his neck and my legs around his waist. He had disposed of the condom so his naked, beautiful cock nestled nicely against my pussy as I scooted closer. I had all kinds of ideas about what to do with that delicious cock.

"Um...Arissa?"

I rubbed my breasts on his chest and was rewarded by the stirring interest of his penis.

"You didn't say you wanted to date me, uh, exclusively."

"I didn't?"

I looked at him and saw the blaze of desire in his eyes and I saw…vulnerability. My heart clenched. I had never thought of Derek as vulnerable but he was—he needed my words just like I needed his. I released my hold on him and pushed on his shoulders until he fell back against the bed.

"Derek," I said as I stretched out on top of him and lowered my lips to his, "I want to date you. In fact, other than work, all I plan to do is date you."

He kissed me, long and gentle and sweet. There was serious like, maybe even love, in that kiss and his lips showed me the bright, shiny promise of our future together. His hands tangled in my hair briefly, then he slowly—well, a girl shouldn't tell everything now, should she?

The End

REDIAL 1-800-SEX4YOU
Chris Tanglen & Michele Bardsley

છ

Chapter One
Drae

ഌ

"Stop with the hair already," I said, batting away Arissa's hands. It was a dangerous thing to do because she had a heated curling iron gripped in one and a prickly round brush in the other.

"Drae Monique Davidson!" she intoned in a mother's fussy voice. "We're in *my* bathroom. *I* rule this domain and all who dwell in it."

I rolled my eyes. We were in *her* bathroom because it was approximately five-hundred times the size of mine. The mirrors were so huge and shiny they put the ones on Hubble Space Telescope to shame and, let me tell you, Cher could hold a concert with the lighting set-up in here. Arissa had the kind of bathroom every woman wanted — the kind you got when you moved in with your very rich, very handsome, very sweet boyfriend. He not only remodeled it to her specifications, he stocked it with every expensive perfume, lotion, makeup and device known to the beauty world.

If I sounded jealous…well, it's because I was jealous.

"Just let me fix that curl," said Arissa. "Then you can finish moping."

"You said that ten minutes ago."

"Stop whining," said Arissa, tugging the brush through my hair. "And stand still!"

I was suffering through this torture of hair, makeup and sexy lingerie because we were preparing for my doom. Er, date. Or, as my disgustingly besotted friend called it — Rendezvous With Erotic Destiny. Being engaged to the man of her dreams had ruined Arissa's perspective. BD (Before Derek), she would have called tonight's appointment with 1-800-SEX4YOU the "Ultimate Fuck Fest".

Six months ago, I forced Arissa to call 1-800-SEX4YOU. Her goal was to get laid and get on with life sans Jeremy the asshole ex-fiancé. Instead, she ended up with her boss and they not only had a night of incredible sex, they went and fell in freaking love. Now my best friend was engaged to the boss, running the public relations firm and living in a big-ass house. Derek insisted that she not only bring her three annoyingly cute cats into his home—he took her to the animal shelter and let her adopt three *more*.

I had no boyfriend, rich or otherwise. Every relationship I have ever had turned out badly. *Every single one.* Yep. I can trace my bad luck with men to the fifth grade when my boyfriend of two whole days, Gregory Meyers, broke up with me by dumping chocolate milk on my head.

"Arissa!" I jerked away as the curling iron descended toward my hair for the hundredth time. "It's going to be tucked under a hood, remember?"

"You don't have to use the half-hoods," she said. "They have silk scarves you can tie around your eyes. Or you can pick out a simple mask. It doesn't have eye holes, of course, but it won't hide your hair."

Arissa and Derek returned to 1-800-SEX4YOU every so often to try out new rooms, new toys and new...whatever else. After six months of hearing about how great her sex life was and how great Derek was and how great being in love was, I figured I had a choice...

Kill my best friend and put her out of *my* misery.

Or make my own appointment with 1-800-SEX4YOU.

I kinda wanted to keep Arissa around, especially since she had the ultimate in bathrooms, an endless supply of alcohol stocked in an amazing bar and a limo at her beck and call. Besides, I really liked Arissa, despite her recent starry-eyed, tongue-tied, kissy-pooed behavior. Hell, I even liked Derek, especially after he humiliated Jeremy and his tramp du jour by firing both of their asses from the PR firm in front of the entire staff. You gotta love a guy who risks wrongful termination lawsuits to get revenge for his sweetheart.

"Done." Arissa stepped back to view her handiwork. I looked in the mirror too. I'm not sure what about my appearance made Arissa's lips curve into a satisfied smile. I looked like me, with more makeup and less clothing. I was pretty, but not beauty-contestant beautiful. I had brown hair and brown eyes, an okay nose, and decent lips. My hair was shoulder-length and, courtesy of Arissa, my usually straight locks were poofed, curled and spritzed.

Thanks to my obsession with exercise, I was in decent shape, and thanks to my mother's breast genes, I had a nice rack. That's not vanity. That's a statement of fact. What I didn't have was height. I am a few inches over five feet tall and there were days I'd gladly hand over some of my excess boobage to get longer legs. I wore high, high heels all the time, because I need those extra inches damn it, and tonight was no exception. The most gorgeous pair of pink and faux diamond shoes showcased my feet, the pearlescent pink on my toenails glittered prettily next to the cubic zirconia that dotted the straps.

Underneath my simple pink dress, I wore a not-so-simple pink corset that attached to silk stockings. I wore a scrap of pink lace that purported to be underwear. I didn't usually like quite so much pink, but Arissa had Derek's credit card and his blessing...so we went to Agent Provocateur and splurged.

"Looks like I'm ready to rock." I sighed.

"You're enthusiasm is underwhelming. You are going to have lots of hot sex. You're going to have fun. And when you're through, you're going to cheer the fuck up. I won't have a depressed maid of honor helping me plan the wedding."

"So this night is about you."

"Of course it is. What did you think? That this night was about you looking good and feeling good and getting over the dry spot in your love life?"

"Har. Har. I got the sexual pun, you bitch. And my love life is not a dry spot. It's the Sahara."

Arissa laughed. She hugged me and left the bathroom.

I looked in the mirror one more time. Okay, I did look good. And I hadn't had anything other than my battery-operated boyfriend to play with in a long, long time.

Oh, what the hell.

It was just a one-night stand, right?

When I strode into the bedroom, Arissa handed me the tiny pink beaded purse that was only big enough to hold my cell phone, driver's license, and one credit card.

"The limo's downstairs. It'll be there at noon tomorrow to pick you up. Your package includes breakfast in bed—which means your new friend will be around for morning nibbles."

"I hope he's donut-flavored," I said.

"Vivian will meet you there." Arissa grinned. "Don't get freaked out if she touches you, okay? Derek says she only likes guys and I say she's into girls. We're both wrong, though. She told me she's bisexual."

"Wouldn't that make you both right?"

"Huh. I guess so."

Without further ado, Arissa hurried me down the stairs, out the front door and into the limo. An uncorked bottle of champagne chilled in a bucket built into the door; Arissa pulled it out along with a glass stored in a cabinet.

Before I'd finished my first glass of champagne, we arrived at the facility, which looked square and nondescript. But I knew from Arissa's descriptions that the inside of the building was anything but bland.

Vivian, who was gorgeous, blonde and *tall,* greeted me in the lobby. She smiled warmly then led me down the hallway to a big, red door.

"This is your room until noon tomorrow. If you need anything, pick up the phone and ask for it. Breakfast is served at 10 a.m."

"Thanks." Suddenly anxious, I stared at the door. "Er…do I just go in or what?"

Vivian leaned close, her perfect face just inches from mine. She pursed her lips and I waited for her to…I don't know…lay one on me or something.

"He's waiting for you," she said.

"You mean he's already here?" My heart jumped then started to pound fiercely. *Oh shit oh shit oh shit.* "I thought I would have more time to prepare." My stomach clenched.

Before panic could claim what was left of my courage, Vivian opened the door and guided me inside. The door shut behind me and I stood there, clutching the teeny tiny purse and trying to calm my nerves.

Sitting on the edge of a monstrous four-poster bed was a man.

He wore a black half-hood…and nothing else.

Chapter Two
Kevin

$\wp$

As the door opened, my stomach did this weird thing where it was sort of bouncing and twisting at the same time, I was terrified that I would start sweating in a most profuse and unattractive manner, I just *knew* that I wouldn't be able to get it up and my disgrace would be a legendary tale in the annals of 1-800-SEX4YOU history. ("Hey, remember that doofus whose penis remained shamefully flaccid? Hee hee hee hee hee!")

I was kinda nervous.

A little-known fact that you won't find in any textbooks is that if you go without sex for three years, your virginity is restored. So I'd been a born-again virgin for, oh, about eight weeks now, which I'm sure is what accounted for my stomach's energetic gymnastics routine.

Before that, I'd only been with one woman. *The* woman. My wife, Tara. We met at fifteen, fell in love at seventeen, got married at nineteen and had six amazing years together.

I wish I could say that she left me or that I came home from work early one day to find her in bed with my best friend and/or his brother. But that's not what happened.

She died. Cancer. The doctors gave her six months, but we only got four. She didn't even get to see our daughter's first birthday.

Don't worry, we'll get back to my comical impotence anxiety in a moment. I just need to explain the source of it. This won't be a bummer story, I promise! After all, you already know that I end up on a bed wearing nothing but a half-hood, right?

Anyway, I was so devastated by my loss that if it weren't for my daughter Melissa, I'm not sure what I would have done. What I did do was throw myself entirely into being Super Dad, soothing a crying baby and changing poopy diapers with superhuman skill. I would have given anything not to have to raise her alone, but I can say with no false pride that I was damn good as a single dad.

Interesting Sidenote – A single dad pushing a stroller through a park is an absolute babe magnet. A single dad who struggles not to break into tears when explaining that his wife passed away could probably be naked and thrusting away within ten minutes or so. Of course, I was such an emotional wreck that I didn't even realize this until my friend Howard pointed it out, using the word "pussy" more times than was polite.

For three years I raised my daughter and worked at my job on a construction crew, a job that I loved. I could never handle sitting at a desk all day. This kept me outside and allowed me to get plenty of exercise, which kept me in good shape despite some poor eating habits that had developed since Tara's death. It didn't help that Melissa always saved me half of a cookie from day care.

Three years of no sex.

Honestly, it didn't really bother me. I wasn't looking to replace Tara and I was too busy for a relationship anyway. I had no problems satisfying my own sexual needs in the shower, especially since I'm ambidextrous.

The day before my birthday, my friend Jennifer came to visit. She'd been Tara's best friend since the two of them were eight, and we'd always gotten along really well. Our friendship had strengthened after Tara died. Nothing romantic, of course (Jennifer had a husband and two kids) but we'd shared a lot of tears together and genuinely enjoyed each other's company.

She seemed really nervous.

"Hi," she said. "Happy birthday!"

"You're a day early."

"I know. But I brought you your present!"

"Where is it?"

"Let's sit down."

We walked into the living room and sat down on the couch. Jennifer, an admittedly striking blonde, crossed her thin legs and smiled at me. "Feeling old yet?"

"Nah. Twenty-nine is no big deal."

"Remind me of that when I'm sobbing next month. So, Jeff and I were talking, and you know, you haven't dated since Tara died."

"I do know that."

"She wouldn't want that. She'd want you to move on with your life. In fact, she'd probably kick my ass if she knew I let you go this long without trying to meet somebody new."

I had a horrifying feeling that I could see where this was going. "Please tell me you didn't set me up on a blind date."

"No…not exactly."

"What havoc have you wreaked with my life, Jennifer?"

"No havoc. Have you heard of 1-800-SEX4YOU?"

I shook my head.

"It's anonymous sex. But classy anonymous sex, not like sleazy back-alley sex or anything like that. They get your profile, hook you up with a sexually compatible match and then you meet in one of their elegant rooms and…you know, have sex."

I wanted to ask her what the hell she was talking about, but settled for staring at her in shocked silence.

"I've got the brochure," Jennifer said, opening up her purse and rifling through the contents. "You're already pre-paid."

"You've already signed me up for this?"

"I know, I know…it's a bit presumptuous…"

"A *bit*?"

"Look, I wanted to set you up on a blind date with my needy friend Helen, and Jeff wanted to hire a pair of bisexual hookers for you, so we compromised." She fished out the brochure and handed it to me. "We're not saying that you should find a new mother for Melissa or anything like that, but that maybe…you know…you should get out and have a little fun."

"Bisexual hookers? Really?"

"Yeah. I'm not sure if he was joking or not."

"Well, I appreciate the thought, but there's no way in hell that I'm going through with this." I glanced at the model on the front of the brochure. "Damn. Will she be there?"

"Just read it," said Jennifer. "If you're not cool with the idea, we can get a ninety percent refund and you can buy yourself some new ties."

"I can't believe you signed me up for a sex service. I can't believe you even know about this place. How *do* you know about this place? Are there secrets about your relationship that I'm just now learning that I don't really want to know about?"

"Jeff's uncle is one of the owners of the place. He got us a great deal."

"Ah."

"You don't have to do it. But you need to go out and enjoy yourself. Whether you decide to use 1-800-SEX4YOU or not, your birthday present includes a night of free babysitting."

"Now *that* I like!"

After Jennifer left, I threw away the brochure.

Then I dug it back out of the garbage and read it.

It really *didn't* sound sleazy. In fact, it sounded kind of exciting. And Jennifer was absolutely right…it was time to have some fun. Despite my attempts to keep the romance fresh and exciting, the spark between myself and my hands was fading.

After two solid days of "I don't want to do that...yes I do...no I don't...yes I do...no I don't..." I caved in to temptation and went to the 1-800-SEX4YOU offices to fill out approximately 35,000 pages of questionnaires that asked about my sexual interests in ridiculously specific detail. I didn't even realize I *had* that many sexual interests, but a lot of the stuff in those questionnaires sounded pretty damn good. I got tested for various STDs (considering my long dry spell, I was confident that I'd be fine in that arena) and was told that they'd be in touch.

And after they called me, I made an appointment.

I wandered around my apartment, unable to believe that I'd actually made an appointment.

On the day of the appointment, I took a long, thorough shower, still unable to believe that I was going to do this.

I dropped Melissa off with her beloved Aunt Jennifer, who was grinning more than necessary.

I drove to 1-800-SEX4YOU, unable to believe that I was driving there.

I signed in, unable to believe that I was signing in.

I was shown to the room and given a quick tour that primarily focused on the impressive collection of sex toys contained in the dresser drawer, which I was assured were sterilized between guests. I got nekkid. I put on the half-hood that didn't seem like it would do all that great a job of maintaining our anonymity. Now blind, I sat my nekkid ass down on the four-poster bed and waited nervously.

There was still time to wimp out.

The door opened.

There was no more time to wimp out.

Chapter Three
Drae

જી

Heart pounding, I stared at my date for the evening. Half his face might be hidden by a black hood, but his square jaw and angular cheeks hinted at his good looks. Oooh baby. He was in *excellent* shape. Every inch of him was muscular and tan. I noticed his skin was darker from shoulders to waist, as if he worked in the sun shirtless. Oh yummy. Had I gotten a construction worker? God, I loved construction workers. They were big and dumb and eager to please—the human equivalent of Golden Retrievers.

I wondered what color eyes he had. And if he chose the hood so I couldn't see something heinous on the top part of his head like baldness or scars or creepy eyebrows.

Stop projecting, demanded a voice inside my head that sounded amazingly like Arissa's. And get moving, you twit! You're wasting valuable fuck time.

Briefly I entertained the idea of pretending I was a dominatrix. I could stride across the room, my heels echoing on the polished wood floor, and straddle him, demanding that he rip off my dress. I could boss him around and make him my love slave and force him to obey my every sexual whim.

Hmmm…

Then I noticed his hands clutched the bed covers so tightly I could see his knuckles whiten. He seemed to be sucking in breaths at an alarming rate, too. Was it remotely possible this guy was more nervous than I was? My gaze zeroed in on his genitals.

His legs were crossed.

Okay, then. I hope to hell he was covering the ol' family jewels because he was anxious and not because he was trying to hide the size of his package. Not that I'm a girl who's gotta have a big dick, mind you. It's just...difficult to work with a penis that could double for a roll of mints.

I glanced around the room. Candles were everywhere, on tables and nightstands, floors and wall sconces. Their flickering flames offered the only light in the room. The bed was gorgeous, huge and filled with pillows. On either side were nightstands with four drawers each. I knew that every one of those drawers held toys and other sexual tools. Depending on your preferences, you could use anything from a dildo to a flogger to get your groove on.

I looked behind me at the door and yeah, I was thinking about bolting. This guy couldn't see me. He'd never know the face of the woman who'd chickened out. Near the door was a series of hooks. A black mask dangled from one and from another, a pair of steel handcuffs. Handcuffs? *Oh boy oh boy!* To hell with it. I was a healthy, single, disease-free woman who wanted sex. I was five feet away from the guy who could give it to me.

I was staying.

So I hung up my purse on one of the free hooks then turned and considered the naked man who was trying to become one with the bed.

"Hi," I said.

Obviously startled, he almost fell backwards, but managed to right himself. His head twisted toward the sound of my voice. I saw his Adam's apple bobble as he swallowed, then he managed a husky, "Hello."

"My name is Drae."

"I'm...uh, Kevin."

What kind of moron couldn't remember his name? And if he was trying to think of a fake name, he couldn't do better than *Kevin*?

"Can I join you?" I asked.

"Of course," he said. "That's what we're here for, right? To join together...in, uh...fun."

I decided his name really was Kevin. And he was a nervous as a virgin. Wait a minute. Was he a virgin?

The only way to find out if Kevin was inexperienced was to kiss him. Guys who'd spent more time with their hands than with women were easy to spot. When they kissed, they usually opened their mouths too wide, slobbered and tried to suck your tongue outta your head.

Kissing was important. A guy who understood the significance of a first kiss (and every kiss thereafter) was a guy who understood the intricate process of bringing a woman pleasure. And if Kevin's kissing technique didn't melt me like butter in the microwave...

I took off my dress and hung it on the same hook as my purse. Then I walked to the bed, my high heels clicking on the wood floor. It was weird, but because I knew Kevin was really nervous, I didn't feel as apprehensive.

Sitting next to him, I put about six inches between us. To my surprise, he reached out and latched on to my breasts, well, the corset and the top of my breasts.

"I was hoping we could kiss first," I said dryly. God, he was *soooo* cute.

His hands dropped away. "I was going for your shoulders."

"They're not as much as fun as my breasts."

He grinned. "I suppose not." He turned toward me, his head tilted. "You said something about kissing?"

I'm a girl of action, so I leaned forward to press my lips against his. Unfortunately, he leaned forward at the same time and we smacked foreheads.

"Ouch!" Pain ricocheted through my skull then settled into a dull throb between my eyebrows.

"Oh Jeez! Sorry! I thought you wanted me to kiss you."

"How are you supposed to do that when you can't see where my lips are located?"

"Oh. Good point." He sighed. "This isn't going as well as I had hoped."

His shoulders slumped and his head bowed, and he sat there looking like a dejected puppy. I couldn't stand it. He was sweet and cute and…did I mention how muscular this guy was? I mean, rock solid. And suddenly I was itching to get my hands on those broad shoulders and fabulous chest and…ooh, ooh…those thighs. And I definitely wanted to see his package. I suspected I would *not* be disappointed.

"Let's start over," I said. "I'm Drae. You're Kevin." My hands coasted along his shoulders. Warm, smooth skin tantalized my fingertips. "Would you mind if I sat on your lap?"

He jolted. "What?"

"I want to sit on your lap. And that means you have to uncross your legs so I can slide onto your thighs."

He uncrossed his legs so fast that his half-erect penis sprang free. Oh my God. I stared at his cock and drooled. He was circumcised, which as a spoiled American woman, I appreciated. He was also huge. Not average. Not better than average. *Huge.*

"Is everything okay?"

"Uh huh."

"Were you kidding about the lap thing?"

God, no. I forgot all about doing a sexy, slow slide across his lap. I leaped onto his thighs and wrapped my legs around his waist. His penis aligned with the wisp of panties covering my pussy, and it seemed happy with this arrangement because I felt it grow. And grow.

And grow.

Like a fucking beanstalk.

Kevin's arms glided around my shoulders as I cupped his face. I leaned forward and pressed my lips to his.

He opened his mouth, just a little, and matched my gentle assault with one of his own. He tasted like cool mint. And his lips were soft and warm and patient. Whatever shyness he might have harbored melted away. I felt his hands in my hair, tugging me closer.

I think we kissed like this forever. Just with our lips, trying every angle, and leaving every so often to visit other places. I nibbled his jaw, he nuzzled my neck. But always, always, we returned to Lip Central.

Then, just when I was butter in the microwave, Kevin's tongue slipped into my mouth.

And my world tilted on its axis.

Chapter Four
Kevin

ဢ

When I agreed to write about my experience with 1-800-SEX4YOU, I was told to read the account written by Drae's friend Arissa and her boss Derek, to give me an idea of what the publisher was looking for. I did and enjoyed it a lot, but I thought it was kind of tacky of Derek to point out inconsistencies in Arissa's story. A gentleman wouldn't do that, right?

This attitude puts me in an interesting predicament, because when I read Drae's version of the events, I smiled at the memory but also shook my head a couple of times. For example...

Oh yummy. Had I gotten a construction worker?

C'mon now. There are plenty of explanations for being well-tanned above the waist. I could mow lawns. I could play sports. I could like to show off my nipple rings. (I don't have a nipple ring, but at this point Drae hadn't been close enough to either of my nipples to discover the absence of holes.) Was her first thought *really* that I was a construction worker, or was she just retroactively placing that lucky guess in her mind?

I mean, it's not a big deal, but just something that bugged me a bit when I read her section. Moving forward...

Obviously startled, he almost fell backwards, but managed to right himself.

Yes, I was nervous. I freely admitted as much in my own section. But I did *not* almost fall backwards. I flinched. There's a pretty big difference between flinching and almost falling backwards. I mean, c'mon, why not just say that I let out a girlish squeak?

Again, not a big deal.

He was also huge. Not average. Not better than average. Huge.

Okay, she did get this part right. Heh heh.

Like a fucking beanstalk.

Yep. Green with lots of leaves.

Okay, I'll be serious now. Sorry about the nitpicks above, I just want to make sure that you're getting an accurate version of the story. When she left off, my tongue had just slipped into her mouth...

Obviously, I'd been wasting valuable energy worrying that my penis might not function at its full potential. I was hard enough to break plywood with my cock. (*Note to Drae. Don't correct this in your section, I'm exaggerating for comedic effect.*) This woman I'd never even seen was turning me on so intensely that my concerns about not being able to perform immediately transformed into concerns that my performance might be all too brief.

Her kisses were completely different from Tara's. This was raw, carnal, about nothing but the sex. I can't deny that my subconscious mind still felt a bit guilty, but consciously I knew that I wasn't doing anything wrong. I deserved this. I was going to have one hell of a good time, and make this mystery woman come until she lost her freakin' mind.

Our kisses grew even more intense.

She began to stroke me with her fingers. "I didn't even know they came in this size," she noted. "I mean, you know how sometimes you'll order a sandwich and it's so big you can't even get your mouth around it? We may have some technical difficulties, Stud."

I leaned forward to kiss her again, and our foreheads collided even harder than they had the first time.

"Ow, dammit!" I tore off the damn hood and tossed it across the room. Then I realized that I'd just done something extremely stupid and quickly closed my eyes. "I'm sorry! That

203

was uncool! I didn't see anything." I sat there, eyes closed, feeling like an idiot.

We sat in silence for a long moment.

"Are you married?" she asked.

"No."

"Girlfriend?"

"No."

"Are you a celebrity?"

"I wish."

"Then what say we ditch the whole anonymity thing and assume that we're mature enough to enjoy this sexual adventure for what it is?"

"Sounds good to me."

We sat in silence for another long moment.

"That means you can open your eyes," she said.

I did, and was absolutely entranced. She was gorgeous. She had brown hair and brown eyes, an okay nose, and decent lips. Her hair was shoulder-length and, courtesy of Arissa, her usually straight locks were poofed, curled and spritzed. (Why write new description when you can swipe it from Chapter One?)

But seriously, she was one of the most beautiful women I'd ever seen. She had hungry eyes, borderline predatory. An unbelievably sexy crooked smile. And a *spark* about her, an almost visible energy as if she had an electrical current running through her. Sort of like the Bride of Frankenstein without the funky hair.

Oh, I wanted her bad.

"Hi there, cutie," she said

And then we started kissing again. This time without any inconvenient forehead-whacking. We clutched each other tightly, reclined on the bed and put in a good five minutes of ravenous kissing, which was quickly accompanied by substantial groping. I joyously caressed her large, full breasts, sliding my fingers along the undersides and then stroking the nipples.

My mouth really needed to be on those nipples.

It was important.

Essential.

A matter of life or death.

"I need to taste your breasts," I told her. "It's a matter of life or death."

"Is it, now?"

I nodded. "Yes, ma'am."

"Well, I wouldn't want to be responsible for interfering with a matter of life or death. Why don't you taste these breasts and let me know what you think?"

I lowered my head and began to move my tongue in circles around her right nipple. The taste of her combined with the scent of her perfume was almost putting me in sensory overload. I moved to the left nipple and licked it as she sighed happily.

"Kevin?"

"Yeah?"

"On the questionnaire, there's a section about talking dirty. Did you say that you were for it or against it?"

"Very much for it."

"I'm only asking because I was getting ready to ask if you'd put that warm tongue on my hot pussy, and I didn't want to offend you with that kind of comment."

"No, I'd be completely in favor of that kind of comment."

"You're sure? You won't storm out of the room in a huff?"

"Definitely no huff."

"So lick my pussy. Now."

I kissed my way down to the requested destination. To call what she was wearing panties would be like placing a single piece of confetti on your head and calling it a hat. These panties covered *nothing*. I didn't even have to push them out of the way before I covered her pussy with gentle kisses.

She was wet, wet, wet. I kneaded the inside of her thighs as I slowly ran my tongue over her. It was hard to control myself... I wanted to just dive in there and give her the most passionate, frantic licking of her life.

Drae moaned loudly as I went down on her, offering such subtle phrases of encouragement as "Oh, yes, lick that pussy!" and "Lick it! Lick it! Lick it!"

I moved my hands from her thighs and slid them under her buttocks. God, she had a firm ass. Sure, I'd only handled one other ass in my life, but still, Drae felt fantastic.

I licked. She whimpered.

"This is fucking great," she said. "But we're not being nearly kinky enough."

"No?"

"No. Lie on your back. I'm sitting on your face, big boy."

Chapter Five

Drae

It's a terrible shame that I have to interrupt this narrative at the part where I get to re-live (and you get to read for the first or maybe second time) the incredibly wonderful oral sex Kevin bestowed upon me.

I'm sorry. Really.

Kevin is a Nice Guy. A very sweet, kind, nice guy. I know, I *know*. I didn't think the Nice Guy existed either, despite the proliferation of romance novels and smarmy reality TV shows marrying off bachelors, but I've since learned that just because you don't see them around anymore doesn't mean they're an extinct species. Then again, I probably got the last Nice Guy on the planet…so *nyah, nyah, nyah*. (It appears Kevin wasn't as lucky in the Nice Girl department, but he didn't complain when I was doing that thing to his…oh, I'll get to that later.)

I did make the clever sandwich comment. And it certainly doesn't hurt to stroke your soon-to-be lover's ego by claiming "technical difficulties" in relation to his large penis. And I will admit he did say the word *uncool*, which is *soooo* 1950s.

As for my assumption he was a construction worker…honey, I know the difference between the tanned physique of a man who builds things and a man who mows lawns. There's a difference, believe me. Any woman regularly reviewing physiques of men who do outdoor labor knows what I'm talking about.

Oh, one more thing. I did not ever, during the course of our, er, intercourse cry "Lick it, lick it, lick it". *Puh-lease.* Other than that, he mostly got things right. Except…

He forgot a very important part. You see, I was wearing a pink corset. Now, corsets are the sexiest piece of lingerie ever made. Yeah, I know all the bitching women these days do on behalf of their sisters in centuries past who wore the damned things. Corsets, worn correctly, do not pinch and do not inhibit breathing. They squeeze in the waist and push up the breasts. I had a very nice shelf going on, too.

I guess my new pink corset didn't make much of impression on Kevin. But, really, getting me *out* of it should have. I mean, the minute I removed the first steel clasp, the others followed in short order and *wham*, off came the corset and out shot my considerable breasts. I almost knocked out the poor guy.

Then again, he became so enamored of my nipples (given his astounding introduction to them), he probably just forgot that I nearly blinded him with a flying corset and bouncing boobs.

He didn't seem to notice that the corset was attached to my stockings and while he was distracted with removing my panties with his tongue, I unsnapped the stockings.

I'm not sure what happened to the corset after that. The next morning, we found it across the room hanging on a mirrored sconce. I have no idea how *that* happened.

Anyhoo…to resume…Kevin was between my legs doing things to my clitoris that made stars dance before my eyes. He was eager. No, voracious. And if I didn't slow him down, it was going to be all over for me. Okay, yeah, I was expecting a multi-orgasmic night. But I had lost control really fast and I needed to regain my senses, just a little.

He licked. I whimpered.

"This is fucking great," I said. "But we're not being nearly kinky enough."

"No?"

"No. Lie on your back. I'm sitting on your face, big boy."

He rolled over, panting, his lips glistening with my juices. He lay near the end of the bed. I looked up and saw two red sashes hanging from the ceiling, inches away from his head. Oh good. I was gonna need those. (Convenient, wasn't it, how I noticed those sashes at the moment I would require some leverage?)

I got rid of the panties, but kept on the heels and hose. Thinking I would do something shocking and sexy, I shimmied down Kevin's torso, dragging my pussy along his heated skin.

"Ow! Ow! OW!"

Those weren't exactly the romantic sounds I was going for. I stopped, mid-drag, hovering above his solar plexus. I looked down and saw Kevin's face contorted in pain.

"What's wrong? Cramp?"

"Shoesinmyhips," he gasped.

"What?"

"Heels…hips…*pain!*"

"Whoa, buddy! I'm not into that kind of stuff. I know I said kinky—"

His hands grabbed my ankles and pulled them away from his sides. My legs went out and I lost my balance. I fell, pussy first, onto his chest and flopped forward. Once again, Kevin got a face full of my breasts, which I'm not sure he appreciated since, at that moment, I heard the breath leave his lungs in a giant *whoosh*.

I tried to scramble off, but he grabbed my ass and I took that as a sign he wanted me to stay put. He inhaled a breath and with it, one of my nipples. I probably should've spent more time saying things like, "Are you okay? Did I maim you?" But with Kevin attached to my nipple and one of his hands slipping between my thighs to play with my pussy, all that came out was, "Ooooooh."

He sucked my nipple hard, grazing it with his teeth, and little lightning bolts of pleasure zinged from my breast to my pussy. Then there was that thing he did with his finger, flicking and rubbing my clitoris until an orgasm threatened...then sliding away, tracing the inner folds, then...oh then...he thrust inside my pussy, fast and rough, pushing up just the right way...

He switched breasts. Damnation! I was getting his chest wet, and his finger was mean and stingy with its pleasuring/torturing and I really wanted him to finish licking my pussy and...oh wow.

"You...uh... God do that again...wait, no... *yes*." I felt the coiling of my ecstasy (oh, c'mon, how many ways can you say orgasm?) and I knew I was going to come soon. Too soon. "You promised to lick my pussy."

"Hmm-hmm."

"Remember that dirty talking thing?"

"Hmm-hmm."

There went his finger again. Thrusting inside, pushing on that one spot that felt so damned good. His mouth had switched nipples again, too. "Kevin?"

"Hmmm?"

"Fuck my pussy with your tongue. I want to come on your face." My intent was to impart this information in a throaty whisper, but I think I screamed it. I startled him long enough to get my breasts away from his mouth. I scooted up, careful of my stilettos this time, and put my knees on either side of his head.

I grabbed the sashes and tested them (though I'm sure 1-800-SEX4YOU probably installs these things to withstand the weight of an elephant), then readjusted my position over Kevin's mouth.

I held on to the sashes.

He held on to my ass.

His mouth latched onto my very wet pussy.

He didn't bother licking. He went straight for the prize, suckling my clitoris *hard*, and baby, it was over.

There is no description for the orgasm. It was unfuckingbelievable. I went blind with it, lost the ability to think and almost suffocated Kevin when, in my enthusiasm, I let go of the sashes and squashed his face.

"Sorry," I said, though I did notice that even though he didn't have the ability to draw breath, his tongue wiggled along my labia, lapping up my juices.

I scooted forward (and his tongue did not stop until it could no longer reach me) until I had room to sit down. I promptly took off my gorgeous, but apparently lethal, high heels.

"Stockings too," he gasped. "Get naked."

I rolled them off and tossed them to the floor. Then I went to inspect the damage to Kevin's hips. Each side had a gouge mark.

"Holy crap!" I was impressed he hadn't demanded medical attention. I touched one owie and he flinched. I leaned down and inspected his left hip. "I think that's gonna bruise."

My gaze sidled to the impressive hard-on just centimeters from my face. It's not that I was concerned about his cock fitting inside my pussy, I couldn't wait to try it, but...*okay*, I was a little nervous. I looked up at Kevin. He was watching me, smiling.

"I'm sorry I gave you boo-boos," I said.

"Well, you know, I think the pain traveled."

I grinned. "Really? Where did it go?"

His hand wrapped around his cock. "Right here."

I crawled between his legs and pried his fingers off *my* new toy. Maybe I was nervous about how Mr. Big would fit inside me, but I had no worries about how it would fit in my mouth.

And I intended to make sure he forgot his pain…and his own name.

Chapter Six
Kevin

ഔ

What the hell was my name again?

Bob? Hugo? Licky the Amazing Tongue-Boy?

Kevin. I'm pretty sure it's Kevin. At least that's what the name under the chapter heading says. I'll go with that.

As far as I know, Drae's version of the last set of events was completely accurate. I can't confirm everything, because my view was often obstructed by her pussy, but there's nothing she wrote that I can dispute. I will say that the stiletto heels hurt like *hell*, and the fact that I was immediately able to tend to her nipple-stimulation needs is proof that I am truly a MAN!!!

Not that I'm bragging, but seriously…whack a pair of stiletto heels into your sides sometime and see if you're able to launch right into a nipple-licking frenzy (it's useful to have a pair of willing breasts handy for this experiment). It's not a sensation I feel any great need to repeat.

The licking, though…

I couldn't get enough of it. I was instantly addicted. It was like crack cocaine in pussy form. Had she not moved out of range, I would have gleefully licked her until there was nary a speck of feeling left in my tongue, and then I would've probably pinched my tongue between my fingers and continued licking manually.

Or maybe not. That's a weird-ass image, isn't it? Sorry.

Anyway, it was no longer my turn to lick.

Drae ran her tongue up the entire length of my shaft, grinning and maintaining eye contact as she did so. Then she kissed the head of my penis. "My tongue has never had to make such a long journey before," she informed me.

I chuckled. "Yeah, right."

"Do you think I'm kidding? Do you not realize that your cock is a natural treasure? After we're finished I'm going to have the damn thing bronzed. Why aren't you a porn star? Or *are* you a porn star? Am I fucking a porn star?"

"Nope, I'm not a porn star."

"You should look into it." She kissed the head of my cock again and then ran her tongue down my length until she reached my balls. She cupped them in her right hand and began to gently tend to them with her lips and tongue.

It felt incredible. I told her so. Several times. Quite loudly.

After she'd lavished a generous amount of attention on my testicles, her tongue made a return journey up my shaft and then swirled around the head of my cock, flicking against the tip. Then she took me inside her mouth, just a couple of inches, and sucked.

I closed my eyes and moaned.

Blowjobs. I remembered blowjobs now. Blowjobs were good.

And Drae was good at it. She stroked the rest of my cock with her hand as she sucked, and I just lay there, basking in the incredible sensation and saying "Oh, God" once in a while.

She picked up her pace.

I opened my eyes and watched her. The woman was practically *glowing* as she went down on me. Her wonderful breasts moved back and forth against my thighs. She was treating my cock as if it were her most prized, beloved possession.

I made a mental note to buy Jennifer a car.

"I need to lick you some more," I said to Drae.

She pulled her mouth away from my penis and vigorously shook her head. "Nuh-uh. Sucking cock." She went back to work.

"I didn't say you had to stop."

She quickly got the idea. Keeping her lips firmly wrapped around my penis, she moved around so that she was straddling me, that glorious pussy hovering right above my face. She gently lowered it to my lips, and I licked that warm, wet flesh as she continued sucking me.

We kept that up for a good long while, communicating only through soft moans, sighs, and the occasional request to go faster and/or harder.

1-800-SEX4YOU was the greatest invention in the history of mankind. I was going to become their official spokesperson. I was going to design billboards, wear sandwich boards, shout endorsements from open windows…whatever it took.

Drae said something, but I couldn't understand it because her mouth was still full and her thighs were blocking my ears.

"What was that?" I asked, my words equally muffled.

"I said, fuck me!" she gasped.

I could do that. As Drae got on her hands and knees, I reached over and grabbed a condom from the bedside dresser. Drae glanced back at me as I tore open the foil wrapper. "Do those things even come in your size?"

"You'd be amazed what fits in one of these."

"So hurry up and amaze me."

I put on the condom and got behind her. She wiggled her ass playfully as I placed my hands on her hips.

"Oh, I do need you to be careful with that thing," she said. "At least at first."

"I will, I promise." I gently pressed the head of my cock against her wet vagina. It offered no resistance. Very slowly I slid inside her, not much, just enough to give ourselves a wonderful sneak preview of upcoming events.

"Oooooooh…" she moaned.

"Does it hurt?"

"No, that was 'oooooooh' as in 'holy fucking shit I can't believe how good this feels'."

I slid in a bit more.

"I do seem to be sufficiently lubricated," Drae noted.

"Looks that way."

"Maybe you don't have to be quite as careful."

I slid in her some more, and then began working my cock back and forth inside her. She was so hot and so tight and so breathtakingly beautiful when she looked back at me.

I fucked her with long, slow strokes, keeping a tight grip on her hips. I looked at her luscious ass, wanting to sink my teeth into it.

How could I have gone so long without this kind of pleasure?

I kept thrusting, still moving slowly and still being careful, though it didn't seem that Drae was in any way uncomfortable. I did wish that there were a mirror to the side so I could watch her breasts sway, but you can't have everything.

"This feels *so* good," she said.

I gasped in agreement. And yet, as good as it felt, I was in total control of my body. I felt like I could keep this going for as long as necessary to make Drae come over and over and over. Whatever record number of orgasms she'd had in previous sexual adventures was going to be shattered.

Apparently, though, this total control of my body did not extend to my mouth. And as I thrust deep into her, I fucked up really, really bad.

"Oh, Tara!"

Chapter Seven
Drae

ဢ

I can't take issue with Kevin's version of events, especially the part where he screamed, *"Oh, Tara"*.

There's not a bigger mood killer in the world than to hear the man fucking you scream the name of *another* woman in orgasmic ecstasy.

Guys who play around a lot have at least learned to cry out vague terms like *baby, honey, sweetheart, darling* and *hey, you*.

Any man who screams an actual name is a cheater and a liar.

"Get out of me, you shit-eating prick!"

He obliged, scrambling backwards.

"Where are my shoes?"

"I can explain," he said, looking all cute and sincere. "Please don't go."

"I don't want my shoes so I can leave," I said, getting off the bed. "I want to use the heels to gouge out your adulterous eyes."

"Honest to God, I'm not married. Not now. Not for three years. I guess I always feel married, even though Tara isn't—"

"Shut up." I heard him inhale a breath as if he intended to speak. "I mean it, Kevin or whatever-the-hell-your-name is. I have heard the married-man song-and-dance too many times not to recognize it."

I rounded the bed, trying not step on candles. Who the fuck needs this many candles? I was writing that in the comment form, by God. TOO MANY FUCKING CANDLES.

"She doesn't understand me," I said in an ultra-whiny voice. "We're separated. I'm getting a divorce. I don't love her. Blah, blah, blah."

"How many married men have you dated?"

"None! Well, none on purpose." I glared at him. "And this isn't about *me*. This is about *you*. How dare you come off so sweet and unsure and 'oh I'm so nervous'. "

Shocked at the tears in my eyes, I stopped talking and tried to calm myself. I liked him. We'd been rolling around on the bed for less than an hour, and had not one, *not one*, conversation that could be construed as heart-to-heart, and I *liked* him.

Well, well, well. My bad luck streak with men continued unabated. What a surprise.

"Drae. Please. Just listen."

"Fuck you." Apparently, my heels had been sucked into an invisible vortex. Aw, shit. I stalked toward the door and yanked the dress off the hook. "I'm telling Vivian that you're married. I hope you get arrested for falsifying information. And I hope she calls your wife and tells Tara what a lying, cheating scumbag you are."

Then a thought occurred to me. I held the dress out, like a very flimsy shield and looked at Kevin. "Does she…know? Please don't tell me you have one of those bullshit open marriages. Because that's such crap! If you're going screw other people, what's the point of committing to one person?"

He shook his head, looking miserable. *Good.* I did not feel pity. Or the tiniest bit of doubt. So what if he looked earnest? And despondent? I had been fooled before. Still, my anger faded—just a little.

Unable to stop myself, I looked at his genitals. The cock I had been enjoying mere seconds ago had softened. Sometime during my diatribe he'd disposed of the condom. Now he sat on the bed, watching me, his eyes dark with pain, and *oh goddamnit*, I felt sorry for him.

"Okay. Here's the deal." I folded the dress over my arm. "You have thirty seconds to tell me the truth. If I believe you, I'll give you five minutes to prove it's the truth."

"My wife, Tara, passed away a little more than three years ago. She was my high school sweetheart and the only woman I have ever made love to. I...I haven't been with anyone else. Not until you."

He looked me straight in the eye the entire time. His words were heartfelt and he seemed...genuine. My stomach dropped. Oh. My. God. Please tell me I did not just scream and rant at the cute, sweet widower. I did *not* just throw a big ol' hissy fit at a guy who had loved his wife so much, he had mourned her for three years. And the *first* time he gets up the nerve to have sexual relations, the poor son-of-a-bitch ends up with me.

"I hope you're lying," I said, shame heating my cheeks. "Because if you're not, then I'm going to feel like the biggest bitch that ever walked the Earth."

"Would you believe Vivian?"

"What?"

"You said I had five minutes to prove the truth. I could call Jennifer—she was my wife's best friend—but she'd just be a voice on the phone. But if Vivian vouched for me...or would you rather see Tara's gravesite?"

He meant it. What was wrong with this guy? He was so nice. I just spent the last five minutes ripping him a new asshole and he wanted to show me his wife's grave just so I wouldn't feel bad about sleeping with him.

I felt sick.

He was telling the truth.

I *was* the biggest bitch to ever walk the Earth.

"I'm so sorry, Kevin." I figured I could apologize another hundred times, but I could never make up for raving like a lunatic about gouging out his eyes and tattle-telling to Vivian.

I put on the dress and grabbed my purse.

"You still don't believe me?" He sounded hurt.

"Yes," I said softly. "I believe you."

"Then where are you going?"

"How could you want to spend another second with me after the way I just treated you?"

"How could you want to spend another second with me after I called out someone else's name?"

"If Tara was the only woman you've ever been with, it's understandable that you would call out her name." I clutched the purse so hard, the beads bit into my fingers. "I feel kinda...honored in a weird way. It's nice to know that you felt something with me that reminded you of her." I grimaced. "I told you it was weird. But I hope you understand what I meant."

I turned, grasped the doorknob, and blinked away the tears in my eyes. *Again.* Oh, what a schmuck I was.

"Drae."

I didn't turn around. I couldn't. To be honest, I was so wrapped up in my misery, I didn't hear him move. The next thing I knew, big manly arms swept around me and he was lifting me up, taking me away from the door and back to the bed. The purse fell from my hand, but I didn't care. I wanted to make up for hurting him. For not listening to him when he tried to explain about *Oh, Tara*.

He laid me on the bed then settled next to me. With his thumb, he wiped away the tears and I sniffled like a big baby, feeling sorry for myself, for him and for the *coitus interruptus*.

"Let's start over," he whispered. "I'm Kevin. You're Drae." His hand slid under my dress and I eagerly parted my legs for him. The same thumb that just wiped away my tears now did its work against my clit.

I pushed away his hand then I rolled on top of him. With his help, I took off my dress and tossed it at the door, missing the candles. All we needed to totally ruin the rest of the evening was a fire. We'd already had head-conking, hip-gouging, adultery-accusing...I didn't want to see the room go up in flames.

At least, not until Kevin and I did.

Chapter Eight
Kevin

ഔ

Huh?

I've re-read Drae's last chapter at least ten times now, and the only possible reaction is…

Huh?

That, ladies and gentlemen, is *not* how it happened. I don't know if she hoped that I'd just wink and go along with her version of the events or what, but I'm afraid that in this case a complete do-over is required. Sorry.

"*Oh, Tara!*" I moaned.

I instantly caught my faux pas from hell and tried to pretend it didn't happen. I didn't hear that, didn't hear that, nope, didn't hear that, la la la la la la la…

"*Get out of me, you shit-eating prick!*" Drae shouted. She apparently was not going to try to pretend it didn't happen.

I got out of her. Quickly. I have a large penis, and it was currently at maximum strength, but I had no doubts that she could pop it off like the flower of a dandelion if I didn't withdraw ASAP.

"Where are my shoes?"

"Let me explain. You don't need to leave."

"I don't want my shoes so I can leave," she said, getting off the bed. "I want them so I can…*poke* you with them!"

"Poke me?"

"Yeah!" Drae mimed a jabbing motion.

I tried very hard to stifle my smile, because I knew my penis was still in mortal danger. It wasn't easy. She looked so...well, *adorable*.

"Don't grin at me, you fuck! Or...*non*-fuck, because you're not getting fucked anymore tonight! At least not by me. Go home and fuck your wife or girlfriend but I hope they don't fuck you because...*fuck*!"

"You're very flustered," I said. "I think you need to take a deep breath."

"I'm *not* flustered! You're the one who's flustered! You flustered fuck!"

"Honest-to-God, I'm not married," I said, keeping my voice calm. "Not now. Not for three years. I guess I always feel married, even though Tara isn't—"

"You flustered fuck!" Drae repeated.

"You really should calm down."

"I'm not gonna calm down!" She dabbed at her eyes and her voice cracked. "I really liked you, and every time I like somebody he turns into complete shit, and you had the best cock I'd ever seen, and...*fuck*!"

"I'm not married," I insisted.

"So Tara's your girlfriend."

"No."

"So then she's your fuck-buddy! I don't play around with guys who have fuck-buddies! Or maybe I do. I'm not sure."

"I don't have a fuck-buddy."

Drae suddenly looked horrified. "Is Tara a blow-up doll? Do you have pet names for your blow-up doll?"

"Tara's my wife."

"Ha! I knew it! You gave yourself away, Kevin...if your name *is* Kevin!" She pointed an accusing finger at me, and then pointed that same finger at her crotch. "Well, you can kiss this pussy goodbye! But not really kiss it...in fact, you can just

223

not kiss this pussy goodbye! In fact, I don't want you to even *look* at this pussy!" She covered it with her hand.

I raised my voice just a bit. "Drae? Calm down."

"No! And stop looking at my ass!"

"Your ass isn't even facing me!"

"Stop looking at it in the mirror!"

"There's no mirror! What the hell are you talking about?"

She quickly looked around for a mirror, found none and then let out a choked sob. "It's just not fair. I was delirious with you inside me. It's hard to coast down from that, okay?"

"Tara was my wife. She died three years ago."

Drae gaped at me. "What?"

I found my own eyes welling up with tears. "She died of cancer. She was my high school sweetheart and the only woman I have ever made love to. I haven't been with anyone else. Not until you."

"What?"

"Is that a good *what*?"

"Why didn't you say that before? Why did you let me scream and cry like a crazy woman? When you moaned *'Oh, Tara'*, why didn't you just follow it up with *'Ooops, sorry, Tara is my dead wife'* and not make me look like an idiot?" Her face fell. "Oh my God, that was cold. I'm so sorry."

"It's okay."

"No, no, it's not. I just…I was just out of my mind with lust, and when I heard you moan her name I lost it. It was stupid. We're here for an anonymous sexual encounter so it doesn't even matter."

"It freaked me out when I said it," I admitted. Then my damn grin came back. "And you looked so adorable when you were ranting."

She glared at me. "I did not."

"Oh, yes you did. I know it's a cliché, but you, Drae, are fuckin' *cute* when you're pissed!"

"Screw you."

"See? Cute."

"Don't make me slap the shit out of you."

"That's a different room."

"Ha-ha."

"Look, I'm really sorry about the misunderstanding, and I'm sorry that I let you make an adorable ass out of yourself. But you know, make-up sex is the best kind."

"Is it, now?"

I nodded. "Wanna make up?"

"Hell yes."

She returned to the bed. We kissed gently, and I knew everything was going to be all right.

We kissed less gently, and I knew everything was going to be even better.

Chapter Nine
Drae

ဆ

What did I tell you about construction workers? Big, dumb and eager to please. The human equivalent of Golden Retrievers. And so cuuuuuute.

Granted, Kevin was better than a Golden Retriever because he had opposable thumbs and decent breath. But there is so much wrong with how he remembered the *"Oh Tara"* incident, I could waste this entire chapter pointing out each and every incorrectly reported detail. (By the way, I am not cute when I'm pissed-off. I'm *not*.)

Suffice it to say that *my* recall of the incident was what *really* happened. Kevin's version was fictionalized. (Who's a good puppy? That's right, sweetie, *who's a good puppy?*)

I think he was embarrassed to admit that he's not only a Nice Guy, he's a *Romantic* Nice Guy. Maybe he thinks that if other men read this (and they will because it's in the annals of 1-800-SEX4YOU history now), they'll think he's a wimp.

Or maybe he was just embarrassed to write about what happened after we stopped kissing and started...but that's for later.

Really and truly, I suspected it took so much blood to raise his Penis Titanic, Kevin simply didn't have enough left in his brain for other functions, such as memory.

Given how much pleasure his cock gave me, I was willing to sacrifice the truth every now and then. If Kevin believed that I asked him if Tara was a blow-up doll (oh puh-lease!) or that whole looking-at-my-ass-looking-for-a-mirror incident occurred...well, I all I can say is, "I forgive you. Now show me the cock, baby."

Okay. We can resume the real story…

Kevin laid me on the bed then settled next to me. With his thumb, he wiped away the tears and I sniffled like a big baby, feeling sorry for myself, for him and for the *coitus interruptus.*

"Let's start over," he whispered. "I'm Kevin. You're Drae." His hand slid under my dress and I eagerly parted my legs for him. The same thumb that just wiped away my tears now did its work against my clit.

I pushed away his hand then I rolled on top of him. With his help, I took off my dress and tossed it at the door, missing the candles. All we needed to totally ruin the rest of the evening was a fire. We'd already had head-conking, hip-gouging, adultery-accusing…I didn't want to see the room go up in flames.

At least, not until Kevin and I did.

Before I could do something sultry and sexy, Kevin flipped me onto my back and rolled on top of me.

"Kevin! I was going to do something sultry and sexy."

He took my nipple into his mouth, sucked it between his lips and flicked his tongue. "Um…never mind."

My arms wound around his neck, encouraging his delightful torture of my breasts. I stroked his back. Wow. Every part of Kevin was muscled. My palms coasted over his firm backside down to cup his first class booty. He clenched his ass (show-off), and those motions pushed his hardening penis along my pussy.

With Kevin attending to my breasts (you'd think they were made of chocolate) and his cock revving to full capacity, I didn't have much to do except wiggle and moan and enjoy.

"I want your cock inside me," I gasped as he began another kissing assault from neck to breasts.

He slipped his arms under my shoulders and rolled so that I was, once again, on top of him. "Sheesh. Would you make up your mind?"

"I just wanted to give you the chance to do that sultry and sexy thing you promised."

I looked down at the cock trapped between his stomach and my thighs and lost my train of thought.

"I was hoping whatever you had planned required movement," said Kevin, bucking his hips to indicate which parts he hoped would be part of said "movement".

I leaned over to the nightstand to grab another condom. Kevin took advantage of the breast dangling over his face to do some more nipple licking. My pussy contracted, getting wetter—and I didn't think that was possible.

I retrieved the condom and scooted between Kevin's legs.

"Now who's changing positions?" he asked.

I put my mouth on his balls and licked.

Kevin shut up.

He was hard (I mentioned that, right?) and warm, a little salty too, thanks to contact with my aforementioned wetness—and as I sucked the tip of his cock, I tasted some of *his* desire (and it was salty, too). I once read that if a guy ate enough pineapple, his semen would taste sweet. I wondered if Kevin would be willing to experiment…then I remembered he was only a one-night stand.

What a disappointing realization.

I liked Kevin. A lot. More than I should given that all we'd done…er, tried to do…was fuck each other senseless.

Speaking of which…I couldn't get his cock all the way down my throat. I've never been adept at the whole deep throat blowjob anyway, but even if I had been a porn star, with the talent to take every inch of this bad boy, chances were good it would have pierced vital organs.

Kevin seemed happy with my efforts, though, if his closed eyes, fisted hands and constant moaning meant anything.

God, I was getting hot. I'd felt horny almost the entire time, except for those ten minutes of ranting and explaining (the *"Oh Tara"* incident), but now all I wanted was to feel that cock buried inside me, thrusting.

I tortured Kevin a little while longer though, with lots of kissing, licking and, his apparent favorite, sucking. Then I rose to my knees, tore open the condom and...

"Can you put these things on backwards?" I asked.

I held the rubber and realized I had rarely — okay never — actually sheathed a cock before. I wasn't sure which way it went. How stupid was that? It would be really helpful if there was an arrow or a "this end down" sign or *something*.

Kevin answered my question by sitting up, plucking the condom out of my hand and rolling it onto his cock.

"Get on, Mistress" he said. "I'll pleasure you."

Okay, he didn't say that. Remember, I was entertaining those dominatrix fantasies, earlier? I figure if Kevin can fictionalize, I can, too.

What he really said was, "Would you please accept my invitation to sit on my cock and fuck me senseless?"

Snicker. Okay, okay...he didn't say that, either. He didn't really say anything. He grunted and pointed.

I took the hint.

I put my knees on either side of his hips, planted one hand on his chest for leverage, and while Kevin amused himself by playing with my breasts, I used my free hand to guide him into my pussy.

Oh. My. God.

I had to stop about halfway through the process because it felt so good. Oh baby, it felt GREAT. Slowly, slowly...*slowly*, I lowered myself onto his cock until finally it was all the way inside.

Then I started to move.

Chapter Ten
Kevin

ഇ

I could dispute some of what Drae said in the last section, but that would take time away from writing about the hot sex. And that would be silly.

I will say that "Then I started to move" does not come *close* to describing the bucking, gyrating, bouncing and thrashing of Drae's body as she rode me. Nor the gasping, moaning, panting and squealing that was coming from both of us (though not so much squealing from me).

There simply aren't enough thesauruses in the world to describe how incredible this felt. Granted, most thesauruses have pretty much the same content, so I guess the *quantity* of them wouldn't really matter, but I will say that all of the words in one of those big-ass hardcover thesauruses would be woefully inadequate to fully describe the sheer bliss of Drae riding my cock.

It felt really, really, *really* good.

And believe me, she was showing me no mercy. Nary a speck. In fact, to keep this whole experience from ending sooner than I wanted, I had to resort to counting imaginary turtles. "One turtle...two turtles...three turtles..." (Rest assured that the counting was strictly in my head.)

My, how this woman could fuck.

I looked at where we were joined, where her pussy was keeping my cock as a happy hostage.

I looked at her wonderful breasts, bouncing and shining with perspiration.

I looked into her eyes. They were feral, almost a little frightening...but frightening in a good way.

"*Oh...*" she gasped. "*Oh God*!"

I gave a sharp upward thrust with my hips and I'm pretty sure that her eyes literally crossed.

"Do that again!" she demanded. "Lots of times!"

I obeyed her order, counting mental turtles the whole time.

"*Oh...oh, wow...I...I think...*" She trailed off and then fixed her hungry eyes on my own. "I think I could fall in love with you."

"Really?" I asked, genuinely surprised.

"Your cock," she hastily amended. "I could fall in love with your cock. I already have. I love it. Love, love, love it."

We continued abusing the bedsprings (fortunately, 1-800-SEX4YOU had invested in good bedsprings) as I pondered this new piece of information. I mean, I knew she wasn't seriously falling in love with me...it was just sex talk. But I just couldn't imagine saying goodbye after we were done and never seeing her again. We'd already botched the whole anonymity thing, but we were fucking in an environment that was exclusively devoted to the idea of one-night stands. That was the whole *point.* If I said that I wanted to see her again, would it end things on an uncomfortable, unpleasant note?

I wouldn't worry about that for now. I'd focus on the fact that a beautiful naked woman was riding my cock and loving it.

We kept this up for...I don't even know how long. At least two-hundred and sixteen turtles. Then I decided that it was my turn to be on top.

"Your turn to be on top," Drae gasped, climbing off me.

I'd had the idea before she spoke up. Seriously.

She lay on the bed and spread her legs wide. I climbed on top of her and thrust inside, correctly assuming that there wasn't going to be much in the way of resistance. Drae let out a shrill cry that would have shattered every mirror in the room, if there'd been any. She wrapped her legs around me and we resumed the "fucking each other's brains out" portion of our time together.

We kissed deeply, and she slid her tongue into my mouth. I could feel her breasts mashed tightly against my chest, the nipples rock-hard. I fucked her with a force and pace that I *would* liken to that of a jackhammer, but since I'm a construction worker that's just far too easy.

Drae screamed. An honest-to-goodness *scream.* I assumed that the 1-800-SEX4YOU designers had taken such noise into account and provided adequate soundproofing, but I still kinda expected somebody to throw open the door and say "Keep it down in there, dammit! Other people are tryin' to fuck, too!"

Our bodies slapped together with each thrust, and our lips were crushed together so tightly that it almost hurt.

I was getting close.

Drae pulled her lips away from mine. "I'm getting close!" she screamed.

"How close?"

"Really fucking close!"

And so I just let loose, fucking her as hard as I possibly could and desperately hoping that by "really fucking close" she meant "within the next few seconds".

That's *exactly* what she meant.

She came so loudly that I half-expected the walls and ceiling to come crashing down around us. Not that I was quiet myself. I let out an actual howl. It was an orgasm of such force and ecstasy that…well, I'm not going to say that it completely made up for my three years without sex, but it did wipe out at least a year and a half of that dry spell.

My orgasm subsided. Hers kept on going.

When it was finally over, I pulled out of her, eliciting a disappointed whimper. I hurriedly took care of the condom removal and then returned to bed. She draped herself over me and we just lay there, enjoying the afterglow and the silence.

She gently kissed my shoulder.

As my mind and body gradually returned to a state that couldn't be defined as "absolute sexual frenzy", I couldn't help but feel a sadness. No, our erotic adventure wasn't over...we still had several hours, and there would *definitely* be an encore. But though I barely knew Drae, several hours just didn't seem like enough.

Epilogue
Drae & Kevin

ප

Drae

Okay, I screamed. And *maybe* I squealed. But any woman in the world would have made the same crack-the-ceiling noises if she were getting fucked by Kevin. Except that, of course, should I ever find a woman trying to get so much as a peek at his cock, I will have to wield the Heels of Death and gut her.

Because you know where I said, "I think I could fall in love with you"? And so very cleverly covered it with, "Your cock"? Well…I kinda, sorta meant it. Without the "your cock", added to the "fall in love with you".

At the beginning of this narrative, I would've said that what Kevin and I did for the rest of the night (with occasional naps) qualified for the description "ultimate fuck fest". But in the morning, after waking up in Kevin's arms, I found myself thinking of it in more romantic terms…such as Rendezvous With Erotic Destiny.

You can't spend all night with a guy and not figure out a few things. For instance, Kevin has a corny sense of humor.

And he's nice to me even when I'm bitchy to him.

And he doesn't snore (and doesn't care that I do and deny it vehemently).

Kevin told me he had a daughter, Melissa. When he talked about his little girl, his eyes lit up and he smiled wide, and I knew he was a great dad. He showed me a picture of her and told me how she'd started preschool and could already say her ABCs.

But, well, what was the point of thinking about how great Kevin was and how much I wanted to see him again…when he hadn't given a single hint that he'd want to see *me* again?

Maybe all he wanted from this evening was to prime himself for the dating game.

I tried not to think about him dating other women, much less sleeping with them. I decided just to enjoy the time we had left.

For breakfast they served mimosas and all kinds of pastries, including donuts. I put one on Kevin's erection, but it broke on the first push so I just licked off the crumbs. Then I licked him.

And that started approximately an hour's worth of licking, sucking and thrusting that led to sweat, moans and orgasms.

Which is really much better than eating a whole donut.

All too soon, though, it was time to get dressed.

It was time to say goodbye.

Kevin

And we did.

We parted ways and never saw each other again. I pined away for what could have been, sitting in my darkened attic for days at a time. I lost weight, forgot to shave, bathed rarely and howled at the moon. I was fired from my job and banished from the city. Melissa was sent to an orphanage run by a cruel headmaster who sold the children on the black market if they asked for seconds at dinner. I slept in the nastiest parts of our nation's sewage system, crying myself to sleep, living off bugs (and not even the good-tasting ones), screaming "Why? Why? *Why*"? at my new imaginary friends.

Or…I told Drae that I wanted to see her again.

It had the potential to be a terrible *faux pas*, but I could handle it. If she was looking for absolutely nothing more than a one-night romp, it was cool. Worst case scenario, our awesome experience ended on a socially awkward note.

She squealed and threw her arms around me.

We kissed.

We continued kissing until some jerk from 1-800-SEX4YOU knocked on the door and rudely informed us that we were going to be charged for additional time if we didn't vacate the room immediately, so we got the hell out of there.

Drae and I have been seeing each other for two weeks now, and though I really never thought I could be happy with another woman after Tara died, I can definitely see this becoming a lasting relationship. Despite some factual errors in her storytelling, she's an *incredible* lady.

Tonight, she's going to meet Melissa. Am I sweating buckets over this? Oh, hell yeah. Do I think it'll work out?

Oh yeah.

Big time.

The End

Also by Chris Tanglen

&

A Third Party
A Third (and Fourth) Party
Aunt Penelope's Harem
Luck of the Irish
Mistress Charlotte

Also by Michele Bardsley

&

A Taste of Honey
Bride Portal
Two Men and a Lady *(anthology)*
Shadows Present
Wizard's Moon

About the Author

∞

Chris Tanglen writes sexy comedies for Ellora's Cave. Chris is a fan of energy drinks, red licorice, gummi bears, short walks on the beach, and intercourse.

Multi-published in several genres, award-winning author Michele Bardsley spends her days creating fictional worlds because, let's face it, reality sucks. A prime example is that no one has yet to figure out how to make calorie-free chocolate. What's up with THAT?

Michele lives in Oklahoma where she is held hostage by her two children, her husband, and three cats. Occasionally her family remembers to feed her, but mostly she's forced to nibble on copy paper while eking out her next story. The manacles make it difficult to type, but she manages.

Chris and Michele welcome comments from readers. You can find their websites and email addresses on their author bio pages at www.ellorascave.com.

Tell Us What You Think

We appreciate hearing reader opinions about our books. You can email us at Comments@EllorasCave.com.

FROG PRINCE OF PLANET MARECAGE

Samantha Winston

ഔ

Part One
Planet Marécage

ဢ

Princess Shari gave a very unladylike curse as her private spaceship, the *SS Marissa*, hit a zone of turbulence due to a small, magnetic storm. Not that she couldn't handle turbulence. Shari, an ace pilot, could fly anything from one of her father's intergalactic warships to the half-rusted antiquity called a shuttle that brought the grain in every morning for the castle's weir-cattle. No, she cursed because she hadn't dressed for piloting. She'd hardly dressed at all. That morning, out of sheer boredom, she'd gotten into a huge fight with her nanny and then had stormed off and climbed aboard the *SS Marissa*.

Her nanny, arms folded across her chest and a mulish look on her face, had called after her "You'd better be back in time for dinner!"

"Huh!" Shari had snorted. Then she'd zoomed off into the vastness of space, and for some reason, headed towards the Bud sector—a part of space that not too many tourists ventured into...for good reason. The Bud Sector had no fabulous planets or stunning sights. Planets abounded, but they were mostly uninhabitable being devoid of atmosphere, swathed in poisonous clouds, or covered in ice thousands of meters thick. Only a few, horrid planets supported life in that sector.

Shari cursed again as the turbulence shook the small craft.

"Serves you right," said the spaceship. Endowed with an artificial intelligence, the *SS Marissa* could talk, sing, and even tell jokes on occasion. Her voice was high and fluty, but with a definite metallic twang.

241

"Up yours," said Shari, one hand on the control stick while her other hand tried to restrain her breasts—the turbulence made them bounce like melons on a trampoline.

"Are you sure my golden space ball went that way?" Shari added, peering at the navigational data Marissa called up.

"Of course." Marissa sounded miffed. She was never wrong.

Shari uttered a whole string of curses and Marissa said in a prissy, "told you so" voice, "I told you not to launch your ball so close to that sun. Its gravitational force caught it and drew it in, and now that little planet seems to have captured it. You'll never get it back."

"The hell I won't!" Shari said furiously. Her golden space ball was worth a fortune, but more than that, she truly enjoyed playing space tag with it. The rules of the game were simple: launch the ball into space—preferably where no planet or sun could affect its trajectory—then it was just a matter of catching it. Once you did, the ball became "it" and tried to catch you. Made with advanced technology, the space ball was small, but a homing device kept it in touch with the spaceship. Other devices kept it from hitting the ship as it shot through outer space, and still others made it weigh little more than a silk cushion. Her father had given it to her for her eighteenth birthday, and she adored it.

She'd had endless hours of fun, zipping across the galaxy, twisting and turning her maneuverable little spaceship. And now she'd gone and lost the ball. Furthermore, her breasts hurt from all the bouncing around. The whole day seemed pretty much ruined.

"Let's go and see if we can get it," said Shari, frowning at the huge swaths of cloud covering the planet. "What is this place called, anyhow?"

"Planet Marécage," said Marissa. The spaceship gave a delicate little cough. "Ahem. This from the *Galactic Dictionary* compiled by explorers Desjardins and Wirber, published in the year 46-776. Hmm, it's a bit outdated. I'll have to download a more modern galactic dictionary. Let's see, page three thousand and seven, paragraph…"

"Just read about the planet, you stupid heap of tin," snapped Shari.

"Excuse me!" Marissa sniffed. "Our little highness is in a bad mood this morning."

"If you don't hurry, I will rip out your memory with my bare hands," snarled Shari.

"Oooh, I'm scared. Well, if you insist. Planet Marécage. Three quarters unbearably smelly swamp water, one quarter horribly stinking mud. No solid land, vegetation includes a variety of skunk cabbage and marsh weed. No spacefaring life, but the natives—a sort of amphibious life form, are semi-intelligent and practice a type of low magic. See 'Appendix C,' page…"

"Enough already. No solid ground. Fine. We'll get as close to the ball as possible, and you'll hover while I go get it."

"Sounds like a plan," said the *SS Marissa*. The ship hummed a bit as they descended, and then they hit the clouds.

"I wish you'd gotten your in-ship stabilizers replaced," moaned Shari, cradling her breasts.

"They should have been replaced this morning, but Miss Royal Highness was in a tearing hurry to get away from her nanny." The ship sounded smug.

"Oh, blow it out your propulsion tubes," muttered Shari.

The ship had come to a complete stop, and Shari stood up, stretching a bit. Outside, nothing but deep mist could be seen. The ground beneath them, just barely visible, was effectively nothing but one colossal, humungous swamp. Shari rubbed her breasts and sighed.

She caught sight of her reflection in the full-length mirror by the portside door. Her long, dark red hair fell in a tousled cascade to her waist. Her hairdresser hadn't had time to comb it. She was still dressed in her nightie—a sheer, lacy number that showed everything.

Well, of course it showed everything. She never wore underwear to bed, and her enormous breasts lifted the front of the nightie higher than the back. Her curly auburn pubic hair peeked saucily from the front, and her ample buttocks, well— Shari bit her full lower lip—she was quite sure that the smooth, round and delightful globes would have driven any male crazy with lust.

The whole fight had been about that. Shari—as Princess Royal of the House of Teres—would never be allowed to see, talk to or even think about a male. She would have to wait to be married until she reached the ancient age of one hundred and fifty, because she could never legally have any children.

The House of Teres, by tradition, was ruled exclusively by a king—a *male*. Shari had three older brothers, and the House of Teres did not marry its women to other houses. Teres males governed the Teres solar system—their planet and *all* the planets of the solar system. The Teres males married powerful women from other houses, and thus the Teres kingdoms thrived.

Raised in luxury, spoiled, and kept in the nursery until past childbearing age, Teres females inspired curiosity and pity, but no one had ever tried to change the rules. When the Teres princesses passed childbearing age, they could marry and leave the kingdom if they wished.

All this had been drummed into Shari's head since birth, and for years she'd been the docile princess, bounced on her mother's and father's knees—the king was the only male she would ever be allowed to see!—and raised by an endless stream of nannies. Hairdressers, manicurists, and stylists groomed her, and tutors taught her all about math, history, poetry and astronomy. Swimming instructors and piano teachers made sure she could swim and play music. But they were all women, and Shari was now twenty years old and in the prime of her physical life.

Every part of her screamed, "Take me!" but only her own hands ever touched the auburn brush between her legs when the peculiar, aching sensation overcame her. And when she tried to appease that ache, someone would always rush in and pull her hands away from her throbbing body. "No, no!" someone would chide gently, and read her a story about three bears or some poor child lost in the woods.

Even the *SS Marissa* had been carefully programmed to watch her. She couldn't even enter the atmosphere of a planet where there might be males. So, while Shari stared at her image in the mirror and longed for a warm hand to stroke her breasts or nestle in the rich curls between her long, shapely legs, she kept her hands to herself and only clenched her bottom a little in frustration. The fight had been epic—but just one in a long line of many, and Shari supposed she'd best resign herself to getting old, fat, and staying single—like all the royal princesses in the House of Teres.

Her aunts and great-aunts sat around dressed in pink and lilac pastel silks, stuffing themselves with sweets while listening to soft music. They loved when Shari visited their quarters, but it gave Shari nightmares for weeks when she saw her fat aunts lying like beached whales on their beds. She thought bleakly of her fate, then turned her gaze back to the mist outside the spaceship. The one game she loved, chasing her space ball, kept her spirits high.

She'd get her golden space ball back. Her love of space-sports had set her apart from her sluggish aunts, and she meant to keep it that way.

Sighing deeply, she cursed again, but without much energy, and opened the hatch.

"The golden ball is somewhere in a fifty meter range." Marissa's metallic voice came from behind her.

"Oh, just perfect," said Shari.

"Do I detect a bit of sarcasm?" asked Marissa primly.

The spaceship—too heavy to land on the surface—hovered carefully just above the mud. Stairs unfolded from the hatch and lowered to the ground. Shari stepped off the ladder and promptly sank to her knees in muck.

Schluff, schluff, schluff, went her feet, as she lurched through the deep mud. The explorers Desjardins and Wirber hadn't been exaggerating. The murky air was so thick she could barely see a yard in front of her, and the mud was unbearably vile. The stench made her stomach heave, and she was grateful she hadn't had time for her usual, abundant breakfast. Of course, just the thought of the abundant breakfast brought on a bout of dry heaves—she had to stop and let loose a string of loud expletives until her stomach settled.

That's when the skunk cabbage on her left rustled.

Shari let out a shriek.

A small head popped out from between two leaves. Two, globe-like yellow eyes stared at her from within a round head. The creature looked a bit like a cross between a frog and an elf. Shari had a book with elves in it—the only male creatures allowed in her fairy tales. All the pictures of the various princes charming, for example, had been carefully excised. Frogs she knew from the swamp near the palace. She'd caught enough of them, kissing them in hopes of finding out what a prince charming looked like. But she'd grown out of that habit. Now she and the creature stared at each other.

"Do you understand Confederate speech?" Shari asked. She didn't actually expect an answer.

"*Oui, Mademoiselle,*" the creature croaked. It had an incredibly huge mouth—wide like a frog's mouth.

Shari blinked. "That's French," she said, feeling her eyebrows lift in surprise.

"*Oui, Mademoiselle.*"

Shari rolled her eyes. Obviously Desjardins had spoken French to these creatures and they had copied him. No real intelligence, just mimicry. She took another step and sank into mud to her thighs. As she got deeper, the mud in the swamp stank even worse, if that were even possible. She gagged, and tears filled her eyes as foul-smelling gas rose from the muck. She'd never in a million light years find her space ball.

Well, she would have to try to communicate somehow with the stupid creature. "Have you seen a lovely, golden ball? About this bog—I mean, big?" Shari held her hands roughly twenty inches apart.

The creature's eyes opened wide. "*Oui, Mademoiselle.*"

Shari felt about to cry. "Please, I'll give you anything—I swear—anything. Just give me my ball and let me get out of this horrible place!"

Now the creature looked interested. "Anything?" it croaked.

"Yes, *anything*. Just, find the ball. Fetch the ball. There's a good, um, creature. Fetch—*apportes! Apportes*," she cried, remembering a bit of her French.

The creature sprang out of the cabbage and sniffled about. Now Shari got a good look at it. It had webbed feet so it didn't sink into the mud, and green legs just like frog's legs—long and muscled. No hair covered its body, but it was not scaly. Its hands and arms were cream-colored like its chin. Its belly was cream-colored too. When it blinked, its oversized eyes popped out a bit, and its huge, wide mouth was set in a permanent grin. In fact, it resembled nothing so much as a huge frog...except for its clothes.

It wore a little shirt and shorts. The shirt had three big buttons, and the whole outfit looked very quaint and old-fashioned. Shari concluded that the frog-creature came from an extremely primitive society.

For a minute it hopped about with great agility. Then suddenly it croaked hoarsely and disappeared into a deep fern bank. All sound ceased. Shari waited for a few minutes, peering into the heavy mist, and then decided the creature probably had forgotten what she'd asked it to do. She tried to turn around, but found herself firmly stuck in the mud.

It took her nearly an hour to get loose, with much thrashing and cursing and wishing she were anywhere but on Planet Marécage. She finally made it back to the stepladder and she looked upwards towards the ship, still hovering patiently in the air. There, in the hatch, sat the creature. It clutched her golden space-chase ball in its little hands.

"Oh! You found it! Thank you!" Shari cried.

"*Oui, Mademoiselle,*" the creature croaked. Then it hopped right up into the ship.

"Oh, no you don't," Shari said. She scrambled up the lowered steps and into the hatch. She looked around the narrow hallway, but it was empty.

Dripping mud on the carpeted floor, she strode into the ship. Her temper boiled as she looked in the tiny but well-stocked galley, under the marble navigation counter, and peered into the small chrome-lined sonic shower stall. Hands on her hips, she whirled around. She felt her eyes narrowing in displeasure as she searched the small, round ship's interior. The polished wood and bright gold trim didn't calm her nerves. Neither did the feel of the soft, hand-woven carpet beneath her feet nor the sight of the luxurious, leather pilot seat. Where was that frog? Something moved in her pilot's seat. Shari's eyes widened in shock.

There! The creature had the gall to be sitting in her pilot's seat!

"What is that stench?" cried the *SS Marissa* in a scandalized tone, as Shari passed in front of a sensor device.

Shari grimaced in disgust. Black, stinking mud covered her right up to her thighs. Her arms and face had suffered the same fate. "Me, I suppose," she said. "I'm going into the sonic shower right after I get rid of our unwanted guest."

She marched over to the chair and said, "You'll have to go back to your planet now. It's time for me to go home."

"*Oui, Mademoiselle,*" it croaked. But it stayed put.

Shari made a face. "Out!" She pointed to the door. "Out you go!" In a minute she would lose her temper, lift the slimy frog by his collar and toss him right out of the ship.

"You promised," said the creature.

"Wha—what did you say?"

"You promised anything I wanted." The frog creature looked suddenly very stern.

"I did?" Shari blinked. "Well, maybe I said something sort of like that, but only because I was in a temper and wanted my ball back. So, thank you, and you can go now."

"You promised."

"I did not!"

The spaceship *SS Marissa* gave a little cough. "If you'll excuse me, Your Highness. I recorded your entire conversation. I'm afraid you did promise him anything. As a matter of fact…"

"Stay out of this!" cried Shari.

The creature gave a little croak and said, "A promise is to keep."

Shari put her hands up in the air. "All right, you win. What do you want? Gold? A new hovel—I mean, house? Some decent clothes?"

"I want to live with you for a while."

Shari stared at the creature. "You have to be out of your little amphibian mind," she sputtered.

"A promise is to keep," it said stubbornly.

"Especially a promise made by a royal princess. You are bound to fulfill his wish," said the *SS Marissa*. There was definitely a note of triumph in her metallic voice.

"Listen, Marissa," said Shari desperately, "I'm sorry I said I wanted to rip out your memory. I was just teasing. You know that! Look, why don't you erase that recording and I'll give you…" she hesitated. What could one offer as a bribe to an imperial private spaceship? She already had weir-leather seats, green sea-wood paneling, premium quality fuel, tinted ports, and mechanical servants that washed and waxed her every day.

"Forget it. You made a promise. You'll have to work things out with your father, the King. Now, let's leave this stinking atmosphere and go home." Marissa's voice held a note of finality.

Shari knew better than to argue. Marissa was programmed to return to Teres before dinner, and it was getting late.

The hatch closed with a loud clank and Marissa said crossly, "Can you do something about that dreadful smell?"

Leaving the creature sitting in her seat, Shari went into the sonic shower. Soon squeaky clean, including her negligee, she went back to the pilot room and attempted to convince the creature that she should be the one to drive the ship. "Look," she said, "I think I know my ship better than you, besides, your legs aren't long enough to reach the floor." Shari thought she was being very reasonable, especially since all she wanted to do was strangle the creature, then junk Marissa, and then maybe scream for a little while.

"But I want to steer!" the creature croaked, its mouth curled in a wide grin.

"No, you sit here!" Her hands shaking a bit with disgust, Shari strapped it into the passenger seat.

The creature stopped arguing and clutched her golden space ball. When his seatbelt was fastened, it croaked, "*Merci, Mademoiselle*," and then fell asleep.

Shari gritted her teeth, charted her course for home, and hit the accelerator.

Part Two
The Royal Nursery

∞

Shari stared at her unwanted guest. It had the most revolting table manners. It sat at her table and slobbered all over the dishes. As Shari watched, it gobbled up all food on its plate, then with its tongue, it reached out and snagged a fruit from the centerpiece for dessert. Afterwards, it grinned at her, burped, and leaned back in its chair. "Delicious," it croaked.

Shari's appetite vanished. Wincing, she clutched at her head, which had been aching ever since she'd floundered into the slimy bog. "How did I get myself into this mess?" Shari moaned.

A deep voice answered from the doorway. "You made a promise."

Shari whirled around. "Sire!" she gasped, then she sprang out of her chair and made a deep curtsy. The creature, apparently unaware of the importance of the king, stayed put in its chair.

"Creature, I order you to bow before King Hari, high king of the House of Teres," Shari said in an imperial tone of voice, still in her position of a deep curtsy.

The king looked at the creature. "What is your name?" he asked it.

"My name is Lesally the thirteenth, of the largest mudflat on Marécage," it said in its croaking voice.

Shari tried not to shudder. Mudflat indeed. And she'd waded through half of it. The stench still hadn't quite left her nostrils.

"Lesally the thirteenth, what wish did you make, and what did the princess promise?" the king asked.

"I wished to live with the princess a while and see her lovely kingdom. The princess said I could have anything I wanted," it added.

"Well, you shall be welcome here in the royal nursery for three days and three nights—after which you shall be escorted back to your mudflat on Marécage."

"Fine," said the creature, and it gave a huge grin.

Shari's stomach turned. But her father's word was law. So she bowed her head and curtsied a little lower, and bit her lip hard so that she wouldn't start to cry.

Her father left after a minute. He never stayed long any more. Ever since Shari reached puberty, her father wouldn't even touch her. He just stayed in the doorway and said a few words every once in a while. Her mother, as usual, spent her time on some imperial mission or other—she had been a member of a powerful house, and she'd been trained as a diplomat. Shari wished *she* could be trained to do something useful, but that would never be. Her fate was written, and now she had to spend three days entertaining a frog.

She rubbed her forehead. Maybe it would like to see the swamp in the back garden? "Come with me, um, what is your name again?"

"Lesally," it said with another deep croak.

"Right. Well, shall we go for a walk? I know of a place you might like."

"*Oui, Mademoiselle.*"

Shari led the way. She'd changed out of her negligee as soon as she arrived back in the palace. Now properly dressed in thigh-high boots, a pleated mini skirt that just barely covered her buttocks, and a tight fitting, sleeveless shirt that showed every curve of her tremendous bosom, she felt a little better. Sexy styles suited her curvy figure.

Shari received the latest fashion catalogues and could order anything her heart desired. Of course, her beautiful wardrobe was wasted on Miss Vert, her blind piano teacher, or on Nanny, who simply rolled her eyes and said, "What a waste of honest, taxpayers' money."

Nanny had three dresses. Shari had three hundred, but none of that really mattered. She wore them a few times then donated them to charity, and so saved her conscience. She was almost glad to be showing the frog around the gardens. Her wardrobe would be put to some use, finally.

No one else noticed her clothes. Her swimming teacher made her wear an unflattering one-piece suit and a swimming cap that pulled most of her hair out when she removed it. Her tutor, Ms. Keenee, looked as old as a dinosaur, and it seemed a miracle she even lived to the next day. When she spoke, it sounded like dry leaves rustling on cement.

"Do you like my dress?" Shari asked the frog hopefully.

"Great," said the frog. Or at least, she thought he said great. It could have been just another croak.

Shari shrugged and led the frog to the swamp. Once there, she pointed, and to be polite, said, "*Voila.*" She figured its French would be better than its Confederation speech.

The frog looked shocked and said, "This is a swamp."

"Yes, I thought you'd like it. Remind you of home—you know."

"I want to see beautiful sights," said the creature in a mournful voice. "I see swamp every day." He sat down and put his head in his hands. He looked miserable.

Shari blushed. Her protocol and manners lessons had been for nothing. She hadn't been thinking. She should have asked the creature what he wanted, not just assumed what he'd like to see. "I'm so sorry," she said. "What would you like to see?"

"Can we go to the beach?" the frog said, looking up at her. "I've never seen clear blue water."

"The beach?" Shari's brows drew together. "Where did you hear about beaches?"

"We are not without some learning," said the creature. It grinned, stretching its mouth wide.

It looked awful. Shari felt her stomach heave, but she took a deep breath and said, "We can go to my private beach."

"Private? How lucky for you!"

"No, not at all. I wish I could go to a public beach, but because I'm a Princess Royal of the House of Teres, I'm not allowed to go to anyplace where there might be males around."

"Males?" The creature looked puzzled.

"Male—female. You know, mating and having babies. Um, in your case, eggs maybe?" Shari frowned. She didn't know anything about this creature. It might even be a male! She hadn't thought of that. "Are you a male or a female?" she asked.

The creature ignored her and gave a great jump into the air. When it came down, Shari saw it had a dragonfly in its mouth. It crunched it up and burped. "Yum. Good," it croaked.

"Ew!" Shari cried, closing her eyes. "How could you eat that? That's disgusting!"

"It's very delicious," said the frog. "You should try something before making an assumption about it. Just because you don't like dragonflies, doesn't mean they don't taste good to someone else."

Shari sighed. "You're right, I never tasted a dragonfly. But I don't want to try one," she hastened to add, seeing the frog eye another dragonfly hovering nearby.

"Let us go to the beach now," said the frog, ignoring her question about males and females. It probably had no idea what she was talking about.

Princess Shari nodded, and led the frog to her room in the palace.

"Pretty princess," said the frog, sitting down in front of her and tilting his head. "Thank you for letting me stay with you."

"You'll have to thank my father," said Shari, digging through her drawer for her bikini.

"Oh, I will," said the frog seriously.

It was a nice enough creature. She was getting fond of it, and might even get used to his crunching up insects. But it didn't have to sit and stare at her with those big eyes all the time. "Turn around a minute while I get dressed," she said.

The frog just sat there, so after a minute, Shari shrugged and took off her boots, her stockings, her skirt and her shirt. She stood a minute, naked, in front of her looking glass, then turned, admiring herself from all angles. She hadn't had time to get fat yet like her aunts—though traditionally the royal princesses grew enormous, thanks to nothing to do and wonderful cooking. But she was definitely as her French teacher would have said *en chair,* 'in the flesh'. Fully in the flesh.

She had big breasts and long, dark pink nipples. She had a nice waist, then her hips flared out into an hourglass shape. Her buttocks were her favorite part of her anatomy. She turned and admired them, leaning over a bit to show off their splendid curve. She lifted her breasts in her hands and weighed them. Heavy and round as ripe melons, their sensitive nipples grew even longer and hard when she stroked them.

"Princess Shari!" Her nanny came in and scolded her. "You'll catch a cold! What are you going to wear, child?"

"My bathing suit. I'm going to take the frog to the beach."

"Where is that horrid creature, anyway?" Nanny asked, looking around.

"Right here a minute ago. Oh look, there he is, sitting on the windowsill. He's probably looking for flies."

"Yuck! Now, get dressed." Nanny's voice brooked no argument at all.

Shari took her sexiest two-piece suit and squeezed into it. It was a string bikini, and she loved how it fit into the crack of her butt. The bra barely hid her nipples.

"That looks disgustingly uncomfortable," said Nanny, pointing to Shari's buttocks, her mouth twisted in an expression of censure.

"You shouldn't make an assumption about it until you've tried wearing one," said Shari haughtily.

"If you think I'd put something like that on, you're very much mistaken," snapped Nanny. "And it makes you look ridiculous."

"Oh thanks very much. It wouldn't suit you anyway," said Shari, exasperated. Nothing she wore found favor with Nanny. She was tired of arguing though. What difference did it make? "I could go around stark naked for all it mattered," she said stormily.

"You ought to be spanked," cried Nanny.

Shari stuck her tongue at her. "Just try it. You never spank me any more."

"You naughty girl," Nanny stormed. "Just wait until I tell your father."

"Come on, let's go!" Shari said to the frog. She fumed as she walked down the long hallways. When she was younger, she used to get the strange, aching feelings in her nether regions. When that happened, she discovered that Nanny's spankings made the feeling so intense it would burst inside her and then go away. She used to provoke Nanny terribly, just to get a spanking. When Nanny discovered this, she stopped touching her altogether. No one touched her anymore, except the royal doctor when she got her once a year health exam. It was bitterly frustrating, but just one more lesson she had to learn as Princess of Teres.

The frog followed her to the transport room, which looked like a little elevator. Buttons on the wall said, "Beach," "Forest Path," "Flowery field," "Mountain view," "Geyser," etc. Hundreds of them dotted the wall. Shari couldn't say that she didn't have some very nice places to visit. She despaired though, because each of the places was deserted and extremely well guarded. She could go to anyplace, but would always be alone. When she pushed "Beach," the transporter gave a little jolt, then a flash of light, and the door slid open.

"Here we are!" Shari cried. "Last one in the water is a rotten egg!" She dashed across the hot sand, her breasts rising and falling with each stride. She hit the water and dove into the surf. Thanks to her swimming instructor, she swam very well. She ducked under a wave, and then swam out to calmer water. Next to her, the frog ducked and dove easily through the waves.

It pointed to a shimmer on the horizon. "What is that?" it asked.

"The force-field. It keeps intruders out while I'm here. When I leave, it disappears. It goes all the way around, see? Even overhead. No one can get near me."

"How sad," said the frog. "You're alone forever."

The thought depressed her, so Shari, to take her mind off it, took a deep breath and dove under the surface. She opened her eyes and vaguely saw the white, sandy ocean floor beneath her.

Darn, she'd forgotten her goggles. She loved to snorkel. Well, next time.

She was about to come up for air, when a sight made her gasp. Of course, when that happened she swallowed a lungful of water and ended up choking and flailing back to the surface.

She barely made it back to the beach, where she collapsed on the sand. The frog joined her a few minutes later.

"What happened?" it asked.

"I don't know." Shari coughed up some more seawater and then for some reason, started to cry. Maybe it was just nerves. After all, the day had been rotten all along and she'd rarely fought so much with Nanny.

"I saw something incredible. A male—I think," she said, "I've never actually seen one, but I'm sure that's what I saw." Wiping her eyes, she tried to remember what exactly she'd seen, but the image had been too fleeting.

She shook her head. "It must have been a hallucination. I'm not supposed to think about males and I guess my brain is playing tricks on me. A male can't live underwater." She sighed and looked out towards the indigo sea. Nothing moved except the waves. Not a sign of life to be seen—and she knew that if, by any chance, someone did outsmart the force-field, its sensors would pick up the life form and a deadly ray would make whoever or whatever it was toast.

That had actually happened one or two times. First came a puff of smoke, then a robot guard—sexless, of course—appeared and ordered her back to her room in her father's stern voice.

Shari wiped away her tears. The horizon mocked her. Her nursery might be vast, but it was a cage from which she could never, ever escape.

The creature seemed moved by her tears. It drew nearer, and reached up to touch her cheek. Its fingers were not slimy, as she'd feared, but its touch felt alien and she flinched.

"Sorry," it croaked, hopping backwards.

"It's not your fault." Shari lay down in the warm sand. Her whole body ached. The day had been long and harrowing. She wanted nothing more than a cup of hot chocolate, then maybe she would listen to some soft music, and crawl into her bed.

"Shall we go, Princess?" The frog's voice held a note in it that Shari had never heard before.

She got to her feet and nodded. "It's time for dinner anyhow," she said. They stepped, well, she stepped and it hopped, back into the transporter. From the beach, or anywhere outside, it looked like a door standing by itself in thin air. Shari pushed "Castle," and there came a bump, a flash of green light, and the door slid open with a soft hiss, letting them out into the transporter room.

"Bath?" croaked the frog.

Shari looked at her sand-covered body and nodded.

She had a vast bathroom, and her sunken tub—made of green marble to match her green eyes—could easily have held a group. As if she would ever be allowed company. Shari filled it with warm water and added jasmine-scented bubble bath so that the tub filled with white, fragrant foam. She took off her bathing suit and slid into the water.

The creature sat on the edge of the tub, and then asked, "Me too?"

Shari nodded. "Whatever." She watched as it jumped in and disappeared beneath the foam. At that moment, Nanny walked in.

"A bath so early?" she asked.

"I was covered with sand," said Shari. "I just want to lie here and relax a while."

"Well, I'll just sit here and wait until you're done. Put your hands on the edge," said Nanny.

Shari did as she was told without comment. After all, she'd heard those words every time she'd had to take a bath since...forever. She closed her eyes to better relax and hopefully chase away the depression that threatened her mood. It did no good to dwell on things she couldn't change.

"Where is that frog?" Nanny asked.

Shari's eyes flew open. She'd forgotten about him. The water in the tub didn't move, and she couldn't see beneath the foam. Where had he gone?

At that moment, a little spark of rebellion flickered in her mind. It flickered, but for once, it didn't fizzle away. For the first time ever, she decided to lie. "I'm not sure. Last I saw him, he was in my room on the windowsill again. Why don't you go look for him?"

Nanny's eyes narrowed. "No, I'll stay here."

"Whatever." Shari put her head back down and let the water buoy up her body.

Something under the water touched her. She jumped, but remembering Nanny, kept her eyes closed.

"Anything wrong, Princess?" asked Nanny.

"No, nothing," said Shari. She squeezed her eyes shut. A light touch slid across her breasts. What was that little frog up to?

Whatever it was, she loved it. It stroked her breasts, and then something fastened onto one of her nipples. After a slight pause, a sort of suction began. Shari stifled a gasp. Her nipples hardened so fast they ached.

The sucking went on, while the light touch traced a line down her hips, and reached towards the place between her legs. It was just at the place where her body sometimes felt odd, where pangs of yearning shot through her at times when she thought about males and why she'd never be able to marry. Sometimes the feelings made her feel like screaming. This evening, the feeling tingled into her belly and bloomed upwards and downwards, and made her feel like singing.

Shari opened her legs wide. She also opened her eyes a crack, to see if she could see anything, but the bubbles were still high and thick, and the water only trembled a bit. If Nanny knew what the frog was up to under the water, she'd make a big fuss. Shari wondered briefly if what she was doing was terribly wrong. But it felt so wonderfully right. Her whole body was shivering with delight.

Something reached between her legs now. It found the two lips of flesh around her slit and parted them, teasing them gently as it did, and then there came a soft pressure on a part of her that she'd never dreamed she'd owned. A little nub — and when the touch reached it, an electric shock shook her whole body. She felt an unbearable aching within her. It felt as if her insides all swelled and wanted to burst.

Something smooth kept fondling her nub, and the gentle suction never let up — first one breast, then the other. Shari's breath came faster, and she opened her eyes to check that Nanny hadn't noticed anything. But Nanny's eyes remained fastened on her hands, and she couldn't see Shari's body. The edge of the tub rose too high. Thank goodness for that.

Shari arched her back a little bit, not enough for Nanny to notice. Something had to give — a terrible pressure had built up in her belly. A sort of electricity coursed through her body and breasts; her head spun now and sweat beaded on her upper lip. The light touch quickened, and something kept on rubbing the nub. It was driving her crazy. She wanted to move, to writhe, to cry out in pleasure, but she didn't dare. She kept her body still, although her heart was hammering so hard her belly throbbed with each beat. And then something began to penetrate her, something velvety yet hard, and far too big to belong to the little frog.

What was happening?

Shari couldn't care less at this point. Whatever the object touching her, she welcomed it. She arched her back higher and opened her legs as wide as she could, begging it to push harder against her aching center. And then she uttered a moan.

"What is it, Princess?" asked Nanny, standing up and leaning over the tub.

The spell shattered. Whatever had been touching her in such a wonderful manner vanished. Shari's heart still hammered, and her body felt as tightly strung as one of her piano wires. "Nothing," she managed to say, and then she reached her arm out. "Bathrobe please," she said.

She stood, putting on her bathrobe, and her knees, she noticed, actually shook. When she walked, her nether regions seemed engorged. Her slit felt inflamed and the swollen lips rubbed against each other. Each step only heightened that full to bursting impression in her body. Her nipples stood so stiffly at attention that she had a hard time pulling her nightgown on. Even the soft brush of the fabric against them made her stomach contract.

Though she tried to appear calm and collected, her heart still beat hard and her body tingled. She had no idea what had happened to her body. To further confuse things, doubts assailed her. Had she been bad? Why did she feel so hot and cold at the same time? Perhaps she'd caught some sort of illness. All of a sudden she just wanted to be alone.

She looked at Nanny and said, "I'm exhausted. I think I'm coming down with a cold. Send my hot chocolate to my room. I'm going to turn in."

Nanny felt her forehead and frowned. "You do look a bit flushed."

"Tell Cook not to bother with dinner," said Shari.

"Very well, Your Highness." Nanny looked undecided. "Where will the creature sleep?"

"Have the maid make up a pallet in my room near the window. That way it can jump outside if it wishes."

"Right away."

Nanny left, and Shari pulled the plug in the tub. The water drained out, but she saw no sign of the creature. The maid came in with a spare mattress and bedcovers, and Shari showed her where to put the bed. She wandered back to the bathroom to put her face cream on, but the frog seemed to have disappeared. When she went back into her room, however, there it sat on the windowsill, staring at the garden.

She was in such a state of excitement that she didn't think. She walked to the frog and said, "Touch me again."

The frog looked shocked. "What are you talking about?"

Shari took its hand and placed it on her breast. "Please," she begged.

The frog pulled away and hopped to the pallet the maid had fixed. "I think I'll sleep now," it said. "You'll do well to do the same." It cuddled in the covers and soon Shari heard little snores.

Stunned, she stared at the sleeping amphibian. How dare that little frog fall asleep? How dare that creature touch her so intimately and a minute later, forget it had ever done it.

She felt her face burning. She'd certainly made a fool of herself. The little frog had probably just been exploring or brushed against her by accident. What should she do? Wake it up and apologize?

Her hot chocolate came before she'd decided what to do about the frog. The servant put the steaming mug on her table—just like she did every night, curtsied and bid her sweet dreams.

Embarrassment made Shari want to crawl under her covers and hide. How could she think that the frog had anything to do with the bath? She remembered her vision at the beach. It must have been another delusion, a tactile hallucination this time. Tomorrow she'd go see the royal shrink. Maybe she could help.

Shari sipped her chocolate and made a face. She didn't want anything—her stomach hurt. She decided to dump it down the sink, and brushed her teeth. She put a light lavender fragrance on her skin to help her relax and sleep, and then she slid under her covers. She kept her hands on the outside. That way, when Nanny stuck her head in at intervals during the night, she'd be reassured that the Princess Royal wasn't giving herself any sort of pleasure.

Nanny didn't want her to touch her own body. That Shari knew. But right now, she longed to reach under the covers and touch the place that had given her so much pleasure. Just thinking about it made a strange wetness appear between her legs. Her nipples stood up again, lifting the sheet, and Shari moaned softly. If she reached beneath the covers, Nanny would come rushing in and scold her, and probably read her some silly bedtime story. That would annoy her so much that the wonderful feeling growing in her belly would vanish. She gritted her teeth in frustration. What could she do?

Just then, she felt a touch between her legs. Gasping, she looked over at the pallet. The little frog had gone. Was he under the covers?

She lifted them, and there, between her legs, was a hand. Attached to the hand was an arm, and her amazed eyes followed the length of the arm to a shoulder, then up to a neck and a face, hidden by shadow, and then down again to a smooth, muscular body, wildly different from her own. Whereas her body was all plump roundness and soft hills and curves, this body looked hard and flat and hairy, with muscles that moved like water beneath its green skin.

Green skin?

Shari blinked, but the skin stayed green. Or rather, it was tan and had a faint greenish tinge to it. The face grinned at her. She could see a flash of white teeth. Oh no. Her hallucination had come back and it was incredibly gorgeous.

"What are you?" she whispered. "Are you real?"

"Hush. Nanny is coming. Close you eyes and pretend to sleep."

Shari did. But she left her eyes open a slit to see. Nanny peered in, and then lifted the empty cocoa mug. "Ahh. She's finished it. She'll sleep like a baby until morning. Take this to the kitchens," said Nanny to the maid standing behind her. Nanny gave one last look at Shari, then left, closing the door.

Shari sat up. "What was that all about?"

She lifted the covers and peered below, but the hallucination had gone. She felt her eyes fill with tears. "I am losing my mind," she whispered.

"No you're not." The hallucination stepped out of the shadows in the corner of her room. Standing in a ray of moonlight, the vision looked even more real than in the water or under her covers. He smiled. "Your cocoa is a sleeping draught. They'll leave us alone until morning."

"Us?" Shari's mouth went suddenly dry. "What us? You're not real!"

"I am." He sat on her bed and touched her cheek. "See? I'm real." He had dark hair, slightly wavy, and his skin was a smooth and warm.

There was a soft tingling on her cheek where his fingers had traced a line. Shari clapped her hand to her cheek and tried to think, but her thoughts clashed and whirled. Fear and curiosity warred with each other, and finally curiosity won. "Who are you?" she managed finally. "Where is the frog creature?"

"I'm Lesally of the Grand Marsh." He gave a wry smile. "This is my real body. That," and he nodded towards the frog's pallet, "was an illusion. As is the mist, the marsh and the mud. It's handy. It keeps people away from our planet. We have no weapons but our illusions."

"An illusion?" Shari shook her head, trying to clear it. The swamp, a figment of her imagination? What did he mean by that? She gaped at him. "Are you a male fantasy?"

Lesally laughed softly. "So, the stories I've heard about the princesses of Teres are all true. You've never seen a male?"

"Well, except my father."

"He wears voluminous robes," said Lesally.

"I've never seen a male otherwise," said Shari. She lowered her eyes, suddenly shy.

"Look at me," said the stranger, tipping her chin back up with his hand. "Never be afraid to look at me. Do I frighten you? Do you like what you see?"

"I love your body," said Shari. She smiled timidly. "May I look?"

"Of course." He lay back on her bed. "My body is your body," he said, his eyes twinkling.

"Are you an elf?" said Shari. "I have this book with elves in it, and they look a little like you, although I'd assumed an elf would be much smaller, and have pointed ears."

Lesally laughed. "No, I'm certainly not an elf. You need a lesson about males," he said.

Shari's heart started to pound. "Only if you'll be my teacher."

"Of course I will be your teacher." Lesally pointed to her breasts. "Those are the most magnificent breasts I've ever seen."

"Where are yours?" Shari asked.

"Men have flat chests, like me." He reached out and brushed his palm lightly over her breasts.

Shari shivered. "When you touch me there, I feel the strangest longing."

"It's not strange, Princess. It's called desire."

"Please, teach me some more about desire."

"No."

"No?" Shari sat up straight. "But, I thought you told me you would teach me all about desire!"

"That's not what I said." Lesally shook his head and then took her chin in his hands. "I want to teach you about love," he said. Then he drew her to him and kissed her.

Shari had never been kissed. When his mouth touched hers, she pulled away in surprise, but he held her chin in his hand and turned her head back towards him.

"Don't be afraid," he whispered. Slowly his mouth took possession of hers. She hardly dared breathe. His soft lips pressing on hers tickled and soothed at the same time. She closed her eyes to better concentrate on the sensations she was experiencing. Rough whiskers rasped softly on her skin as their chins touched, but his lips were satin-smooth. Delight filled her as he deepened the kiss, nibbling on her lower lip, his teeth pulling at the sensitive flesh.

Shari gave a tiny gasp, and a shiver ran up her body. His mouth pressed harder on hers, and then he stopped and whispered in her ear. "Did you like that?"

"Yes." She didn't want it to ever end. Putting her hand on his cheek, she slid her lips over his face, pressing them chastely against his cheeks, his eyelids and his temples.

He let her explore, then he stopped her and pressed his mouth to hers once more. This time, his tongue gently parted her lips, and his mouth opened. Surprised, she opened her mouth to protest, and he clasped her head harder to him, so that his tongue invaded her mouth. Her own tongue met his, the sensation akin to another electric shock. Her breathing quickened as she grew used to his lips and tongue.

She decided her tongue wanted to explore, so she sought out his teeth, discovering a delightful little notch in one front tooth. She'd thought that she'd never tasted anything so fascinating and sweet as Lesally's mouth. Then, far too soon, he drew back. His eyes seemed very bright, and she noticed his chest rising and falling quickly.

She noticed something else, and instinctively, her whole body quivered. "What's that?" she whispered, pointing.

"What does it look like?" he replied, shifting his hips so that she could see it better.

"It looks like an ivory tower with a dark coral tip, growing from a forest of dark, curly hair. It looks smooth, soft, and yet it looks hard at the same time. There are some...*things*

267

behind it. They are round, covered with soft hair, and seem extremely soft. May I touch?" she asked.

"Of course." His eyelids lowered. "It's called a penis, or a cock if you prefer, and those are my testicles. A Princess Royal should know the proper name for everything and know what it represents and for what it serves."

"What does this cock serve?" whispered Shari, running her fingers up and down the velvety shaft. Her fingers tingled at the touch. Such a fascinating mixture of soft and hard, of smoothness and texture.

"This will serve you," said Lesally, drawing his breath in with a hiss. "Oh, Princess, this cock will serve you well."

As she touched him, she felt her nether regions getting inflamed again. They'd grown so wet, she feared something went wrong. With a little sob, she let go of the fascinating penis and lay back on the bed.

"What is wrong, sweet one?" Lesally asked, leaning over her and taking her into his arms.

No one had ever held her, and she stiffened in shock. "I don't know," she sobbed. "I feel so hot, and cold at the same time, and down there…" she pointed shyly. "Is all wet."

"That is called a vagina, and it exists only to be served by my penis." Lesally's voice held no teasing note. He spoke so seriously and softly that Shari felt herself melting into his arms. "It is wet with desire, for it is but a passage to pleasure. Has no one ever showed you or told you the wonders of your sex?"

Shari shook her head. "No one."

"Then I, as your teacher, shall." He kissed her once more and stroked her breasts. His hand moved slowly as he traced circles around her nipples.

Her sensitive nipples hardened and he teased them with his thumb until she trembled and mewed with desire. Nothing she'd ever felt could compare with this. Another wave of heat made her feel faint and she swayed, holding tightly to his shoulders.

"Are you all right?" he asked, cupping her breast in his hand.

"Yes, oh yes," Shari said, her voice ragged.

Then he sat and pulled her up next to him, right onto the edge of the bed, facing the dressing room mirror. "Open your legs," he ordered.

She did, hesitantly. Every time she'd tried this before, a maid or Nanny had come running.

"They think you're drugged and asleep," said Lesally, as if he read her thoughts. "Open wider. I want to show you everything."

She spread her knees wide apart, and her auburn brush came into view, along with the shiny, coral-colored interior.

"Now, I will show you your wonders," said Lesally. "Look. I call the whole a pussy, but it's got different parts, all magnificent."

He parted her pubic hair with one hand, and gently traced the two lips surrounding her slit with one finger. They were slick and swollen. "These are labia. Outer lips," he whispered. He parted them, and she saw more lips, smaller and narrower, but also bright coral and covered with dewy juice. "Inner lips," said Lesally, "Surrounding your passage which is that little hole." He dipped the tip of his finger into it, making Shari jump.

But when he withdrew his finger, she could only think that she wanted more. She longed to take his hand and press it hard against her pussy. As if to agree with her, her pussy suddenly clenched a bit, and a rush of hot liquid moistened her passage.

Lesally smiled at her. "You like this." It was a statement, not a question, but Shari nodded anyway.

Then he showed her a small protuberance, higher up. "A clitoris, or clit for short, is so sensitive, that one must touch it gently, and it's best touched with a velvety tongue," he told her. Then he lowered his mouth to her body and kissed her there. "Ambrosia," he said.

His tongue darted out and he touched her clit. Shari felt a now familiar pressure building in her lower body. When he tongued her clit, she could hardly breath. Her heart started to pound, and her hips lifted off the bed by themselves, pressing her body harder against his mouth. She never dreamed her body could be so complex and beautiful, or that she even had a secret passage that she could now see as well as feel. It throbbed, tightening then gaping, opening like her mouth, seeking...something.

His tongue drew circles around her clit, and at the same time his fingers stroked her, coming nearer and nearer her center, then, one entered her passage, and she moaned in relief.

Shari fell backwards on the bed, spreading her knees wide. She raised herself on her elbows so she could see her body reflected in the mirror, and she could see Lesally as he lapped at her pussy. The sight made another rush of heat flood her passage.

With one hand, Lesally reached up and took hold of her breast, and with the other, he penetrated her, softly stretching her. Her juices covered his hand, and she could see how shiny and slick she was in the mirror. His finger disappeared into her passage. For a minute he held it still—and then he moved it gently back and forth. Tickling aches spread through her. Heat rose from her belly. She felt a wave of pleasure rising from her belly, and now something extraordinary started to happen. Her heart pounded so hard she thought she might be dying. A hard, strange pulsing grew and grew deep inside her, and she couldn't stop her hips from rising off the bed.

In the mirror, she saw Lesally's finger working in and out of her tight passage. The feeling in her pussy was building to a crescendo. Little spurts of electricity ran through her legs. Her nipples tightened and beads of sweat pearled on her upper lip. She grabbed her covers, the soft sheets bunching in her clutching fingers. Under her buttocks the bed moved — or perhaps her hips moved the bed, she wasn't sure of anything right now. Lesally's fingers plunged deeper, searching inside her, setting her on fire.

"What's happening?" she cried.

"Hush, it's called an orgasm. Let it take you. Let it shake you. Don't worry, I'm here to hold you."

And he did.

His fingers delved into her, his tongue worked on her clit, and Shari felt waves and waves of contractions suddenly shake her belly. Her vagina started to pulse; it contracted on Lesally's fingers. She uttered a cry of sheer delight. Arching her back, she drove herself further onto his hand. "Harder," she begged.

He rose up above her, lowering his body onto hers. Using his hand, he guided his penis to her passage, slowly sheathing himself within her. For a minute she tensed as his hard penis made its way into her tender body.

"Relax. I won't hurt you, I promise," he murmured in her ear.

His voice soothed her, and her body, already on the pinnacle of some kind of release, opened. He slid in to the hilt, his stomach coming to rest on hers. They joined together.

Joined! Shari's head spun. There was a man inside her, his hard penis buried in her vagina, all the way in. He rested there, then, slowly, he moved, sliding back and then slowly pushing back in again.

The movement intensified the frantic throbbing she felt. Her legs opened, her back arched, and she clutched his body to hers. The feeling overwhelmed her. She couldn't begin to describe it. His cock, wonderfully alien, pushed inside her —

271

long, thick, and incredible hard. Heavy, its weight rested against her insides, filling her completely.

For a long time she shuddered, her body shaking beneath his. She sobbed as the contractions grew, and then in a starburst of light, her body seemed to explode. Crying out, Shari flung her head from side to side, her hips bucking, her breath coming in gasps.

"Hush, it's all right." Lesally said when it was finally over. He cupped her face in his hands and tenderly kissed her lips.

"It was incredible," she said, laughing weakly. "Is it done? Is that it?"

"No, not at all." His chuckle tickled her ear.

Then, Lesally started to move again. Slowly at first, then faster, he penetrated her. His shaft moved within her body, and she met his thrusts with little cries of delight. Again, she felt herself getting swollen, and again the feeling grew in her chest and belly until she burst, once more, into an explosion of mad pulsing, into a spiral of pleasure.

And this time, she felt Lesally start to tremble in her arms. His face, pressed into the crook of her neck grew damp with sweat. He drove his hips into her, and low moans came from his throat. He wrapped his arms around her, and suddenly he gave three massive thrusts, driving himself into her deepest depths, and she felt something spurting inside of her. He uttered a loud cry.

"Are you all right?" Shari asked. "Did you hurt yourself?" Fright made her voice high. Had he burst something? "It's all wet!" she cried.

He gave another mighty shudder, and collapsed against her. "It's all right," he gasped. "My pleasure made me cry out. Don't worry, it..." he gasped again and then gave a soft laugh. "It is a man's pleasure to spill his seed. It is a bit wet," he said apologetically.

Afterwards, they lay in each other's arms. Shari's hands roamed over his body, and over hers, gently exploring, touching, feeling her now tender breasts and the satisfying soreness between her legs.

"Now, Princess, it's time for a bath," said Lesally.

"No, I want to sleep," she said. Her whole body felt like liquid honey.

"I haven't finished my lessons yet," he said.

Her eyes flew open. "There's more?"

"Oh, much more," he told her, a chuckle in his voice.

Part Three
Lessons in Love

ஐ

Lesally ran her bath. He slid into the tub and waited until she joined him. Then he took some of her soap and gently rubbed it all over her body. She did the same to him, lingering on his long thighs and flat stomach, and over that fascinating part of his anatomy that seemed to change shape and size whenever she touched it.

In fact, his whole body fascinated her. The hardness of his muscles and the dark, curly hair on his chest and legs astounded her. Shari made him stand up so that she could see and touch him all over. His flat, hard chest was soon decorated with her soapy handprints, and then she rubbed her way downwards until she came to his thighs. Hesitantly, she touched the equipment between his legs. So many different things to explore! His cock grew hard when she touched it, yet his testicles remained soft. And when he grew hard, his body trembled a bit at her touch.

He had to sit down after a while, after she'd pushed and pulled, tickled and touched his cock. His face was flushed and he seemed out of breath. "Are you all right?" Shari asked.

He grinned. "Of course. Your touch excites me, can't you see?"

"I do see." His cock was poking like a sea monster out of the water. Shari laughed.

"My turn," said Lesally, and Shari stood while he rubbed soft soap over her body.

Now, both covered with fragrant lather, wherever their bodies touched, they slid. Sensations were different now. Hands and arms felt slick, and when Lesally nudged her legs apart with his thigh, they opened as if buttered. His penis pressed against her belly, and she raised herself on tiptoes a bit so that he could slide into her. It hurt a bit—she was sore and still very tight, but the feeling turned to pleasure under Lesally's skillfully gentle thrusts.

He withdrew and turned her around, so that her marvelous croup faced him. He parted her legs and touched her sopping wet pussy. "Do you want me?" he asked.

"Yes! Please," Shari begged, bending over. He took her from behind, curling over her body, his chest pressed to her back. How could anyone have hidden all this from her? It was incredible. The fullness of his cock entering her, his hands clutching at her waist, the words of love he whispered in her ear—it was breathtaking. Her whole body expanded to meet him, and when his cock plunged inside of her, she never wanted it to end.

He drove his cock deeper inside her, each thrust nearly lifting her off her knees. One hand massaged her breasts, and the other hand reached under her belly to tickle her clitoris. Shari braced herself on the edge of the tub and pushed backwards, feeling the waves of pleasure clenching her stomach and thighs. But Lesally stopped his hard thrusts and withdrew, teasing her, circling her labia with the tip of his penis until she begged him to take her once more. Now that she knew what the outcome would be, her body shivered in anticipation.

"Please, take me," she begged.

"Oh, I will, Princess," he said, his voice thick. "Now I shall show you another passage to pleasure, and then I will let you sleep."

He parted her buttocks, and slowly, ever so slowly, pushed his finger into her butt, all the while rubbing her clit skillfully with one finger, another finger deftly plunging into her throbbing vagina. Shari gasped as her body's senses seemed to go into overdrive. She'd always loved Nanny's spankings, and having her temperature taken was terribly exciting, but this was incredible! Her luscious croup rose and fell, pressing harder against Lesally's fingers. And she wanted more.

For a while he teased her, stretching her gently, making her want to scream with frustration. She tried to gather her thoughts to tell him, but all she could feel was his agile fingers probing her body, touching her in places that both tickled and ached. Pressure built in her belly, a pressure that made her pant, that made her nipples so hard they hurt, and pressure that made her want to feel something huge penetrate her body. She needed something bigger!

"More," she managed to gasp, rubbing her magnificent butt frantically against his belly. She felt his erection and caught it between her thighs and squeezed.

Lesally uttered a moan and withdrew his finger. He put more slippery soap on her ass. Then Shari felt the thick head of his penis pushing against her tight muscles. The tickling push of his penis as it slowly moved into her sensitive anus drove her wild. Lesally moved slowly and gently, but it felt all the more exciting for it. Inch by inch, she let him past her tight ring of muscle. As he eased into her body, he softly touched her clit. The sensations threatened to overwhelm her. Her body was at a fever-pitch, she didn't know anymore where his body left off and where hers began.

Once he'd half-sheathed his cock within her magnificent bottom, he gently moved it in and out, until Shari suddenly bucked against him and started to shriek, her vagina and her buttocks pulsing in unison on his cock and on his fingers. Lesally cried out too, holding her tightly to his chest as he ejaculated into her, his body thrusting and thrusting, his hips grinding into hers.

Shari realized that he'd shared her pleasure. She didn't worry that he'd hurt himself anymore, even when he cried out. She was also glad that her chambers were soundproofed. The vision of Nanny rushing in and seeing them was disastrous.

Lesally would be executed on the spot. She shivered, and pulled away from her lover.

"Your life is in danger," she said. She didn't want to say it, but she had to. "You must leave here immediately."

Lesally got his breath back and looked at her. They were sitting in the tub, face to face now, arms and legs entwined. "How could I leave you now? Your lessons are going so well," he said, a note of teasing in his voice.

Shari's hands trembled and she clenched them in her lap. Her heart was breaking, but she couldn't bear it if the guards toasted him. "Please. You must go. Your life is in danger."

"No." His smile grew wider. "I'll be all right, I promise. You'll see."

Her head was swimming from fatigue and too much excitement. She tried to argue, but it ended up as a yawn. She sighed deeply, and leaned against his broad chest. "Promise you'll be careful," she said.

Afterwards, he rinsed her off and carried her to her bed. Shari was vaguely aware of his hands, smoothing the covers over her body, and then she fell into a deep, dreamless sleep.

* * * * *

Lesally lay next to her, his body sated but his mind too full of what he'd seen and learned to sleep. He'd always heard about the House of Teres—who in the galaxy had not?—but he'd never dreamed he'd be there one day, lying in silken sheets next to a beautiful princess. The princesses of Teres were legendary, their seclusion, their enforced innocence, and their youthful beauty renowned—however, nothing he'd heard had prepared him for his feelings upon seeing Princess Shari. He raised himself on one elbow and peered at the sleeping woman.

Moonlight streamed in the window and cast a faint, silver light upon her face. In repose, her face was as pure as a work of art. When awake, a hundred expressions chased themselves

277

across her face. Curious and intelligent, her forced confinement hadn't made her capricious or whiny. She both accepted and rebelled against her fate.

Accepted because, Lesally sensed, she recognized tradition and respected it by her nature. She also liked to please. He smiled as he thought about that. She seemed anxious to please, and in every way. His penis stirred and he shifted in the bed.

She had a streak of rebellion in her too, though. Her actions earlier in her bath proved it. She hadn't said anything to her nanny about him being in the tub with her. What fun that had been!

He too had a streak of rebellion—it had made him leave his sod-fish traps and go spy when he'd spotted the spaceship. Despite his best friend Brant's horrified protests, he'd donned his frog disguise and hopped out to see the visitor. Brant had tried to stop him, and no doubt he'd ridden his marsh boat as fast as he could back to the palace to tell Lesally's parents. But that hadn't stopped Lesally.

When the hatch had opened, and Shari's long legs had descended, he'd barely been able to keep his disguise. He'd wanted to leap out then and there and present himself to her. Only the insignia on the ship stopped him. The Royal House of Teres. The spaceship would never have landed if it had suspected a humanoid male in the vicinity, so he'd kept his disguise and played along.

He hoped his parents wouldn't worry too much. They'd know where he was, of course. Right now, they were probably praying that he wouldn't create an intergalactic scandal or war. The powerful House of Teres had weapons that could wipe out his world. That gave him a pause. But only a pause. He was no fool, and he would think of a way to turn the tables in his favor.

His parents often despaired of him. He'd paid far more attention to his magic teachers than his math or history classes. Math bored him, but the art of illusion delighted him, and he adored fun. Now, few on the Planet Marécage could match his skill. He knew that the rest of the galaxy called it low magic, and that amused him. Low magic indeed, as if there could be high and low, or some magic better than other magic. The best magic of all came from the heart though. He knew this instinctively.

He had never ignored his heart, though it often caused trouble. Like the time he'd brought the wounded water tiger home. He'd nursed it to health, hiding it from his parents, and when it recovered, it nearly ate the entire flock of swans in the palace garden—now that had netted him a punishment to remember! But a year later, when he'd been cornered by that savage selkie—who had saved him? Why, the water tiger. It had come roaring out of the swamp, teeth flashing and claws ready to tear the selkie apart.

He grinned at the memory, then leaned over and kissed Shari on the cheek. She stirred but didn't waken.

"I will not put your reputation or my people at risk," he whispered. "But I love you. I loved you from the moment you stepped out of your snooty spaceship onto my muddy planet. How lucky you came in over my marsh, and that I was out with Brant fishing for sod-fish. My frog form may be an illusion. However, my love for you is real. I will find a way for us to be together, I promise." He kissed her again, breathing in her sweet, warm scent. Going to his pallet beneath the window, he curled up in the blankets. He stared at the stars and thought of a plan.

* * * * *

The next day, Lesally donned his frog illusion and hopped about the nursery, getting into nanny's way, slobbering all over his food, and breaking no less than five priceless vases. He croaked his apologies, explaining that he'd been trying to catch the flies near the flowers. The maids, furious, shooed him outside.

Lesally looked around him. He'd been hoping to explore the rest of the palace. The royal nursery, however, had only an extensive garden in the back. The same force-field that kept Princess Shari safe from prying eyes at the beach or on a forest trail acted here too. He could see its faint glow in the sky.

He toured the gardens. The stables housed some sleepy-looking, fat, docile horses. All mares, he noticed. A female cat sat in a patch of sunlight. He bet that in the sky only girl-birds were allowed to fly by. A sudden feeling of anger shook him.

He had to stare very hard at a yellow butterfly to calm his nerves. He could not imagine how Shari felt, being a prisoner for life. He knew she accepted her fate, but he didn't. The thought of her being forced to live all alone depressed him. He thought of his plan to save her. That helped him regain his temper.

For a second there, he'd wanted to shed his disguise and storm into the royal palace, shouting at the king. That, he reflected wryly, would have gotten him vaporized on the spot. A vaporized frog would be of no help at all to Princess Shari.

He glanced again at the shimmer marking the boundary set by the force-field. He had to be very careful in keeping up his disguise. The same power that fed the force-field made the weapons work here. One flicker of his real identity and *Zap!*, he'd be water vapor. His parents should be glad now he'd studied magic so hard, forsaking math, for it kept him alive. It would be magic, along with a bit of trickery, which would enable him to save the princess. And he excelled in trickery. Why, just look at his disguise!

In his present form, he stood roughly three feet high. He could appear bigger or smaller, but the smaller he made himself seem, the harder it was to keep up the spell. Bigger would have made him appear too imposing and he didn't want to frighten anyone—he knew he had to appear completely inoffensive and sexless.

The frog was perfect. He knew from fairy tales that frogs often hid princes, and the irony made him grin. He also knew that he had to act quickly, for his three days were almost up and he couldn't bear the thought of leaving Shari behind. He'd fallen completely head over heels in love with her. Her concern for his safety, the sweetness that he saw in her smile and in her eyes, and her respect for duty and tradition had captured his heart. She was everything he'd ever wanted in a woman.

He remembered her uninhibited lovemaking and his cock grew stiff. He had to concentrate to keep his illusion in place. His whole body reacted to thoughts of Shari. He'd always wanted to penetrate a woman's ass. Shari had let him, and she'd loved it as much as he had. The recollection of her tightly muscled anus massaging his cock made him swallow hard and stare some more at the butterfly.

"Pretty yellow butterfly," he chanted, until his raging hard-on subsided.

The gardening staff—three women dressed in overalls, heard him talking about the butterfly.

"What is that creature still doing here?" one woman asked.

"The king has let him stay, more's the pity," her companion answered with a shrug.

"A stupid toad," said another. "Poor Princess Shari, having to put up with that slimy beast."

Lesally gave a deep croak and made an illusion butterfly, which he ate with great relish and much crunching. "Yummy yellow butterfly," he chanted, as he hopped back to the palace. He thought of his plan to liberate Princess Shari and gave a loud croak. If he could keep up the deception another day and cast an illusion on...He stopped thinking about it. Too much thinking could ruin his illusion, especially if it involved Shari's exquisite body.

To cool himself off, he dove into the royal pool.

"Whoosh!" He gasped and swam to the surface then hopped out. "Don't they heat their pools?" He eyed the icy-cold water and sighed. Actually, he needed just that. He jumped back in.

* * * * *

Shari woke up late, so sore she could hardly walk, but the soreness faded after a little while, only to be replaced by a dull ache. She ached with longing, she knew now. Longing for her lover's long, smooth, greenish-tinged body. When she looked at Lesally in his frog disguise, he winked at her, and she felt a sharp tingle in her nipples.

When he accidentally brushed against her, her labia swelled instantly and that made walking difficult. She felt drunk on love. All day long she wandered about, her body tense as a bowstring, her nipples erect, her pussy so excited that if she just leaned against the arm of a sofa it began to pulse madly. When her nanny or the maids spoke to her, she would blink and come out of her trance a bit.

But all she could think of, all she could do, was wait for evening.

* * * * *

"Can we go for another ride in that magic elevator?" Lesally wheedled as they sat down for lunch with nanny.

The Princess blinked and looked at him. "Of course," she said.

"It isn't magic," said Nanny with a sniff. "Only backwards planets use magic. We have technology."

"Of course," croaked Lesally. "Oh mighty House of Teres. I bow to your superior technology." He got off his stool and bowed in exaggerated fashion to the portrait of the king hanging on the wall.

"It's good to show respect," said Nanny.

"You want to go now?" Lesally asked, hopping about like a demented rabbit.

"All right." Princess Shari said, smiling at him. "How about we go to the beach again?"

"No, Lesally wants to go to the enchanted forest!" cried Lesally. He wondered if he were overdoing his silly frog act.

But Nanny rolled her eyes and said, "I told you before, there is no magic here. It is a forest, nothing more or less."

"How exciting. On Planet Marécage, we have great massive swamps. We know nothing about forests," Lesally explained. "You should come and see sometime. I will give you a guided tour," he said to Nanny. "If you stay on the trail, you won't fall into the quicksand."

Nanny winced. "I thank you for your invitation, but I prefer to stay on Planet Teres."

"Well, I need to get my hiking boots," said Shari. She dressed, and soon they were in the elevator with the buttons.

"Where to?" she asked.

"The enchanted forest," said Lesally with a wink. It pleased him to see her blush.

She pushed "Forest" and there came the usual flash of light and jolt. The door slid open and they found themselves standing on a wide, sandy path. On either side of them tall trees cast a cool shade.

"How lovely," said Lesally.

"It is peaceful here. I often come when I need to...calm myself." Shari said, looking at the tall pine trees.

"Princess, are you happy?" He watched her face closely as he spoke. He wanted to rescue his princess, but only if she wanted to be rescued. He would never take her away from her home if she truly loved it here. He did not think she did, but he had to be sure.

"No." She smiled, but it was a sad smile. "I thought I had learned to be content with what I have, but lately, I find myself dreaming of another life."

His heart gave a glad leap. "In what way?"

"I want to make a difference in this world, or in some other world. I don't want to waste my life being a decoration. A princess should help others. I have been taught that Teres is a powerful, wealthy empire. But there are other places that need our technology. My mother is a diplomat and she meets with people from everywhere. She can do things, help others...Why can't I?" she finished plaintively. "I accepted the fact that I was trapped here for so long, but now I'm beginning to hate it."

"Perhaps I can help you," said Lesally. "But we shouldn't speak of this anymore. It might seem strange to anyone listening that you're confiding in a frog."

"There is no one here. You can change," said Shari.

"I dare not," Lesally said, looking around. "I have heard tell that there are always spies and guards—even ones you can not see. The princesses of Teres have always been protected thus."

Shari reddened. "I'm sorry. It's probably true," she said. "I nearly cost you your life with my thoughtlessness." Tears filled her eyes.

His heart ached for her. "No! Do not cry, Princess. Come, let us walk a while."

They did, hiking up the gently sloping path. The forest hardly changed. It had some birds and a few insects, but otherwise it was still. Lesally didn't doubt for a minute that it had a sophisticated survey system there. The same force-field as at the beach also surrounded the forest, and the path curved in a circle, so that eventually they would arrive back at the doorway. When they'd walked for about thirty minutes, Lesally turned to the princess and said, "You can relax here, and if you like, you can lay down in a clump of sweet fern, and I will sit on that log and sing for you."

"Would you do that?"

She lay down in the soft fern, and Lesally concentrated very hard. What he was about to do was difficult, but he had to practice, because tomorrow, it had to be perfect.

He left an illusion of the frog sitting on a nearby stump. He created the pretense of a song, to cover up any loud noise Shari might make. Then he made himself invisible. He sat next to the princess, and all the while keeping the illusion of her clothes intact, undressed her.

Shari's eyes opened wide in amazement. "Where are you?" she put her hand out. "I can't see anything, but I hear your breathing, and I feel your hands. How can I be naked and yet appear fully clothed?"

"It's the magic of my planet. We are masters of illusion, I told you this. I can make anyone see or hear what I want. They won't hear me speak. They will only hear me sing. They can't see me. They can only see the frog. And they will see you lying here, taking a nap, fully dressed."

"What should I do?" she asked.

"You mustn't move or make a single sound that might be heard over the singing. Is that clear?"

"But..."

"Hush! Just close your eyes and pretend I am singing to you," said Lesally. Then he lowered his head and took one of her nipples in his mouth. It hardened instantly and Lesally groaned. This would be some test for his capabilities.

His penis grew so hard it ached. He wanted to thrust it right away into Shari's hot cunt to ease his need, but he knew he had to move slowly. He parted Shari's legs and his mouth left her nipple with regret, then traced a trail from her breasts to her parted thighs with his tongue. He stopped there, getting a firm hold on himself, and kissed her inner thigh. Her flesh felt as smooth as the finest satin. His tongue followed the curve of her thigh to the hollow near her hip, then he slid down to her pussy.

She gave a mew of impatience and thrust her hips upwards.

"Stop!" he ordered, giving her a strong shake. "If you move or speak, I will be vaporized. Do you want that?"

"No," she whispered. Her eyes widened and she stopped writhing.

"If you don't obey, I will spank you," he said, his voice stern.

Shari stiffened. "Yes, Nanny," she whispered.

Lesally nearly lost his illusion. "Did you like it when she spanked you?" he asked a little breathlessly. Did she hate being spanked? Or would she let him do it?

"Sometimes." Shari sighed. "She'd put me over her knees and spank me when I was bad. Sometimes I'd be bad just to get a spanking." She looked archly at Lesally from beneath lowered eyelashes. "Would you ever give me a spanking?" she murmured.

"I'll do just that if you disobey me," said Lesally. He shivered. The thought of bending her over his knees and slapping his hand against her smooth buttocks was making his cock twitch.

"Oh yes, please do," she whispered, arching her back a bit.

Her body gave off a heady scent and her cunt looked slick and swollen with desire.

He checked to make sure the illusion was still perfect, then put his mouth to her pussy, greedily sucking and licking. She bucked against him and he held her still while his tongue flicked over her clit. It grew larger and harder. She writhed against him now, little cries coming from her throat.

"Harder! More! Faster!" she gasped.

"Quiet!" he begged, holding her still.

She tried to stay still, but he could tell his teasing set her on fire. It amused him to be in control of her splendid body.

He held her still, leaning on her with his forearms so she couldn't move. Dipping his fingers into her cunt, he watched as her flesh swelled and reddened. He used his tongue to tickle her clit, and her breathing grew labored as she tried not to wiggle. But her heart was pounding madly against her ribcage, and little tremors ran through her arms and legs.

He drove his tongue into her cunt, delighting in her taste and perfume. She was so wet his face was soon covered with her juices, and he knew that in a moment he would explode. He wanted to keep on teasing her, but aching pressure was building in his loins. Soon he would be unable to control himself. His cock throbbed in time to his pounding heart and his head started to feel as if it would fly off his shoulders. The frog on the stump wavered for a minute, as Lesally raised himself on his elbows and guided his cock into Shari's hot pussy.

She came at once, crying his name so loud he nearly had a heart attack trying to overcome her cries with a singing illusion. When she finished, he let himself go, ejaculating into her body with all the force built up since that morning. All the energy he'd managed to accumulate holding his illusion together made his orgasm explosive. He had to hold onto Shari to keep himself from flying to pieces. For the first time ever making love nearly made him weep. He shuddered against her, his seed spurting out, and he felt each spurt like an electric jolt. Finally his body stopped convulsing and he managed to raise his head.

He knew Shari couldn't see him. He was invisible. But he could see her. With her flushed face and her hair tangled, she looked like an adorable goddess of love. The pale green ferns contrasted with her dark red hair and fair skin, and the sharp fragrance of the crushed plants beneath her mingled with the muskier, sweeter scent of their lovemaking. He kissed her mouth, parting her lips with his tongue, and felt his penis stir once again. As he was still inside her, it was no effort to wait a bit then thrust again, slowly, then more urgently.

"You cried out," he whispered.

"Sorry."

"I am going to have to spank you."

Shari kept her eyes closed, but her mouth curved in a wide smile and her body rose and fell beneath his as she met his thrusts.

"Spank," said Lesally, thinking how much he would enjoy doing just that, the second he had her somewhere her cries wouldn't get him vaporized and he could revel in the sight of her reddened buttocks and in her lusty, pleading cries.

Her body quivered. A wash of heat flooded her vagina.

"Spank, spank, spank!" he said into her ear.

Her eyes flew open. "Oh!" she cried, and he felt a hard throbbing in Shari's cunt. A low moan escaped her lips.

He wanted to make it last, but the sun had started to set. He knew that his energy was flagging and he had to save himself for the morrow. When he felt his orgasm coming, he didn't try to control it. He let it wash over him and he held himself still while his penis twitched madly as he ejaculated. Afterwards, he held the illusion in place while he dressed her, and he reintegrated the frog illusion. It drained him. So when they regained the palace, Lesally had to lie down for a long nap.

Shari tucked him in, and although he was almost asleep, he whispered, "I love you. See you tonight." She paused, and then whispered, "You owe me a spanking."

His frog illusion shivered.

* * * * *

That night, when her cocoa came, Shari only pretended to drink it, then she poured it down the sink. After that, it was just a matter of making believe she slept and waiting for Lesally to appear in his real form.

He did, as soon as the door closed behind Nanny.

288

"My princess," he breathed, sliding in to the bed next to her. "All day I've been waiting for this moment."

A rush of heat submerged her, and she nearly gasped for breath. "Me too," she managed to say. She wrapped her arms and legs around him. "Even though the forest was enchanting, I wanted to see you. Now I may. Why do you fear to be spied upon here?"

"Because, no one would ever think to spy upon you in your own room, Princess. You are prisoner, of course, but that would be invasion of privacy. Even a Princess Royal cannot be treated in such a manner."

"I'm so glad!" she said.

"Me too." He smiled and kissed her lips.

"You still owe me a spanking," she said, looking at him mischievously. She was interested to see that her words had an immediate effect. His cock stiffened visibly.

He swallowed, sitting up on the side of the bed. "Come here," he said, his voice masterful.

Shari felt a rush of wet between her legs. She lay on his lap and didn't try to hide her arousal. She rubbed her breasts against his thigh and moaned in anticipation.

His hand came down on her buttocks with a little slap.

"Harder!" she cried, writhing her body. He complied, and the next slap stung.

His erection was now poking her in the stomach. His cock was getting very hard, and it got harder each time his hand hit her buttocks. Shari cried out in a mixture of pain and pleasure. Her buttocks were getting hot, and the stinging heat was spreading straight to her aroused pussy. She could feel her flesh swelling and moisture leaked onto her thighs.

He stopped spanking, and then she felt his hot breath on her buttocks as he leaned over to kiss her. He slid her off his lap and onto the bed so she lay on her stomach. He then straddled her body and ran his lips over her skin, kissing away the sting. As he kissed her, his hand crept between her legs and his fingers found her clit and massaged it. A bolt of desire shot through her body.

That did it. Shari rolled onto her back, opened her legs as wide as she could, and said, "Take me right this minute, or I'll scream!"

This time, he didn't make her wait and he didn't tease. Shari felt his erection pressing into her pussy, and she opened her legs, using her hand to guide him.

"That's right," approved Lesally, kissing her mouth again and whispering in her ear. "Put me where you want me."

"After last night, I want you everywhere," she moaned. She took his penis and placed it in her swollen pussy, slipping it between her labia.

Lesally drew his breath in with an audible hiss. "Oh Princess," he breathed. His hands trailed over her sides and slipped underneath her. One finger started to tickle her ass, prodding gently, slipping in and out as waves of ecstasy washed over her.

"Now, please!" she cried, arching her back to give his hands full access to her body.He thrust into her, slowly at first, and not all the way in.

"Harder!" she begged.

"I don't want to make you sore," he answered.

"I can take it!" she insisted.

He went slowly though. Easing his cock into her sensitive flesh then pulling it out again when it had barely penetrated her. She felt her excitement build, felt her flesh expand and get slicker as he drove himself to the hilt, faster and faster. At the same time, his fingers filled her ass, thrusting in time with his cock. Rushes of electric shocks ran through her, tearing ragged cries from her throat. She bucked against him, holding his hips, digging her fingers into his buttocks, loving the feel of his hard body arched over hers. She felt his belly contract, and his breathing quickened.

"Wait," she said, panting.

"Wait for what?" He held himself still though.

"I want to feel you." She closed her eyes, trying to imprint the feeling of his body on her mind so she could recall it later, when their three days were up and he'd left her. She wanted to tell him about her sorrow, and at the same time, she didn't want to think about losing him just yet. It felt good holding him, feeling him inside her. She never wanted this moment to end.

Her body betrayed her. Her nipples, rubbing against the wiry hair on his chest, tingled and her belly clenched. Her hips lifted off the bed, driving his cock deep inside her. It plunged into her sensitive flesh, stretching her, filling her. His fingers slipped from her anus, and with a strangled cry, she felt herself shatter.

They cried out in unison, their bodies shaking. Shari's legs opened as wide as they could, as her orgasm shook her. Lesally dug his chin into her shoulder and held her tightly while his seed left him. Shari loved it when he came. She could feel his orgasm inside her. Little spurts of energy seemed to leave his body and shoot into hers. His penis twitched and jumped in her body, driving her right over the edge of pleasure into the deep well of her own orgasm.

Shari breathed in deep gasps. Her body glistened with sweat, and the urgent need she'd felt all day was finally assuaged. Her heartbeat returned to normal, and then she turned to Lesally, lying on his back next to her.

She feasted her eyes on his magnificent body. A male! And a fine specimen indeed!

She let her eyes wander from his navel to the nest of dark curly hair, where his penis lay at rest. She had no basis of comparison, not even photos or pictures, but she knew he had a perfect cock. It brought her intense pleasure, being long and thick enough to fill her completely. Just looking at it at rest made her want to tickle it so that it expanded. She loved the soft, hardness of it. And she especially loved feeling it plunge into her pussy.

He raised himself on his elbows and kissed her, then trotted off to the royal bathroom to wash. She heard the water running and splashing. He came back a moment later with a soft wash cloth.

"Here, let me," he said. Tenderly he cleaned her body, and the light scent of roses and lavender filled the air as he drew the wash cloth over her breasts, her belly, and then between her legs.

His hands were strong and capable, and yet they could be so gentle, like now, when he patted the damp cloth over her sensitive skin. He tossed the cloth on the floor and lay back on the bed, stretching his long body out beside her. She admired his sleek midriff.

The rest of him wasn't bad either. He had a keen gaze, and his light brown eyes crinkled with laughter when they shared a joke, or grew dark with desire when he looked at her. He had a sensuous mouth and a firm chin. He had a noble air, and Shari felt that she could rely on him in no matter what situation. His shoulders were broad and his arms muscular. He had a flat stomach, with the muscles nicely defined. His long legs were perfectly proportioned, as was his whole body. Just looking at him made her mouth water.

A male! She blinked, and a tear rolled down her cheek. He was a male, and she was a Princess of Teres. Tonight they would spend their last night together. Despite the growing love she felt for him, she knew it could never be. Despair threatened to submerge her, but she tried to keep it in check. Tonight—she still had this one night. She would lake it last forever.

To take her mind off her pain, she looked more upon her lover, upon Lesally.

He seemed to be dozing. Emboldened, Shari reached out and touched his penis. It stirred a bit. In her hand, it lay like a tame creature, although she knew just how wild it could get. She glanced at Lesally. He slept on, a faint smile on his lips.

She squeezed his cock a bit, and then touched his testicles. They were so soft and fragile seeming she hardly dared lift them. Instead, she took his penis again and examined it. She remembered Lesally's mouth on her sex, his tongue on her clit, and an idea occurred to her. She lowered her lips to his penis, and slid her mouth over it. With her tongue, she stroked its shaft.

Almost at once, it sprang to life in her mouth. She ended up with just the round tip between her lips, the shaft held in her hands. She sucked on it a bit, stroking him and pumping with her hands. She tried to imagine what would feel best for her lover, what he would like. Did he like it hard, soft, fast or slow? She wasn't sure, but she wanted to try everything.

A sound made her look up. Lesally had his head thrown back, and his hands clutched at the sheets. As she sucked, he arched his back and thrust into her mouth. He dug his heels into her bedcovers, a low moan escaping his lips.

"More," he gasped out.

His excitement was infectious. Shari felt her own body respond and soon she was so wet and slippery that she touched herself to ease her desire. Lesally trembled with the effort of holding himself still. Shari licked and sucked, and rocked back and forth on her own hand.

Shari felt herself for the first time. Her fingers dipped into her passage, and she found that nub of pleasure and rubbed it. In her mouth, Lesally shivered with pleasure. Little spurts of juice filled her mouth, and then he uttered a loud cry and pushed her head firmly to him.

Surprised by the sudden gush of fluid, Shari pulled back slightly. But the taste of his seed was not unpleasant. It was very salty, and had a slight metallic tang. His pleasure filled her mouth and she swallowed it, thinking that now she knew him, all of him. She knew the sight, the sound, the feel, and the taste of him. And she would never get enough of him. Tears of self-pity filled her eyes, but she rubbed them away before he could notice. She lifted her head up and licked her lips.

"Let me," said Lesally, drawing her to him and kissing her thoroughly. His tongue smoothed her lips, dove into her mouth, and lapped up his own seed.

Now she could no longer hold her tears back. They flowed down her cheeks and ran into her mouth. Tears, his seed, all mingled as they kissed.

Lesally drew her close and held her tightly against his chest. "Don't cry," he said.

"Only one more day," whispered Shari. "I won't be able to live without you, Lesally." She hadn't meant to say it. She had decided to be strong. But lying in his arms, so close to him, she had realized the truth. She couldn't live without him. "For the rest of my life, I'll be nothing but an empty shell. I'll have my memories of you, and I'll treasure them, but I will be the most unhappy princess in the galaxy until the day when I can be with you again."

New tears spilled down her cheeks. "When I'm old and wrinkled, will you come and get me? Will you take me away from here?" Her voice broke.

He sighed, his breath warm against her cheek. "I'd have come and gotten you, of course. But I can't live without you either, so I have a plan."

Shari felt a wild spark of hope. "What is it?"

"You'll see. Tomorrow morning. When you wake up, get ready for a bit of a shock. Just remember, I am a master of illusion. Just go along with whatever I say, and you and I will be able to stay together forever."

Shari stared at him. "Please tell me that you're not just teasing me. I couldn't bear it," she said. "You're the first person to ever ask me how I felt. No one else wants to know. When I tell Nanny I'm unhappy, she scolds me and tells me about starving children on far-off planets. She says I have to be glad I'm so well fed and have such lovely clothes. But I don't care about all that."

"Hush, I know."

"I can't hush," she wailed. "I have to tell you this. You're the one I want to spend the rest of my life with. I don't want you to save me just so that I can leave this palace. I want to leave it to be with you."

He took her face in his hands and kissed her. "I love you, Princess Shari. Trust me. We will be together always, one way or another."

"One way or another?"

Lesally sighed. "If I fail, we will both certainly be executed. Do you still want me to go through with my plan?"

"Yes. A thousand times yes," she said. "I would rather die in your arms tomorrow than live a hundred years without you."

He smiled. "Then I shall try."

Part Four
Happily Ever After

ഇ

A loud scream woke Princess Shari. She blinked, trying to get her bearings. The last thing she remembered was lying in Lesally's arms, her whole body sated. She smiled and stretched, and hit something next to her.

Her eyes flew open. Lesally, in his three-foot frog form, lay in bed with her.

There came another sharp scream, and then she recognized her nanny's voice. She cried, "What has he done to you! My poor darling!"

Shari sat up. She felt fine. But when she glanced down, she saw her stomach was enormous. It looked like a big bump in the middle of her body. She sat up higher, and was amazed to see herself stark naked in bed. Lesally, in his frog illusion, was naked too. He was sitting in the bed, and between his legs, Shari saw a perfect, green penis and testicles. Lesally gave her a wink.

Shari was too flustered to wink back at him. How had her stomach gotten like that overnight? Gingerly, she touched it. It felt like her stomach, only huge. She looked at Lesally, who was grinning widely. He winked at her again, and whispered, "Remember, illusions seem real." That went a long way towards reassuring her, and she managed a shy smile in his direction.

Nanny rushed about, calling for the royal doctor, the royal guards, and the king. Everyone came running at once.

"What is going on here?" The king's voice boomed. He strode into the nursery, and stopped as if he'd run into a glass wall. His face became almost as green as Lesally the frog.

"What are you doing in my daughter's bed?" he cried. That he'd brought his courtiers with him—all males—was a measure of the situation's gravity.

"You invited me," said the frog, in a perfectly reasonable voice. "The king's word is law here. You told me to be welcome for three days and three nights."

"But, but…you are a male!" shrieked Nanny. "You should have told us!"

"No one asked me," said the frog coldly.

Everyone now stared at Shari. She looked at her enormous stomach. It was an illusion, but it felt real. This must be Lesally's plan, so she would go through with it. She put her hand on her now huge stomach and rubbed. Her nipples, as soon as she touched herself, hardened. Between her legs, she felt a familiar ache. Just the sight of the frog's penis made her hot. She tried to think of something else.

"What has he done to you?" roared the king.

"I don't know," said Shari. "I had no idea he was a male. No one explained to me about males," she added.

"But I can show you what he did to me, if you like. It's quite fun, and I think you should try it," she told Nanny.

Shari reached over and stroked Lesally's penis. "It gets hard when you do this," she informed the watching crowd.

"Great Galaxies!" Her mother's voice pierced the stunned silence.

Lesally the frog, his penis now quite erect and just as large as a human's penis, stood up and bowed. "I would like to claim the princess Shari as my wife. She will come back to my planet, and we will breed many baby frogs, such as myself."

Shari's mother rushed into the room. She hadn't set foot in the nursery for ten years, but she must've leapt into the nearest transporter as soon as she heard the news. "My daughter can't marry! She's a princess of Teres!"

"A very pregnant princess. You'd better get a couple more nannies. She'll be laying her eggs very soon," said Lesally.

"Oh my poor baby!" screamed Nanny.

Shari pulled a sheet over her body. She didn't feel embarrassed, but she didn't like the way the king's courtiers ogled her breasts. One of them, she saw, had a rather huge erection pushing against his velvet pants.

"We have to do something!" cried the queen.

"I suggest you let her marry me, and that we go back to my lovely planet. I promise we'll send you lots of letters, as soon as we manage to build a spaceport to accommodate the spaceships. Of course, it may take a while. We're still in the Middle Ages compared to you, and the planet is mostly swamp. However, my house is warm and snug, so you don't have to worry about your princess. She will be quite happy there, I assure you."

Shari held her breath. Would it work? Would her father really let her go?

There was a deep silence, while everyone thought about this. The king whispered to his courtiers, noticed the one with the erection, and got so angry he kicked the poor fellow in the shin. The queen went to Shari and stood by the bed, not touching her. No one touched a princess of Teres.

Shari lumbered to her feet, the sheet wrapped around her, and said, "I want to go with Lesally. Post the wedding banns, Mother." Her stomach stuck out in front of her, and her mother, the queen, took one look and burst into hysterical tears.

The king, his temper more or less under control, snapped, "Nanny! Get the princess a decent wedding dress. Post the banns in a public place no one will ever see, and let's get this wedding over with!"

* * * * *

The wedding was hasty. Shari wore a satin sheet with a hole cut in the middle, like a poncho. Lesally, as a frog, wore his little shorts and shirt. Shari felt odd with her stomach sticking out so far. She kept telling herself it was an illusion, but it felt very real! She was afraid it was a dream, and she was afraid she'd wake up. She, a princess of Teres, getting married and about to leave her planet, and not even old and wrinkled yet!

Standing next to her frog, in front of the royal judge, saying, "I do," she thought she was the happiest woman alive.

Lesally croaked, "I do."

And Shari's nanny burst into tears.

Then the king signed the marriage license, and the queen gave Shari a wedding present. A whole suitcase full of gold. The queen, obviously, suffered pangs of regret.

The king had no such pangs. He stood amid his courtiers—one with a cast on his shin—and didn't wave as the spaceship, the *SS Marissa*, lifted off Planet Teres once more.

The ship spoke in a prim voice. "I have orders to leave you on the planet and to depart right away."

"Fine," said Shari. "You don't mind if I make love to my husband, do you?" She parted her knees and scooted her butt down a little in the seat so that the frog illusion could reach her.

The ship gagged. "You can wait until you disembark," she managed to snap.

"I can't wait," said Lesally. He kept his frog disguise, of course. He hopped off his chair and stood between Shari's legs. Her stomach still resembled a huge mound. Lesally lifted the satin wedding dress sheet and slipped beneath it. A moment later, Shari felt an agile tongue touch her. It was a hot, velvety tongue, and it ticked, licked and stroked her clit until she was wet and shaking with desire, then Lesally the frog hopped onto her lap. Or at least, it looked like he did.

"That is strange," said Shari.

"What?" The whisper came from next to her ear.

"I can't feel you sitting on my lap." She kept her voice very low. The *SS Marissa* had electronic ears like a bat.

"It's just an illusion. I'm here, but invisible." Lesally breathed and a touch as light as a breeze stirred her hair. Then his touch descended and Shari felt his fingers parting her labia. One finger drew light circles around her clit, and Shari moaned. Then he penetrated her with a finger and thrust in and out.

She looked down and saw that the frog illusion had introduced his penis into her vagina and was frantically thrusting while crouched on her lap. It looked very strange, even though it felt incredibly sexy. "How odd," she gasped.

"Close your eyes," Lesally said.

Shari did, and when she did, she felt his presence as he stood between her legs. The frog illusion on her lap imitated Lesally's movements.

"That is the most disgusting thing I've ever seen," huffed the *SS Marissa*. "I can't believe you're doing that."

"I hope you're not getting your circuits overheated," said Lesally innocently. He paused, then Shari felt his cock sliding into her tight passage. Slowly he entered her, gently pushing, so as not to hurt her. When fully sheathed, he thrust, and Shari shuddered with pleasure. Her hands gripped her chair's arms and she opened her legs wider so that Lesally could penetrate her fully. He did, his cock filling her completely and hitting her womb with every stroke.

"Yes!" she screamed.

"Yuck!" screeched the *SS Marissa*.

"I love you," Lesally whispered in Shari's ear, and she smiled though tears of happiness poured down her cheeks.

Lesally paused his thrusting, much to Shari's dismay. She tightened her thighs around his waist. "Why are you crying?" he asked, concern in his voice.

"I'm so happy and it feels too good," she whispered.

As the ship made its way through space in an icy silence, Lesally made Shari cry out in delight. While the frog illusion sat on her lap and fucked her with enthusiasm, invisible Lesally held her in his strong arms, and kneeling between her legs, drove his powerful cock into her. Shari wanted to hang onto him, but knew it would look odd if her hands stayed in mid-air. She had to hold herself perfectly still so the illusion would look fine.

If she suspected a trick, the *SS Marissa* would turn around and take Lesally back to be executed. So Shari grabbed the arms of her seat and clutched them tightly, while her invisible lover caressed her breasts. When he pinched her nipples, she gave a little gasp. And when he leaned over and whispered, "I want to spank you so badly," she lost control and a massive orgasm ripped through her.

"I'm coming!" Shari screamed.

"I'm leaving," snarled the *SS Marissa*.

They landed, and the ship, without a word of goodbye, streaked off.

Shari stood in the mud, her mother's suitcase beside her. She looked at Lesally. "You know, I don't care if the planet is all mud, as long as I'm with you."

"I know that," said Lesally, and before her eyes, transformed from frog to his handsome self. He stood next to Shari, naked, and held her hand. "Are you ready?"

"Yes," she said.

The next instant, the mud vanished. The sky changed from gray to blue as the mist disappeared. Grass appeared beneath their feet. It was as if a sheet had been whipped off a picture and what had been hidden, came to light.

The fresh, green scent of pine replaced the smell of swamp, and Shari found herself standing in a large clearing in the middle of a beautiful pine forest. They were on the top of a mountain, and could see for miles. Above her, fluffy white clouds sailed in a pale blue sky. A few silver spaceships flew overhead, and she could see gorgeous cities built in the distant valleys, while rivers wound between lush farmland. Lesally was suddenly dressed in rich clothes, and Shari felt shy and awkward around him. She blushed and turned away, ashamed of her satin sheet and huge stomach.

"What is it, my love?" he asked her.

"I'm so ugly, and you're so handsome," she said.

"Look at yourself," said Lesally, a chuckle in his voice. She looked down, and she had own lovely body back. She wore a beautiful gown made of white satin copiously embroidered with pearls. Then she felt something heavy on her head. She reached up, and pulled off a gold crown. She suddenly noticed that Lesally had a crown as well.

"Is this all an illusion?" she asked.

"The clothes are an illusion. I will have to get some real ones for you. It would be an effort to keep up the illusion for both of us for very long."

"But…but this planet! It is beautiful. Is this an illusion too?" Shari shook with emotion. "Everything is so incredibly gorgeous!"

"No. This is the real Planet Marécage, This is how it really looks. Well, on this part of the planet. We also have deserts and high mountains, oceans and beaches where we can swim together. Hold on, I have to contact Brant." He stopped and waved his hands. A floating screen appeared, a young man staring out of it. "Brant! I'm back!" Lesally said.

The young man in the screen made a face. "Well, it's about time. When I told your father where you'd gone, he nearly had me drawn and quartered."

"You look all right to me," said Lesally. He took Shari's hand. "This is the Princess Shari of the House of Teres. We were married this morning."

"Oh, we know about all that." Brant's face split in a huge grin. "When the King of Teres posted the banns, they made headlines all over the galaxy."

"How embarrassing," said Shari. She felt her face grow red. "So everyone one knows about my disgrace."

"Disgrace!" Brant looked thunderstruck. "Your Highness, forgive me, but we are all rejoicing here. Prince Lesally, tell her that we are honored to have her among us."

"Prince? Prince Lesally?" Shari raised her eyebrows.

He nodded at Shari. "My father is King, and I am sure he is looking forward to meeting you."

"Oh he is," chuckled Brant. "He and your mother, the queen, have arranged a royal wedding." To Shari he said, "King Harold had just about given up trying to get Lesally to marry. No one was right for him, much to the despair of the ladies of the kingdom. I see he was right to wait though. Welcome to Planet Marécage, Your Highness. Oh, and hurry up and get home. We're all waiting to meet you."

"I'll take the meadow route," said Lesally. "Send some flyers to get us at the oak tree." Brant nodded, and the screen disappeared.

"Where are we?" asked Shari.

"On a hill, not far from the capitol city, which you can see over there." Lesally pointed to a large, prosperous looking city in the bend of a wide river. "I wanted to take you here first, so that you could get used to the idea, and get a glimpse of what the Planet Marécage looks like without its protective illusion."

"Is there a swamp?"

He chuckled. "Oh yes. Your spaceship came right down over our largest one. That was no illusion. I will show it to you one day—it is not as muddy and smelly as I made it seem though, and you'll love fishing for sod-fish. It is a lot of fun. So, do you like it here?"

"It's beautiful," said Shari. "But why did you choose me? Why?"

"When I saw you wading around in the mud, wearing just a sheer nightgown, your lovely body nearly made me faint. How could I have let you go? And when I saw the emblem on your spaceship, and realized who you were, I knew I'd have to be a frog, and not a prince in order to save you…even though Brant said I was a crazy fool."

"I'm so glad you're a crazy fool, and so happy you decided to save me," said Shari. She kissed him, and pressed her body to his. "Do we have to go to the wedding anytime soon?"

He responded by unzipping her gown and carefully helping her step out of it. "I know it's an illusion, but if I rip it, I'll have to call up another one, and I bet I'm going to be a bit exhausted," joked Lesally.

She wore no underwear beneath her gown. The warm breeze lifted a lock of her long hair, and her skin prickled. She remembered their lovemaking in the spaceship, and she felt a rush of wetness between her thighs. She moaned softly.

"What is it?" he asked.

"I don't know what it is," she said unsteadily, "but whenever I think of you coming, when I think of your pleasure and how you cry out, I get all wet."

Her prince unzipped his pants and pulled out his erection. "Will this help?" he asked.

"Oh yes!" breathed Shari, and she got on her hands and knees, looking at him over her shoulder. "But hurry, I think I'm going to come with or without you in a minute."

"Never without me," murmured Prince Lesally. His hands itched to spank her magnificent ass, but his control was already tenuous. He seized her waist, knelt behind her and thrust into her in one stroke.

Shari's body burned as he filled her, his cock pushing hard right to her womb, his hands clutching at her breasts as he knelt behind her. Shari leaned onto her forearms, on the soft bed of pine needles. As she raised her buttocks higher, she found she could change the angle of his thrusts, making them deeper or shallower.

She was just about to explode, when Lesally withdrew his penis from her pussy. Ignoring her breathless entreaties, he turned her over onto her back and hooked both of her legs over his shoulder. Lying with her legs in the air and Lesally crouching between her thighs, she could look down and see his cock thrusting in and out of her pussy. Her legs held high and spread wide, she had no control now over his movements. It gave him more leverage too, and his cock buried itself to the hilt at each stroke.

He slowed down, drawing his cock nearly all the way out. Then, after hesitating with the tip of it just barely touching her labia, he thrust down again, holding her legs even higher. He slammed into her, and she felt his balls slapping against her rear. Torn between sharp pleasure and pain, Shari gasped as each thrust seemed to reach the very center of her being. Her legs were spread so wide she could see everything. The view made her mouth go dry and her pussy spurt juices. Several strokes later, Shari screamed for release, and when she finally came, her vagina pulsing wildly, Lesally exploded with a great cry.

Shari loved when he came—a part of him went into her body and became part of her. She clasped him in her arms until he'd stopped trembling. Whenever he came inside her, she felt stronger and more beautiful than she'd ever felt before.

The pine needles prickled against her back, and she pushed him off her regretfully. "I think we'd better get going."

Lesally got up and helped her to her feet. "Your crown is crooked, Princess," he said with a grin.

"Yours fell off," she answered, pointing to the ground.

"Shall we go now?" asked Lesally, putting it back on and helping her into her dress.

"Yes, we shall. But you know what?"

"What?"

"I will be looking forward to our wedding night," said Shari. And she turned around so that Lesally could zip her up. "Now don't get any ideas," she said, as his hand touched her bare buttocks.

"I can't help it," whispered the Prince. "When I see your body, I can't control myself. The touch turned into a little spank.

They were very late for their wedding. And then they lived happily ever after.

The End

Why an electronic book?

We live in the Information Age — an exciting time in the history of human civilization, in which technology rules supreme and continues to progress in leaps and bounds every minute of every day. For a multitude of reasons, more and more avid literary fans are opting to purchase e-books instead of paper books. The question from those not yet initiated into the world of electronic reading is simply: *Why?*

1. *Price.* An electronic title at Ellora's Cave Publishing and Cerridwen Press runs anywhere from 40% to 75% less than the cover price of the exact same title in paperback format. Why? Basic mathematics and cost. It is less expensive to publish an e-book (no paper and printing, no warehousing and shipping) than it is to publish a paperback, so the savings are passed along to the consumer.

2. *Space.* Running out of room in your house for your books? That is one worry you will never have with electronic books. For a low one-time cost, you can purchase a handheld device specifically designed for e-reading. Many e-readers have large, convenient screens for viewing. Better yet, hundreds of titles can be stored within your new library — on a single microchip. There are a variety of e-readers from different manufacturers. You can also read e-books on your PC or laptop computer. (Please note that Ellora's Cave does not endorse any specific brands. You can check our websites at www.ellorascave.com

or www.cerridwenpress.com for information we make available to new consumers.)

3. *Mobility.* Because your new e-library consists of only a microchip within a small, easily transportable e-reader, your entire cache of books can be taken with you wherever you go.

4. *Personal Viewing Preferences.* Are the words you are currently reading too small? Too large? Too… ANNOYING? Paperback books cannot be modified according to personal preferences, but e-books can.

5. *Instant Gratification.* Is it the middle of the night and all the bookstores near you are closed? Are you tired of waiting days, sometimes weeks, for bookstores to ship the novels you bought? Ellora's Cave Publishing sells instantaneous downloads twenty-four hours a day, seven days a week, every day of the year. Our webstore is never closed. Our e-book delivery system is 100% automated, meaning your order is filled as soon as you pay for it.

Those are a few of the top reasons why electronic books are replacing paperbacks for many avid readers.

As always, Ellora's Cave and Cerridwen Press welcome your questions and comments. We invite you to email us at Comments@ellorascave.com or write to us directly at Ellora's Cave Publishing Inc., 1056 Home Avenue, Akron, OH 44310-3502.

Cerridwen, the Celtic Goddess of wisdom, was the muse who brought inspiration to storytellers and those in the creative arts. Cerridwen Press encompasses the best and most innovative stories in all genres of today's fiction. Visit our site and discover the newest titles by talented authors who still get inspired - much like the ancient storytellers did, once upon a time.

Cerridwen Press

www.cerridwenpress.com

Discover for yourself why readers can't get enough of the multiple award-winning publisher Ellora's Cave.

Whether you prefer e-books or paperbacks,

be sure to visit EC on the web at www.ellorascave.com

for an erotic reading experience that will leave you breathless.